When a Lord
Needs a Lady

More Historical Romance from Jane Goodger

Marry Christmas

A Christmas Scandal

A Christmas Waltz

When a Duke Says I Do

The Mad Lord's Daughter

When a Lord Needs a Lady

JANE GOODGER

KENSINGTON BOOKS
KENSINGTON PUBLISHING CORP.
www.kensingtonbooks.com

KENSINGTON BOOKS are published by

Kensington Publishing Corp.
119 West 40th Street
New York, NY 10018

All Kensington titles, imprints, and distributed lines are available at special quantity discounts for bulk purchases for sales promotion, premiums, fund-raising, and educational or institutional use.

Special book excerpts or customized printings can also be created to fit specific needs. For details, write or phone the office of the Kensington Special Sales Manager: Kensington Publishing Corp., 119 West 40th Street, New York, NY 10018. Attn. Special Sales Department. Phone: 1-800-221-2647.

Kensington and the K logo Reg. U.S. Pat. & TM Off.

First Electronic Edition: February 2014
eISBN-13: 978-1-60183-162-0
eISBN-10: 1-60183-162-5

First Print Edition: February 2014
ISBN-13: 978-1-60183-223-8
ISBN-10: 1-60183-223-0

Printed in the United States of America

The Miserable Marquess

"It's said he never smiles. That he is one of the most miserable men in all of Britain and that his heart—if he has one—is the size of a pea." She held up her thumb and index finger to show just how small his heart was.

Graham, at first horrified, let out a sharp, and rather rusty, laugh. "Do tell me more."

She smiled, her full lips looking incredibly enticing at the moment, so Graham forced himself to look into her eyes. They were changeable eyes, green and gray and blue in a field of golden brown. "It's said—I overheard Miss Wright talking with her mother about Lord Avonleigh—that he will marry the very first girl he smiles at. Not a polite smile. A true smile."

He hadn't heard that one. "Truly? That's what they say?"

"That and the part about him not having a heart. He's known as the Miserable Marquess."

"He has a heart," he muttered. "Somewhere."

"Of course he has one," she said. "He simply has never used it."

Chapter 1

"I'm dying."

At her mother's words, Katherine Wright let out a small, silent sigh as she looked at the crowded beach from their suite in the Grand Hotel. Brighton was nothing like Newport. There was nothing genteel or stifling about this famed holiday spot. It was crowded with what her mother called riffraff. It was raucous and loud. It was . . . wonderful.

"I *am* dying," her mother insisted, removing the cool compress from her forehead and placing it directly over her eyes. "I was led to believe Brighton was the place to go. *The* place. Charles Dickens used to holiday here."

"That was twenty years ago, Mother. And I rather like it. It's so alive. And one cannot find fault with the hotel or its clientele. It's all so very charming. Those bathing machines. Really," Katherine said, looking at the line of small covered wagons that quality women used to change in before bathing out of view. She'd used one just yesterday, curiosity overcoming her. She'd carried her bathing outfit in a satchel, climbed aboard, and changed while the wagon was pulled by a very sad-looking horse, approximately fifteen feet into the water. The driver waded into the water and, with a small splash, dropped a set of stairs. She'd stepped carefully down into the cold water, her slippered feet sinking only a bit into the hard-packed sand. The wagons were in place so that no male eye could spy on a woman while she wore her bathing costume. After a bit of wading, she hauled herself out and was done.

How different from that holiday two years ago she'd spent at her grandmother's home in upper New York when, wearing nothing but her shift, she'd run full-tilt off a broad, flat rock and into the cold lake water with a joyous scream. If Mother had known, she would have fainted. Even there, in that silly old wagon, her mother stood diligently by making certain no man glimpsed an ankle—or worse, perhaps the curve of her calf—as she stepped down the ladder.

Her mother had not joined her, but waited in the bathing machine, complaining about the odd smell in Brighton.

"It's the sea," Katherine had said. "I think it smells rather nice."

Katherine turned from studying the bathing machines to look at her mother. She did look rather awful. She'd suffered from megrims for years, but these bouts seemed to be coming more frequently of late—and just when it was time for her mother to do something she didn't care to do. Today, they'd planned to walk along the pier. The English called it promenading; Katherine simply loved the way the English made everything seem just a bit more special. It was a glorious day, and Katherine ached to go out and join the throngs.

"So many people. Who are they all? I can tell that they're not all the type of people I was led to believe would be in Brighton. I can hear them from here. Close the window, dear." Elizabeth Wright was a good woman, Katherine knew, but she was a terrible snob.

It was true that Brighton attracted an eclectic crowd, and Katherine was beginning to suspect Lady Haversly, who was giving Katherine entrée into society this fall, had simply wanted the pair of them out of her hair for the summer.

"They take the rail here, I'm told," Elizabeth said. "Droves of them escaping the city like rats."

Katherine gave her mother a look, even though the older woman's eyes were still covered with the compress. "I do wish you weren't always such a snob, Mother."

"You'll be glad when you're a duchess," Elizabeth said smugly.

Katherine took a bracing breath. She didn't want to be a duchess or a marchioness or even a baroness. She wanted to go home to New York City and attend school as she'd always planned to do. What was the point of all that studying she'd been forced to do if not to prepare her for a university education? When she'd broached the subject with her mother, she might as well have announced that she planned to become a prostitute. It was then she realized, with a slow build of horror, that all her lessons in language, philosophy, and European history were simply to prepare her for her life as a peer. It had been a well-orchestrated and carefully planned operation—and Katherine almost admired her mother's ability to stay focused on the prize all these years.

"Money is crass, dear. But having a title, that is something you cannot buy. I only wish my own mother had done for me what I have done for you."

It hadn't occurred to her mother that waving her dowry in front of an impoverished peer was tantamount to buying a title. And it also hadn't occurred to her that if Grandmamma *had* married her mother to a title, Katherine would not have existed—at least not in her present form.

"I'm going to my room to read," Katherine said. "I hope you feel well enough to attend supper. I hear the Duke of Monmouth will be in attendance."

That perked her mother right up. "A duke, you say?"

" 'Tis only a rumor." Made up by Katherine about a title that had ended with the infamous Duke of Monmouth's beheading in the sixteen hundreds. She pushed away the twinge of guilt she felt for lying to her mother.

Elizabeth sagged back down into her pillow, grabbing the cool cloth from her head. "If he is in attendance, I will simply have to endure the pain. It is an opportunity we cannot miss. A duke. Now, that would make everything perfect, would it not? Though I did rather have my sights on the Duke of Penfrey. He's supposed to be so handsome and have such a lovely home in London."

Katherine looked at her mother with amused exasperation. She drove Katherine to distraction, but she loved her mother with all her heart. "Yes, it would be nice, wouldn't it?" she said softly.

She walked over to her mother and gently replaced the compress, then kissed her cheek. "I'll see you tonight then, in our little dining room. At eight?"

"Unless the duke is here," Elizabeth said softly, already sounding as if she were drifting off to sleep.

"Unless the duke is here," Katherine said, then tiptoed from the room.

* * *

"Oh no, miss. If you get caught, it's my job that'll be lost." Clara, Katherine's loyal maid and partner in crime, didn't look even a tiny bit worried. Her eyes danced with excitement. Such a bad maid, she was. Katherine grinned.

"That won't happen, Clara. Mother cannot dismiss you because I will not allow it." She looked in the mirror and smiled. She looked so . . . ordinary. Just a girl going out for a stroll. She'd pretend to be looking for someone on the beach, but in reality she would be gloriously alone with no one hovering about, no one keeping an eagle's eye out for any untitled gentleman who might dare look her way.

Yesterday, for the first time, she'd donned her maid's skirt and shirtwaist and a smart little hat with a jaunty blue feather, and walked along the beach all by herself. For an entire ten minutes. It had been glorious and perhaps the most frightening thing she'd ever done. To feel the wind against her cheeks, to pause and watch the children play, to wonder what the sand would feel like between her toes. She'd bought a bit of fried dough laden with powdery white sugar that she'd never seen before in her life. It was heaven in her mouth.

And she was going to do it all again today.

"What if your mother finds out?" Clara hissed rather gleefully. Honestly, a proper lady's maid would go scurrying off to tattle on her. But not Clara.

Katherine shrugged as if she didn't care, but of course she did. She didn't want to upset her mother, truly, but she also didn't want to spend the day staring at the four walls of her room again. She didn't know what had come over her when she first looked out at Brighton Beach and saw all those people, all that activity and chaos. She stood there and felt the strangest impulse to be impulsive. This trip had not been well planned, not at all. They had expected to be in the midst of titled ladies and gentlemen, but instead found themselves surrounded by no one of import. Truth be told, Katherine was relieved. They only needed to stay in England for the Little Season and then they could go home. That meant she could be sleeping in her own bed by Thanksgiving. She missed her younger sister terribly and was simply biding her time until they could return to New York.

Despite the lure of her rather large dowry, no titled gentleman had given her even a passing look except a rather loathsome viscount whom even her mother found extremely disagreeable. The Wrights were wealthy, but they were not part of the New York elite, that *nouveau riche* group of shipping magnates and steel barons who ruled society in New York. No, the Wrights were on the fringes of that group. And while her mother dreamed of becoming close friends with the Vanderbilts and their ilk, Katherine knew that eventuality was unlikely and truly didn't wish for it.

Though her mother dreamed of a title, Katherine knew her mother would never force her into a marriage she found disagreeable. Instead, and this really was so naïve and sweet of Mother, she hoped a titled gentleman would actually fall in love with her daughter. From what Katherine had seen of titled gentlemen thus far, she felt she was fairly safe from that fate. Everyone was so very English, and she was so very American. She didn't see anyone other than a desperate man being interested in her at all.

Katherine was about to step from the room when Clara stopped her. "Oh goodness, I almost forgot," she said, hurrying from her bedroom to a small sitting area. "A letter from your sister." Clara thrust the thick packet in her hand, giving her another cheeky grin.

Katherine smiled again, tucking the letter into her pocket before slipping out the door and into the thickly carpeted hall. They were on the sixth floor and Katherine didn't want to wait for the lift, so she headed toward the massive square staircase, taking the time to look down at the breathtaking view from above. She adored heights.

She took lively steps down and down until she reached the opulent lobby, its marble floor gleaming. She walked through the front door without drawing a single glance, for the moment enjoying the anonymity of appearing to look like a servant. She walked directly out of the hotel's grand entrance and across the street to the soft sands of Brighton Beach, thick with people taking the waters, all dressed from head to toe in their finest bathing outfits. She walked along the beach toward the pier that jutted into the sea, dodged by small children who rushed to the water's edge to collect water for their castles' moats. Breathing deeply, Katherine let out a sigh of pure contentment.

"Miss?"

Katherine looked about for the small voice, but saw nothing—until she looked straight down and spotted a little head poking up from the sand, blue eyes full of mischief.

"Oh," she said. "A sea nymph."

That won her a giggle.

"I'm a little girl, not a sea nymph," the girl said in her charming little English accent. Even though Katherine knew she was in England, hearing those broad vowels from a child made her smile.

"Oh." Katherine hunkered down. "And what villain buried you in the sand like this? Shall I fetch the constable?"

Another giggle. "My brother," she said. "And he only did as I asked. I buried him right proper yesterday. He got stuck."

A bit farther down the beach, a little boy broke from his mother's grasp and ran toward them. "I think your brother is here to save you," she whispered, standing up to greet the boy and his mother.

"She almost stepped on me," the girl announced.

"That is true," Katherine said, with a laugh. "And now that I know you are in good hands, I'll be off. Good-bye, little nymph."

Her brother, nearly covered from head to toe in sand, was already helping his little sister emerge from the sand.

"Good day," she said to the mother, who returned the greeting.

As Katherine was walking away, she heard the mother say, "She was an American lady. Imagine, all the way from America."

Katherine smiled, knowing she'd never have become part of such a charming scene if she'd stayed in her room. The smell of fish and chips filled the air, and not far down, a small band was playing on a pavilion. Stalls with souvenirs and candy lined the beach, and Katherine dug in her pocket for a bit of change. The closest stall was filled with plates and tiny silver spoons with the words "Brighton Beach" engraved on them.

"I'll take this," she said, pulling out one spoon with a charming depiction of the pier. She tucked it in her pocket, liking the small weight of it there.

The beach was terribly crowded, so finding a place of relative privacy where she could read her sister's letter was difficult. Finally, she settled on an old jetty near a tidal pool not far from the pier, her feet dangling just inches from the water. A tiny crab scurried along the smooth sand beneath the calm water of the pool, stirring up a small cloud of silt. "I'm afraid I've eaten quite a few of your relatives," she said as she pulled out her sister's letter.

> *Dearest Katherine:*
>   *It is so completely boring in the city without you here. And scorchingly hot. Yesterday, it was so hot I stayed all day in my room, not daring to move else I'd incinerate from the friction. I imagine you sitting on a terrace at the seaside, a cool breeze making you chilled, and forcing you to send Clara for a wrap. I imagine you eating ices and dipping your toes in the cold English water. Is it cold? Are you baring your toes? Father brought me to Central Park; I fear I'd made quite a nuisance of myself with my complaints. He's been in boring meetings with Mr. Rockefeller since you've been gone. Father's been very busy, and our trip to the park was lovely for both of us.*
>   *Aunt Beatrice stopped by last week with Cousin Jake. He's become so tall. Or perhaps I am shrinking?*

Katherine laughed softly aloud, and unthinkingly placed the page beside her to continue reading. Her poor sister made it sound as if New York was shockingly miserable, but she knew her Lucy was rather dramatic—as most fifteen-year-olds were prone to be. Poor thing. It did sound awfully hot in New York. And she was enjoying a cool breeze at the moment.

A cool breeze that lifted the first page of her sister's letter off the jetty and floated it like a tiny boat in the tidal pool. "Oh drat," she said, glaring at the page. She reached for it, but the page drifted tantalizingly out of reach. Perhaps if she leaned just so, with one hand grasping a post, her feet planted just at the water's edge, she could just . . . about . . .

"Oh," she cried, as her grip on the jetty pole slipped and she began the inevitable headfirst fall into the shallow water.

And then "Oh!" again, as a strong hand gripped her wrist and pulled her back to safety. She looked up into the most beautiful male eyes she'd ever seen in her life. His eyes, an almost preternatural shade of gray, were only partially shielded beneath a thick fringe of dark lashes.

"Thank you, sir," she said, laughing, delighted to be saved by such a gallant and handsome man, who instead of laughing with her, frowned. His hand still gripped her wrist, warm and large, and when Katherine looked down, he immediately dropped it.

"Beg pardon," he said, stiffly.

"I cannot, sir. For if you had not put your hand around my wrist, I would be in the water right now and quite miserable." She grinned up at him, almost willing him to smile back at her.

"You're an American girl," he said, giving her a quick, impersonal look, which no doubt took in the fact she wasn't quality—not even American quality. And in that moment, Katherine knew—she *knew*—that he *was* quality. From the tips of his shiny shoes, to his light woolen trousers and his fine linen shirt covered by an expensive, beautifully cut jacket, this man was quality. Perhaps even the kind of quality who had a title in front of his name. Oh drat.

Graham Spencer, Marquess of Avonleigh, knew the minute the girl in front of him realized, perhaps not who he was, but most certainly *what* he was, for her face lost its light. Her smile disappeared, and her eyes, sparkling not moments before, turned cold. He felt the loss of that light acutely, which was nearly as much a shock to him as his very presence on this beach.

He'd been looking out his hotel window, thinking about a meeting he was to have later that day with Herbert Menders about his latest dismal investments, when he'd spied a young woman, wearing a blue hat with a yellow feather bursting from its band, strolling along the beach. Despite her ridiculous hat, she had an elegance, a carefree grace, which struck him. It made him curious. Why was this girl alone? He watched as she talked to a child in the sand, as she went to a souvenir stand, as she listened to the band for a moment. He felt strangely compelled to go down to the beach and get a closer look. Following this impulse was so out of character for him that the thought alone nearly drove him back to his room and his worries.

And then he was standing behind her, watching her, afraid to breathe lest she turn and see him, when a page of her letter lifted off the jetty and floated on a breeze into the water. He knew by the way she was dressed that he shouldn't approach her—she wasn't destitute by any means, but she certainly was not anyone he could ever seriously consider—but something about her drew him. She was a fine-looking woman, but it was more than the way she filled out that ordinary dress. He couldn't have said why he remained there, standing behind her, feeling a longing that he had no name for. When she nearly fell in, he didn't think, he acted, and found her practically in his arms, laughing and looking up at him. He hadn't wanted to let go—hadn't let go, actually—until she looked down at his hand still clasped around her wrist.

"Allow me to introduce myself," he said quickly, lest she leave. That could not happen. "My name is Gray. I'm a . . . valet for a gentleman staying at the Royal." He nearly winced at the lie, but he knew that if he'd told her the truth of who he was, she would curtsy deferentially or blush or, worse, walk away.

She tilted her head and narrowed her eyes, as if not believing him, though he couldn't think of a reason she wouldn't. She looked past him to the large, elegant façade of the Albion Royal Hotel. "Gray the valet," she said, as if tasting the words. Then she smiled and thrust out her hand. "My name is Katy. I'm a maid for Miss Wright of the New York Wrights." He must have given something away, for her eyes widened. "You know them?"

"I know *of* them. I know they have a daughter they are trying to sell to the highest bidder. Or rather, title."

She looked momentarily shocked, then burst out laughing. "Oh my. I hadn't realized how quickly news travels in England. I imagine every gentleman with a moldering castle is out looking for her. They are fabulously rich, you know, the Wrights. Your employer wouldn't be one of those gentlemen with a moldering castle, would he?"

Graham felt a smile tugging on his lips, but he suppressed the action. "My employer *is* looking for a bride, as a matter of fact."

"A wealthy bride, no doubt."

"How cynical of you. But, yes, a wealthy bride would do better than a poor one, I should think," he said, feeling slightly irritated because it was the truth. Unless his latest investments brought in historic returns, he would be in a desperate state—desperate enough to marry simply for money. And the only families with the kind of money he needed were Americans. One family, the Von Haupts, was already courting him with ferocious tenacity. One of the reasons he was in Brighton was to escape their relentless pursuit. It wasn't that their daughter, Claudia, was ugly—she wasn't. But he simply could not imagine spending his life with a woman who reminded him so much of milk and toast, rather than marmalade and scones. Well-made scones with marmalade were his only weakness. It made him nearly ill to think that his title, steeped in history and revered for generations, would be brought this low.

"And your employer is?"

"Graham Spencer, Marquess of Avonleigh."

He watched as her mouth opened slightly. "Oh, you poor dear," she said.

Now, that, he didn't expect at all. "He's not such a bad sort," Graham said rather indignantly.

"Perhaps not to you, but I've heard things." She shrugged. "I'm not one to gossip."

"But I am, and I'm very curious. What have you heard?"

She pressed her lips together as if such an action would keep the words from escaping. "It's said he never smiles. That he is one of the most miserable men in all of Britain and that his heart—if he has one—is the size of a pea." She held up her thumb and index finger to show just how small his heart was.

Graham, at first horrified, let out a sharp, and rather rusty, laugh. "Do tell me more."

She smiled, her full lips looking incredibly enticing at the moment, so Graham forced himself to look into her eyes. They were changeable eyes, green and gray and blue in a field of golden brown. The two were heedless of the people strolling past, giving curious looks at the well-dressed man and the ordinary girl. "It's said—I overheard Miss Wright talking with her mother about Lord Avonleigh—that he will marry the very first girl he smiles at. Not a polite smile. A true smile."

He hadn't heard that one. "Truly? That's what they say?"

"That and the part about him not having a heart. He's known as the Miserable Marquess."

"He has a heart," he muttered. "Somewhere."

"Of course he has one," she said. "He simply has never used it."

"Would you like to know what I've heard about Miss Wright?"

"Not particularly." And she bent down to retrieve the now-soggy bit of paper the changeable wind had pushed to the sand.

"I've heard she's quite ugly. Has a large wart, right here," he said, pointing at his nose.

"You've heard no such thing," Katy said, standing up quickly. "She's quite lovely, actually. And brilliant. As a matter of fact, she'd much rather go to university than marry some old duke."

Gray gave a mock shudder. "I'm certain Lord Avonleigh could change her mind. He's neither old nor a duke."

She laughed and started walking back the way she'd come, before turning to face him once again. "I'm afraid I'm not in the business of matchmaking. Miss Wright wants nothing more than to return home and get away from all these pompous, self-involved prigs. It was a pleasure meeting you, Gray the valet."

Graham watched her, a bit of panic striking him unawares. "Shall we meet here tomorrow? At the same time?"

She whirled about and tilted her head as if solving some great problem; then her expressive eyes flashed. "If I can get away from my duties, then yes."

Graham smiled, fully and wholly, his cheek muscles straining with the uncharacteristic exercise. He watched her until she was swallowed up by the summer crowd, until even the silly feather on her hat was not visible.

Chapter 2

"Sir, what is wrong. You look . . . happy."

Graham gave his valet, Mr. Chase, a withering look as he removed his jacket.

"I do apologize, sir," Chase said, taking the jacket before Graham could toss it on the settee, "but I happened to look out the window, overcome with curiosity as to what it was that had you in such a tizzy . . ."

"I was not in a tizzy."

"I happened to look out the window and saw you talking to a young lady."

Graham pulled off his tie and threw it on the settee, getting a small bit of satisfaction at Mr. Chase's annoyance. He decided to ignore Chase, even though he realized such a feat would be impossible. For some reason, his valet saw himself more in the role of surrogate father than employee. Perhaps because Graham had so much been in need of a father since his had died tragically fourteen years earlier. Mr. Chase was the only one who knew the depths his despair had reached, the only one who knew the truth about his father.

"The young lady in question seemed to quite engage your attention."

Graham's collar joined his cravat with a satisfying *plop*. "Spying on me, were you?"

"Hardly, sir. But it is one of my duties as valet to ensure your safety."

"It is not and you know it."

"Be that as it may, my lord, it appeared as if you—I can hardly credit it—were laughing."

Graham gave Chase, whom he'd known since he was in short pants, a level look. "And?"

"It was rather singular, sir. That laugh. And that girl. Such an ordinary one, at that."

"She was hardly ordinary," Graham said softly, ignoring his valet's uplifted brows.

"Of course, sir." Mr. Chase was silent for a moment. "Sir?"

"Yes, Chase."

"Such girls, well . . ."

Graham took a deep breath, knowing what his old friend was hinting at. "She doesn't know who I am. She thinks I'm a valet."

Silence. "Sir, if I may speak frankly."

"I cannot stop you, so proceed."

"Why? You are not the type of man to trifle with a young lady who, shall we say, is not a social equal."

Graham shook his head slowly, trying to make sense of what he'd done. "Damned if I know. Something in the sea air, I suppose. I'm seeing her tomorrow." Perhaps he was doing so to disprove the theory that he hadn't a heart, though what he would prove by pretending he was someone else, he didn't know.

"Do you think it wise to see her again, sir?"

"Not in the least."

Katherine walked back to her hotel feeling an excitement stirring in her that she'd hadn't felt for years. What had possessed her to lie to that man? And worse, what had possessed her to agree to see him again? Had she gone mad? No, she realized with honesty, she'd been charmed by a handsome man with a fascinating accent and striking eyes. And if he'd known who she was, he would have changed, treated her as if she were an untouchable bank account rather than a girl.

It was wonderful for a man to see her, to be interested in her, and not her family money. Yes, that was it, the heady realization that a handsome man might actually want to spend time with her. Even though she knew it was wrong, to go gallivanting about on her own unchaperoned, Katherine also knew it would take a hurricane advancing on the shore to stop her. She pushed down a rather strong wave of guilt about lying to her mother. But didn't she deserve a bit of fun? And not the kind of "fun" she'd been forced to endure since her coming out, the endless balls, the boring suppers, the tedious luncheons. No, this was different, this was an Adventure.

Katherine walked into the hotel, completely unaware of the people who looked at her breezing by. She rode the lift up to the sixth floor, humming the same song the band had been playing earlier. Then, seeing no one in sight, she lifted her skirts and ran down the hall to her room, leaving behind a small trail of sand. She burst into her room and started laughing.

"What happened?" Clara asked. "I saw you talking to a man. Who was he?"

"Lord Avonleigh's valet."

Clara furrowed her brow. "It wasn't!" The two of them had shared more than one giggle talking about the renowned Lord Avonleigh, who was said to have never smiled at a female. His legend had grown to the point that debutantes were making complete cakes of themselves in a misguided attempt to make the stone-faced curmudgeon grin. This, she had learned in her two months in England. She shared everything with Clara, and the Legend of Lord Avonleigh, the Miserable Marquess, was the one they enjoyed the most.

"Oh, it most certainly was his valet. He claimed Lord Avonleigh isn't as heartless as his reputation would suggest. And, Clara, you won't believe what I told him. I can't fathom why I would do such a thing. I told him I was Katherine Wright's maid."

Clara's eyes grew even wider. "You didn't!"

"I did," Katherine said, letting out a laugh. "And I agreed to meet him tomorrow. Can you believe I would do such a thing?"

Katherine expected Clara to be just as thrilled with her adventure as she was, but she was surprised to see her maid frown. "I don't think you ought to. It was one thing to walk alone along the beach, but it is quite another to meet a man in secret."

"It won't be in secret. I'm telling you."

Clara lifted her chin. "Will you be telling your mother then?" As a guilty flush stole over Katherine's face, Clara let out an "Aha."

Katherine, feeling much less excited about her adventure, walked to her bed and sat down. "I suppose I shouldn't see him. I suppose it would be wrong." She let out a long breath. "But he was so beautiful. The most beautiful man I've ever seen, and I don't really see what harm could come of going for a walk tomorrow and just happening to run into him."

"Handsome, was he," Clara said, sounding cautious.

"The most handsome. Of course, nothing could ever come of it. I live in America and he lives here. If he knew who I truly was, he'd want nothing at all to do with me. These English are so conscious of class."

"Perhaps . . ." Clara began and stopped. But those two syllables gave Katherine hope.

"Perhaps what?"

"Perhaps it would be all right. You're a good girl, who knows right from wrong."

Katherine grinned. "Yes, I do. And I might never have a chance again to be, well, to be me. At least while we're here in England." She lifted her nose in the air and took on the persona of her hated governess, Miss Smythe. She was English (her mother had hoped she'd acquire a bit of an upper crust accent), and she'd disdained everything American—including Katherine. "Back straight, do not slouch. Do not laugh aloud. Do not cry. Wear your best. Do your hair. Try not to sound overly intelligent. Try not to look too interested. Or interesting." She slumped a bit. "It's all so tiring."

"All those coins just weighing you down," Clara said, then laughed when Katherine frowned.

"I know I shouldn't complain," Katherine said. "I'm luckier than most. I do know that."

"Even expensive shoes can be difficult to walk in," Clara said philosophically.

"You are brilliant, do you know that, Clara?"

"Or dumb as a cow for not running to your mother right now to tell her what you've been up to. And what you're planning."

That night, Katherine had a sedate dinner with her mother, who continued to complain about her illness, which only added to the guilt Katherine was feeling. Her mother, despite her dislike of Brighton, was sincerely disappointed that this trip hadn't been a great success.

Her mother only picked at her food, making Katherine feel worse. Apparently walking in the sea air greatly increased her appetite, and she was famished.

"Are you going to eat your beef, Mother?"

"My stomach just cannot tolerate meat right now. I'll just sip my tea."

Indeed, since coming to England, her mother's headaches had worsened considerably and Katherine had begun to worry. Elizabeth had always suffered from an occasional headache that meant a day spent in bed, but she'd never been one to stay abed for days on end. Perhaps the very air that was making her so hungry was making her mother ill.

"All you do is drink tea, Mother. You'll waste away." Katherine eyed her mother, who looked rather hale and hearty for a woman who'd spent the day abed.

"I have plenty of pounds to lose before I disappear completely," Elizabeth said with a smile. "I believe the sea air disagrees with me, but I won't have to suffer it much longer."

"Oh?" A shot of joy filled Katherine as she hoped her mother was hinting they could return home.

"Lady Haversly sent me an invitation to a house party. We leave in four days."

Katherine swallowed her disappointment. "A house party? How wonderful."

Obviously, she'd failed to fool her mother, who said, "It very well may be wonderful. I've heard there will be quite a variety of people invited."

"Dukes and princes, I suppose," Katherine said on a teasing note.

Her mother raised one eyebrow. "A whole host of titles seeking rich American brides. I'll be in heaven."

She wasn't coming.

Graham stood by his window, looking down the beach, his eyes searching for a yellow hat and blue feather bobbing in amongst the crowds. He tapped his chin softly and relentlessly with the knuckle of one hand, feeling his gut twist in disappointment. And hating that his gut twisted in disappointment. Why would he put so much stock in whether some maid failed to meet him? Perhaps because yesterday had been the first time in years that he'd laughed with such abandon. While those stories about him were surely exaggerated, he was honest enough to realize they weren't so far off.

And then he saw her—not wearing the little hat with the blue feather, but a large one made of straw, affixed to her head with a wide yellow ribbon tied to one side of her jaw. His relief was ridiculous. He smiled as she stopped to help an elderly man retrieve a handkerchief that flew out of his hand in the stiff sea breeze.

"She does seem to have a certain charm about her," Mr. Chase said from behind him. "I'll give her that."

"So kind of you, Chase. I am off. I will be back in time for dinner." Graham couldn't stop the grimace. He was dining with an old Cambridge classmate—Charles Lynch—one he hadn't really cared for then and one he didn't want to spend time with now. They had bumped into one another in the lobby, and Graham could hardly refuse the man's invitation. He hadn't been quick enough on his feet to come up with a viable excuse.

By the time he got to the jetty where he'd met her the day before, she was already there, staring out to sea. She looked like a Monet painting, all brightness against the darker blue of the ocean and sky. A long, curling strand of red-gold hair had escaped her hat, and he had the urge to step close enough to her so that strand would touch his face. She didn't turn when he walked up beside her, but he knew she sensed his presence.

"I think I should like a home on the ocean," she said. "I never get bored looking out. It changes every day."

"I have a home by the Black Sea," he said, then grimaced. "I mean to say, Lord Avonleigh has a home. I have a room. A small one."

She looked up and gave him a curious little smile. "It is difficult not to think of these places as ours, even though we are simply employees, is it not?"

He'd actually never given it a single thought. Chase was such a part of his life, he'd never wondered, not once, whether or not he liked not belonging anywhere, not owning a bit of land. Most people in England did not own land, of course. But did they want to?

"Do the Wrights have a home on the ocean?" he asked, choosing not to answer her question.

"Yes and no. They own a lovely cottage on Long Island, but you can't see the ocean from the house. You have to walk along a sandy path in the woods to get to the water. I think I'd prefer to see the ocean from my window. The Wrights rented a house in Newport last summer, right on the Atlantic. It was lovely."

"And did you like Newport?"

She shook her head. "I didn't care for it, to be honest. And neither did Miss Wright. It's very stifling there. Very proper. And Miss Wright isn't entirely proper. I much prefer Brighton." She turned and motioned down the beach, which was filled with people—some wealthy, but most not.

"Miss Wright isn't proper?"

She bit her lip. "Oh, she's very proper. That's not what I meant. It's just that there are so many rules to follow in Newport and New York, and she doesn't like to follow the rules. But she does follow them in the end." She let out a short breath. "Poor girl."

"Poor," Graham said. "From what I've heard, that adjective does not fit Miss Wright. And the fact that she is here hunting for a title tells me more about her than I need to know."

She turned fully to him, bemused by his passionate speech. "How presumptuous you are. Especially for a man whose own employer is hunting for an heiress. Rather hypocritical, if you ask me."

"Many members of the aristocracy cannot stomach the idea of marrying American heiresses, but they have no alternative."

She lifted one eyebrow. "They could work for a living," she said pointedly. "You do."

Graham felt frustrated and more than a bit angry—with himself and with her. He'd been looking forward to seeing Katy all day, and now that he was with her, they were simply arguing. It was not what he'd imagined. "It would take fifteen men fifty jobs to make the kind of money that is needed to sustain some of these estates."

She dipped her head, her brow furrowed. "It's as bad as all that?"

"Actually worse," he said, his voice softening. "And the aristocracy is not blameless. They squandered money and opportunity. There is a sense of entitlement for many. It can be maddening at times. The fact remains that these estates, including Lord Avonleigh's, are vital to the well-being of hundreds of families—families who are suffering for the aristocracy's mistakes. To be fair, no one accurately predicted the agricultural depression we are having. No one knew the price of wheat and tin and copper would fall so drastically."

Her intelligent eyes moved over his face, and finally she smiled. "It's good to know and understand two sides of the coin, isn't it now?"

"It is. And now that we've attempted to solve the world's problems, I would like to celebrate with an ice cream."

She grinned, her eyes sparkling, and he swore his heart stopped for just a moment. "I adore ice cream," she said, and clapped her hands together. He offered her his arm, and the two walked along the beach toward the pier where the ice cream was sold.

"How long are you in Brighton?" she asked, her hand firm and warm in the crook of his arm. He felt unaccountably happy, to be strolling along with a pretty girl on his arm. It was such an ordinary thing to do, and yet it was the first time in his life he'd done so without the ceremony and watchful eye of a mama or stern chaperone. The band was playing "The Flying Trapeze," and he whistled along with the tune, gaining another smile from Katy.

"Just seven glorious days and three of them have already passed," he said, stopping his tune only long enough to answer.

"I don't know how such a cheerful man can work for such a dour one," she said. "Even when we were debating the cause of the aristocracy's problems, I detected a small smile."

"I am not usually so cheerful," he said ironically. He could hardly remember a time in his life when he felt so content. Not even that depressing thought could stop his smile. "And Lord Avonleigh is not so dour. Not all the time. Especially lately."

"Oh? Has he found himself a rich heiress?" she asked, clearly teasing.

"Something like that, I suppose. He has made no formal offer."

Her eyes grew wide. "Who? I daresay I'll know of her."

"I believe it is a Miss Von Haupt."

Her mouth opened slightly. "Claudia Von Haupt? Oh, that is simply delicious."

"Delicious."

"You see, Claudia has absolutely no sense of humor. Her smiles are as vacant as her head." She pressed her fingertips against her lips to stop from laughing, but a few giggles found a way to escape.

Graham stopped still and let out a laugh, one that sounded not quite so rusty as the previous ones. "What an apt description," he said, still chuckling.

"She is beautiful," Katy allowed. "But isn't it fitting that a man who never smiles should marry a woman who smiles but doesn't understand *why* she's smiling." She squeezed his arm, innocently pulling it against the softness of her breast. It was not a calculated move in any way, but his body responded as if it were. Graham swallowed hard and cleared his throat, trying to get his body in line. Perhaps the ice cream would cool his thoughts.

Katherine waited while he stood in line to get their ice cream. She breathed in the salty air that was tinged with the sweet smell of ice cream, wonderful summer smells. Beneath her feet, little plops of melted ice cream clung to the sand, for it was a warm day. Gray returned, holding two paper cones filled with vanilla ice cream, his knuckles already sticky from the melting confection.

"I've never had a paper cone before," she said. "We've metal ones in America. Or glass."

"These are called hokey-pokeys," he said with a grin. "I do believe ice cream tastes better in paper."

Katherine had no real idea how old Gray was, but at that moment he looked like a teenage boy, his cheeks flushed from the wind and sun, his gray eyes sharp and bright beneath his straw boater. He looked freshly shaved, and his clothes, while casual, were impeccably clean and pressed. She imagined a valet would know how to take care of garments and would present a polished look more so than other working men.

She watched as his eyes dipped to her mouth, and she felt a sudden warmth flood her body. Oh my. Forcing her eyes to the sea, Katherine took a deep breath.

"You have a bit of ice cream on your nose," he said, his voice close to her ear. Too close. Was that his warm breath on her face, or was it the sun? She stayed still as he took an index finger and wiped it away. And stopped breathing completely when she felt him leave the errant drop on her bottom lip.

He stepped back, suddenly, almost violently. "I do apologize," he said, his voice sounding strained.

She turned her head to look at him, feeling confused and embarrassingly aroused. She shook her head slightly, to clear her head. But she could still feel where he'd placed that tiny bit of ice cream, and couldn't help but lick it away. His gaze dipped to her mouth, and his gray eyes darkened. Then, as if to erase what she'd just done, as if they'd kissed, she wiped her hand against her mouth, removing any remnants, trying almost desperately to rid herself of the raw feeling his touch had given her.

"You should only apologize when you offend," she said, shocking herself with her boldness. What had come over her? She was not this girl, this girl who wanted a man to touch her again, who wanted him to lean in and kiss her. She immediately took a step back, her brow furrowed. "I shouldn't have said that. I don't know why I did."

But he took a step closer, his eyes, if possible, even more intense. "I want to kiss you," he said fervently.

"I've given you the wrong impression," Katherine said. She glanced at her hotel, praying Clara was not looking out their window. Or worse, her mother.

"No, you have not," he said, laughter in his voice. "Not at all."

She started to protest, but he interrupted her.

"I can honestly say I have never acted so impulsively in my life. Never. It is the sea air. It makes one a bit freer than one would normally be. I know you are a good girl. And I am a good man. But I am standing here, looking at you and wishing I could kiss you even though I know I cannot. And you are standing there wishing I would kiss you. Even though you know if I did, you would likely slap me for it. Is that about right?"

Katherine nearly denied what he was saying, but instead let out a laugh so full of joy, passersby stopped to stare. She lifted her ice cream in a mock toast. "To the sea air," she said. He bowed slightly and lifted his own, and they finished their treat grinning at each other like a couple of fools.

When the ice cream was gone, Gray handed her a clean handkerchief so she could wipe her face and hands. She tried to give it back, but he shook his head. "You can return it laundered, tomorrow." Another meeting set.

Tucking the cloth into her sleeve, Katherine nodded, trying desperately to retain some sort of dignity when all she truly wanted to do was smile. "I really must be going," she said, again glancing at the hotel.

He nodded, terribly formal. "I was wondering," he said. "Have you ever taken a stroll at midnight along the beach? It's quite different when no one's about. I often do, you know."

It was as if a great bellows sucked the air from her lungs. "Do you."

They stood there, two grins slowly growing on their faces, and Katherine knew that nothing, barring a death or disaster, would keep her from the beach that night.

Chapter 3

As it turned out, despite her mother's claims of imminent death, no one died and the night was clear. Her mother said she was too ill to even eat in their little dining room, leaving Katherine—once again—to her own devices. If she didn't know better—and she did—Katherine would have thought that her mother knew about Gray and was actually sanctioning this wildly inappropriate meeting. All evening, she'd been debating with herself, and her practical, intelligent side seemed to win every argument.

He wanted to see her in the dead of night. At a time when no respectable woman would dare to venture out alone. Never, ever would she even consider such an adventure if she were in the States. What was it about Brighton that was causing her to act so impetuously?

She could not go. Could. Not.

He'd said aloud that he wanted to kiss her. Oh goodness, she thought, her insides melting like ice cream in the Brighton sun, he wants to kiss me. The most handsome man she'd ever met in her life wanted to kiss her. It didn't matter that he was a valet and she was pretending to be a maid. It didn't matter that in just three days she would leave for a house party and never see him again. Why didn't it matter?

Katherine folded her hands together as if she were praying, although holy and chaste thoughts were the furthest things from her thoughts at the moment. Instead, her mind conjured the feel of his index finger upon her bottom lip, the look in his beautiful eyes when he'd told her he wanted to kiss her. The sound of his laughter, the tune that he'd whistled.

No, the sensible, intelligent girl who argued so fervently for her to remain in her rooms was losing this argument. She could hardly hear that girl over the beating of her heart.

"I'll be turning in now," Clara said, eying her suspiciously.

Ever since she'd returned from her walk, Clara had been shooting her disapproving looks. But she didn't care, didn't care, didn't care.

Katherine casually looked at a wall clock. It was nearly eleven. Her stomach gave a wonderful little leap. "All right, Clara. Good night."

Clara took a step, then hesitated. "Good night, then."

She smiled at her maid. "Good night. See you in the morning." And then she sat and picked up a book as if she intended to read for a time. The door between their rooms snicked closed, and Katherine let out a sigh of relief. She'd wait forty-five minutes and then get dressed. And then . . .

No. She couldn't. She could not meet a virtual stranger at midnight knowing full well he would kiss her.

"Yes. I can," she whispered, and felt a thrill go through her.

"Sir?"

"I'm going for a walk, Chase."

His valet snapped his watch, a gift from Graham's father, open and made a great show of looking at the time. "It's nearly midnight."

"I'm aware of the time."

Mr. Chase remained silent for a few, blessedly long seconds. "You'll ruin her."

"One cannot fully ruin a maid, can one?"

Mr. Chase's face tightened, and he compressed his lips so tightly, the area around them turned white.

"Good God, Chase, do you forget who I am? Would I ever compromise a girl, no matter her station?"

Mr. Chase took an angry step forward. "But that is precisely what you are doing."

"No," Gray said with force. And he was honest enough to realize that he was saying it forcefully as much for the valet's benefit as his own. He did not want to compromise this girl. He rather liked her. He . . . well, hell, he didn't want *anything* to hurt her. Not even him.

"Chase, I cannot explain it . . ."

"Oh, good God."

"Don't 'good God' me."

"You're falling in love with her," Mr. Chase said, his voice tinged with something that sounded suspiciously like an accusation.

"Don't be ridiculous. I've only known her for two days."

Mr. Chase sat down, deep in thought. "Sir, may I speak . . ."

"Yes, yes."

"I've known you since you were a boy. You are the most level-headed young man I've ever known. You never act impulsively. Ever. Even on your birthday when you were a boy, you would calmly wait for your presents. You never disobeyed your father. You rarely argued, and when you did, you were almost always on the right side of it." He spoke to himself, as if he were trying to work out a great puzzle. "Let's see how this plays out, shall we?"

For some unaccountable reason, Graham actually felt moved. "I wasn't seeking permission," he said softly.

"Weren't you, sir?"

He probably had been. Damn it. "I won't hurt her."

"At the moment, sir, she's not really my concern."

Graham told himself over and over that she would not be there, standing by the jetty when he arrived. But she was, an oversized jacket over her brown dress. She appeared completely nondescript, until she turned and saw him and smiled.

"Good evening, miss. Care for a stroll?"

"I shouldn't be here," she blurted, clutching her arms about her.

She's nervous, he realized, with a twinge of guilt. No doubt she'd get sacked if the wealthy Miss Wright discovered her maid had sneaked out to rendezvous with a man. What kind of cad was he to put her in such a position?

"No. You shouldn't. More importantly, I should not have asked it of you."

She let out a laugh. "More important is why I am here."

"Why *are* you?"

She shook her head, charmingly bewildered. "I suppose," she said, weighing her words carefully, "it's because you asked."

"Because I asked. If I asked you to go to Scotland with me, would you?"

"No, I wouldn't," she said, smiling. "It's Brighton. It's magical." She turned and looked at the sea, shining in the moonlight.

"And here I thought it was my charming self."

She tilted her head, studying him. "You are charming. Or perhaps it's simply your accent. We Americans think your accents are so appealing. You make everything sound special."

"Please allow me to escort you back to the Grand, Miss Katy. And please accept my apologies for asking you here in the first place."

"Only if you promise not to think too badly of me for accepting. I nearly turned around and then thought of you here, waiting, heartbroken. And so I came."

He held up his arm for her to take. "I'm so obviously smitten, am I?"

"Oh yes," she said. "I pictured you returning to Lord Avonleigh's suite in tears. Perhaps drowning your sorrows with his fine brandy and then getting fired on the spot. How could I live with myself if that were to happen?"

"With great difficulty."

Katy laughed, so glad he was such a gentleman. She'd been completely truthful. She had actually turned around to go back to her room, then forced herself to come, imagining him waiting there in vain.

The street that bordered the beach was busy with traffic, but the beach itself was nearly deserted. Music filtered to them, ebbing and waning as the pub doors opened and closed. A cool breeze buffeted the pair as they made their way slowly to the hotel, brightly lit and welcoming. As they walked, she told him about her summers at a place called Stony Creek in New York. Her summers with her grandparents sounded decidedly middle class, and Graham felt a twinge of guilt. He could hardly regale her with tales of his own childhood, with its lessons, private schools, and long, wonderful days wandering about Avonleigh. He walked beside her, mostly silent, delighting in her stories even though he remained quiet. This was so foreign to him, simply walking beside a pretty girl and listening to her chatter.

"Do you have any stories to share? I fear I'm dominating our conversation. Do you have brothers or sisters?"

"A sister," he said, without embellishing.

"Younger or older?"

"Younger."

Clearly, his limited responses were frustrating her, for she gave him an expression of exasperation. "And your parents?"

"Both dead. My mother died when I was quite young. I don't remember her at all. But my father . . ." He paused, bracing himself for the pain he always felt when he thought of his father. "My father was a great man," he said, softly. "He died fourteen years ago, when I was nineteen."

"You're as old as all that?" Katy said.

"Quite middle-aged," he said lightly, and she laughed.

As they got closer to the hotel, he felt her slow her pace.

"We leave in three days," Katy said. "And we shall never see one another again."

He didn't like that thought, not at all, but he was intelligent enough to realize how foolish he was acting, pursuing a girl he could never have. If he married, and it seemed almost certain that he would be forced to do so quite soon, he would have to marry someone who came with a large settlement. "Are you trying to delicately tell me how foolish it would be to spend more time together?"

She looked at him, giving him a grin. "It *would* be foolish. You already are quite smitten, and this can only end in your heart being badly broken."

He knew she was teasing, and was rather irritated that her words were far closer to the truth than he cared to admit. It wasn't as if she was sophisticated and classically beautiful. If he had to describe her, he might use words more like adorable or charming. She was a maid, for God's sake, and yet she drew him, and he didn't know why. Graham didn't like feeling so at odds with himself. "I had no idea my heart was so visibly on my sleeve," he said sardonically, and she frowned.

"I was only teasing."

"I'm not used to such teasing," he said honestly, sounding very much like the marquess he was, not the carefree valet he was pretending to be. It was almost comforting to remind himself of who he truly was.

He looked up and found himself at the edge of the light emanating from the hotel. He stopped, stepping away from her. "I supposed you expected romance and kisses," he said.

She looked up at him, confusion clear in her eyes at his abrupt tone. She shook her head. "I don't know what I expected, but certainly not the man standing in front of me."

He let out a harsh breath through his nose, frustrated and angry, though he truly didn't know why. "You should not have come."

"I'm fully aware of that," Katy said, her cheeks flushed. "Believe me, I will not be so foolish again."

Graham took a step toward her and stopped abruptly. "Good night," he said, but neither moved.

"Good night."

"Did you expect me to kiss you?" he demanded harshly.

"I . . . I don't know."

"Do you want me to kiss you?" he asked, far more quietly.

She shook her head, looking at him warily, as if he'd gone quite mad. He supposed he had. "No, I don't."

"Can I see you tomorrow then? At one? By the West Pier?"

Her eyes widened, as if she were quite surprised he'd even bothered to ask. "I don't think that is a good idea."

Bloody hell. What had he done?

"But . . ." she said, and paused. "I haven't thought very well since coming to Brighton."

He grinned when he realized she'd changed her mind.

"But you mustn't be so quarrelsome," she said with a warning note.

"I cannot guarantee that. I'm rather a quarrelsome person."

The sound of men's loud voices distracted him, and when he realized who it was, he grabbed Katy's arm and pulled her farther into the shadows.

"What is wrong?" she said, struggling to keep up with his long strides.

"Someone I know walked out of the Grand. He's an acquaintance. Of Lord Avonleigh's. I'd rather not have him see me, if you don't mind." That was all he needed, for Charles Lynch to see him and call out to him. If she was leaving in three days, he had but two full days left with Katy, and he'd be damned if they ended now. He stopped near the edge of the water and stood still, Katy in front of him, facing the sea but close enough that he could feel her warmth, breathe in her soft floral scent. Behind him, he could hear the sound of footsteps in the sand, and the men's voices getting louder. He drew her closer, one hand on each shoulder, his thumbs just grazing the soft skin on her neck. He wondered what she would do if he bent and pressed his mouth against her neck. Graham Spencer was not an impulsive man, but he was finding it rather difficult to resist that delectable bit of flesh just inches away. And so, he pulled her toward him and bent his head and tasted her.

At her sharp intake of breath, he stilled.

"Oh, do go on," she whispered.

He didn't like thinking about how those words made him so damned happy. "If you insist."

Chapter 4

Do go on? Had she gone quite mad? Oh, but it was so delicious to have his hands on her shoulders, his mouth on her neck. She wouldn't have thought such a simple thing would make her insides feel as if she were dissolving. She could feel his breath, warm against her neck, as he slowly made his way to the soft skin where her jaw nearly touched her ear. If these simple kisses made her feel like this, what would a real kiss do? She wondered what would happen if she turned now and let him kiss her mouth.

Such a dangerous thought from a girl who'd never truly been kissed.

He let out a ragged breath, and Katherine had the heady realization that he was as affected by the kiss as she was. "You, my dear, have the softest skin," he said, before trailing his mouth from her ear to the back of her neck. The flood of sensation she felt made her breath catch and her knees nearly buckle.

Male voices nearby made her stiffen, and Gray pulled away, but kept his hands upon her shoulders.

"Poor chap. I'd feel sorry for him if he wasn't such an arrogant bastard," a man said. His words caused his companion to chuckle.

"I'm afraid Avonleigh's not going to get much sympathy if what you're saying is true. He's not a favorite in the ton, is he?"

Katherine felt Gray's hands jerk a bit and knew it was because the men were obviously talking about his employer.

"Hardly. And mark my words, it is true. Heard it from Henley."

"Henley, you say? I'd hardly put much stock in it, then. Henley's just a rumormonger, you know that."

The men moved away, still chatting about Avonleigh and his finances, and Gray dropped his hands as Katherine turned.

"What a nasty pair," she said, searching Gray's expression for his reaction. But his face was impassive, as if the men had been talking about someone else entirely.

"This week has been rather enlightening in regards to my employer's reputation," he said thoughtfully. "No heart *and* no money, it would seem."

Katherine let out a small, uncertain laugh. "You weren't aware of his reputation?"

He shook his head. "Not entirely." He inhaled deeply, his eyes on the men who were now quite far down the beach. "Let me escort you to the hotel." He held up his arm gallantly, and Katherine took it, settling her hand naturally into the crook of his elbow.

He stopped at the edge of the light again and turned to face her, looking stern and almost angry, as he had before. "I would like to see you again," he said. "Tomorrow afternoon. And tomorrow evening." What a strange, commanding nature he had for a valet. Then again, perhaps when on equal footing, this was how all valets acted. Certainly, if he knew she was an American heiress, he wouldn't be quite so . . . haughty.

And then something shifted in his face, and he said, "You did agree." For a fleeting moment she saw a vulnerability that made her heart squeeze just a bit.

"Of course. If I can."

He stared at her grimly for a long moment before shaking his head. And then her heart nearly stilled completely, because he smiled. He was quite stunning when he smiled.

"Good night, Gray," she said, grinning back at him like a fool. He bent quickly and kissed her cheek, and she turned and hurried into the hotel, her entire body singing. She made the trip to her room more slowly this time, as the joy she was feeling started to dim with the realization that this was just a fleeting thing. She'd be gone in just three days.

* * *

Katherine tiptoed into her room carefully and silently closed the door behind her.

"There's no need for your skulking about, Miss Katherine." Clara stood in her room, her nightcap askew, her expression filled with exasperation. "Where on earth were you? I nearly had a fit when I saw your bed empty—and my coat gone. You were with him, weren't you? I know you are bored and I know you are a good girl, but to go out at night and—"

Katherine held her hand up, stopping her maid in mid-sentence. "I'm in love," she said, grinning widely, and Clara squealed and gave a small clap. Then, as if it suddenly occurred to her how ridiculous that statement was, she frowned.

"Oh, posh," she said, waving a hand at her employer.

"I *am* in love," Katherine said, throwing out her arms and twirling back onto her bed.

"You're no more in love than I am."

Katherine sat up and propped herself on her elbows, lifting one brow. "You have become jaded and bitter."

"Taking care of you has done that to me," Clara said, pulling out her button hook and attacking one of Katherine's boots.

"Here, I'll do that."

"Well, if you're going to marry a valet, you'd better get used to doing for yourself, I suppose," Clara said, and handed over the button hook, then watched as Katherine loosened her boots until they both landed with a thud on the floor. A good lady's maid would have immediately pounced on the boots, given them a quick polish, and put them away. Clara kicked them aside and went to fetch Katherine's nightdress.

Katherine pulled a face. "I'm not in love."

"You don't say."

"I'm infatuated. And a bit sad. He is very wonderful, in a dark, brooding sort of way."

"Heathcliff," Clara muttered under her breath. Katherine had read the book aloud with Clara some years ago, and the two of them had nearly swooned at the thought of Heathcliff.

"If he's Heathcliff, I'm certainly not like that Catherine. I'm Katherine with a *K* and we are a much nicer sort."

"Is he like Heathcliff?"

Katherine thought about it. "Well, he looks like I imagined

Heathcliff would look. Gray is very handsome. Probably the most handsome man I've met. But he's not quite as broodingly angry as Heathcliff. Then again, he hasn't fallen in love with me yet. And he doesn't know I'm completely unattainable." She threw the back of one hand against her forehead and collapsed back onto the bed. "So tragic."

Clara plopped down next to her, very unlady's-maid-like. "What if he does fall in love with you?"

"Oh. He won't. We're leaving in three days. He hasn't the time. We've only two nights left, and who knows if I'll be able to see him at all. Mother cannot have a permanent headache, can she?"

Clara muttered something about headaches, but Katherine ignored her. "He wants to see me again." Katherine could see Clara turn her head toward her, but kept her own eyes on the smooth, white ceiling.

"Do you think you should?"

"Absolutely. When will I ever have such an adventure again?"

Tucked in Graham's jacket was a dog-eared copy of a book the concierge at his hotel loaned to him—*Life Beneath the Waves and a Description of Brighton Aquarium*—when he'd informed the man of his plans. He'd wanted to tour the aquarium, opened just one year, ever since his arrival. And now, the prospect of touring it with Katy made him nearly giddy. Graham was a tad frightened by his obsession with the American girl, and thought perhaps it was because she was so completely unattainable. It gave him a bit of freedom to let down his guard, to be the man he perhaps would have been had he not been shouldered with such backbreaking responsibility.

Whatever the reason for this madness, he found himself grinning as he walked toward the Chain Pier, where he knew Katy would be waiting. He knew, because he'd spied her walking toward the pier, which was not far from the Albion where he stayed, her bright blue plume bobbing with every step. He couldn't wait to see her face when she looked at the creatures featured in the aquarium. No doubt it would be a new experience for her. He'd been to the Fish House in London, of course, but Brighton's aquarium was touted as both an architectural and scientific wonder.

The sun was a milky globe in a grayish sky as he approached the pier, immediately spying Katy among the others promenading near the pier. Of course, she wore the same hat she'd been wearing the first time they met, and the sight of it made him smile. If he were her beau, he would buy her more hats than she could ever wear in a lifetime, one more outrageous than the next.

He stood for a time, watching her watch the passersby, and vowed he would keep his title and his arrogance well hidden. He'd been an ass the night before and nearly frightened her away. He could still hear that breathy "do go on" and was amazed that he hadn't "gone on" nearly as far as he'd wanted to. He could not remember wanting a woman as much as he wanted Katy, but was not foolish enough to act on that desire.

"I could spot you in a crowd anywhere with that hat," he said, a smile in his voice and on his face.

She turned, grinning. "I do love hats," she said.

"Perhaps you should have been a milliner instead of a maid."

She looked away, and he thought for a moment he'd insulted her, but she recovered quickly from whatever insult he'd apparently given. "I have absolutely no artistic skill, but I do know how to recognize a piece of art."

Graham held out his arm for her to take. "Shall we? I thought we would visit the aquarium today." He pulled out the book, its pebbled black cover showing signs of wear. "Have you ever been to an aquarium before?"

"When I was a very little girl, my mother took me to the Barnum Museum. It was filled with all sorts of frightening things, and had a small aquarium. I was happy when it burned down, but I did feel sorry for the poor animals that were kept there. I remember seeing that glow in the sky and knowing something terrible had happened downtown. We found out the next day the museum had burned. It had the most gruesome exhibits." She shuddered slightly. "I was perhaps too small to have gone to such a place—I couldn't have been more than eight or nine—but it was all the rage and my father was quite enthusiastic about going."

He squeezed her hand, which rested in the crook of his right arm. "There is nothing gruesome about this aquarium. It's all sea creatures. But . . ." he said, gazing down at her lovely upturned face, "it is a bit dark, so you'll have to stay very close or risk getting lost."

She narrowed her eyes. "It seems you are always conspiring to keep me close, sir," she said, and attempted to maintain her stern countenance before breaking into laughter.

"You have found me out." They stopped, for there was quite a line of people waiting to go into the aquarium.

"It must not be a very large aquarium," Katy said, looking at the small building in front of them.

"The aquarium is below us," Graham said, and tapped his boot on the brick walkway.

After obtaining their tickets, they walked down a wide set of granite stairs that led to an open-air courtyard below street level. It was one of the grandest public buildings Graham had even seen, with a tall, arched ceiling that made the interior look more like a cathedral than a place of amusement. Ornate columns stretched from the gleaming marble floor to the ceiling, which was below the street; it was quite spectacular.

"Oh look," Katy said, pointing to one of the arches. "A mermaid. How charming." Indeed, every keystone in each arch was decorated with mermaids. "Wouldn't it be great fun if mermaids did exist?"

"You mean you don't believe in mermaids?"

"Nor fairies or goblins, either. I fear I'm quite practical."

Katy looked about the expansive room in wonder. Light from the street level, in addition to gaslight, made the cavernous room bright and airy. "It's a wonder that this entire place is beneath the ground. I never would have thought to visit the aquarium had you not brought me here."

As they left the courtyard and entered the exhibit areas, they suddenly found themselves in darkness, the only light emanating from the exhibits themselves. Graham felt Katy squeeze a bit closer to him, and he smiled. He leaned toward her ear and said, "Afraid of the dark, are you?" She looked up at him, her eyes wide, her face only inches from him. The darkness gave Graham a false sense of privacy, and he felt himself lean toward her, his eyes drifting down to her lips. He heard her short intake of breath, and was about to press his mouth against hers when a small child, pursued by his harried mother, brushed by, breaking the spell.

Graham stepped back, appalled by what he'd been about to do. He realized, now that his eyes had adjusted to the gloom, that anyone could have easily seen them had he been insane enough to actually kiss her. It would have been disastrous for both of them if someone he knew—which was entirely possible as this was a very popular exhibit—had seen him.

"That would have been a terrible mistake," he said, his voice low.

"Terrible," she said, her voice breathy and causing a spike of desire so strong, Graham took another step away from her.

Katherine felt as if she'd been drugged. Imagine wanting to kiss him in a public place. While it was quite unlikely that she would know someone in the aquarium, she still felt an odd thrill about the danger she was putting herself in. She was unchaperoned and walking about with a man who could not be more inappropriate. Why, it would be like going on an outing with her father's valet, Mr. Brock. Just the thought of that made her giggle, for Mr. Brock was nearly as old as her father and completely unappealing. She didn't know why she was acting this way, but every time that wave of anxiety flooded her, she pushed it away. She had a devil on her shoulder, whispering in her ear that no harm could come from walking on the arm of a handsome man. No harm could come because, after this week, she would never see him again. No harm because she would return home to America and he would return to his duties as a valet.

Oh goodness, surely she was cursed to perdition for acting this way.

She was keenly aware of his hard muscled arm beneath her hand, of the long, hard length of him as he stood beside her while they gazed at the beautiful dahlia anemones with their delicate pink-orange tentacles that did, indeed, resemble the dahlias they had in their garden back home. It was thrilling to be on the arm of such a man, but strangely comfortable, as if she'd known him for years rather than just two days.

After their tour ended, they had tea in the dining hall, chatting all the while, drawing glances from those around them. They spoke of their sisters, she about Lucy and he about Juliana, his determinedly unmarried sister who lived in Northumberland, shockingly alone in a pretty little house with a view of the North Sea. The two of them were a beautiful pair, and no doubt strangers looking at them would assume they were a young couple, just married, and very much in love. After tea, they went aboveground to find the air had turned a bit moister and a thin fog had settled on Brighton.

Gray looked up at the sky and frowned. "If it's raining, you don't have to come tonight," he said.

"I'm not a lump of sugar, you know," she said. "I won't melt."

"I'm glad you said that, because if you hadn't, I fear I might have barged into your hotel tonight and stolen you away." She laughed, delighted with the image. "My God, you're so beautiful when you smile," he said, suddenly serious.

"Then I shall have to smile all the time," she said with a jaunty tilt of her head. They walked around the outside of the aquarium until they reached a small souvenir stand.

"Shall we make a purchase?" he asked, eyeing the cheap knick-knacks and jewelry with paste stones.

"Her," Katherine said, pointing to a mermaid that appeared to be holding a rather large emerald. "Emeralds are my favorite stone."

Gray made the purchase, eying the mermaid skeptically. "You know, I have a suspicion this emerald may not be real."

"Truly? How much did you pay?"

"Threepence," he said, trying not to smile.

"Well, then, it is most assuredly real, is it not, sir?" she asked, directing her question to the man selling the items at the stand. He was clearly amused by their banter.

"Sure, and I'm the king of England, didn't ya know?"

Katherine gave the man her best curtsy. "Pleased to meet you, your highness."

Laughing, Gray drew her away, the necklace still in his hands. "Here, let me put it on you. I'm afraid the chain may turn your neck green."

"I don't care," Katherine said dramatically. "I shall never take it off."

"Then you will most certainly have a green neck." He smiled down at her as he reached around her neck and fastened the clasp. "Is anyone looking?"

"Why?" she managed to ask. Something strange happened whenever he looked at her the way he was looking just now.

"Because if I don't kiss you, I fear I shall perish."

Katherine looked round, seeing that the souvenir seller was staring at them with interest. "I'm sorry to say you are going to perish, sir."

"Don't stop on account of me," the man called over.

Katherine pressed her lips together, trying desperately not to laugh aloud. "And there are others. Those two women behind you are looking rather sternly at us."

"Very well," Gray said, stepping back with obvious reluctance. "I'll save my kisses for tonight."

Katherine surreptitiously looked at the large, ornate clock that chimed annoyingly on the quarter hour, as she tried to appear remotely interested in what Sir Rutherford Haverhash was saying. Her mother, who sat across from her and at an angle, kept jerking her head toward the man, as if directing her to pay better attention to his monologue on the importance of British sheep to the world economy. He was young, had tragically crooked teeth, and the sort of eyebrows that would one day need a good combing. Her mother could not be seriously considering this man as a possible son-in-law.

She forced herself to look at him and smile, and did acknowledge that he had the most striking pair of gray eyes she'd seen since . . . Gray's striking gray eyes. It was half past ten and they were only on the third of seven courses. She touched the mermaid necklace that she'd tucked beneath her dress. No one at this table would ever mistake it for a fine piece, but she liked that it was there, a solid reminder of Gray. How would she ever be done in time to meet Gray? She could plead a headache. Certainly her mother would empathize with *that* complaint. Miraculously, her mother's headache seemed to have dissolved, and she was having a markedly wonderful time sitting next to a gentleman who wore some sort of uniform. He was very dashing, with thick muttonchops and a mustache as grand as his rank of general. Her mother actually seemed to be flirting with the man, which Katherine found embarrassing and rather puzzling. She supposed a bit of harmless flirtation wasn't forbidden, even for mothers. Still, she wished her mother wouldn't laugh quite so loudly; she was drawing censorious looks from their British hosts.

A beet salad was placed in front of her and she took a delicate bite. Next to her, Sir Rutherford made short work of the salad, chewing noisily and making Katherine slightly ill. The clock chimed. She would have to leave in an hour if she were to have enough time to change out of her gown and into something simpler. At the thought of seeing Gray again, her heart picked up a beat. Silly heart.

"Woolgathering, are you?" Sir Rutherford boomed.

"All the talk of sheep," Katherine said dryly.

"Oh. I do apologize," he said, clearly not getting her joke.

"I was joking. *Wool*gathering. Talk of *sheep*."

He looked at her blankly for a time, then burst out laughing. "Oh yes. Sheep. *Wool*gathering. Oh, I do say that is quite funny. All that sheep talk." He calmed down after a time, and looked rather worried. "I wasn't boring you, was I? I do have a passion for sheep farming. We've been quite successful, you know. Five thousand pounds just last year, which, I don't mind saying, is an impressive income."

"Yes, it is," Katherine agreed.

"I've a nice estate. Nothing as grand as some. Not as grand as what you're used to, I'm sure."

Katherine felt panic growing that he was actually hinting he might want to court her. "I'm allergic to wool," she blurted. "It makes me sneeze horribly. And break out into hives. Can you imagine?"

"No, actually, I cannot," he said slowly, and rather coldly. Katherine realized, to her shame, that while Sir Rutherford might be a foolish man when it came to her and sheep, he was not a stupid one. He was angry with her and she couldn't blame him, but she didn't know how she could make amends without making him even angrier. Instead, she turned slightly to her left and pretended to be listening to a conversation her mother was having with another woman.

The clock chimed again, the salad was removed, and Katherine began her plan to have a bad headache come on very quickly.

It was drizzly outside and she was late. Thank goodness Clara had decided her adventure was more important than propriety. She would have to give Clara a spectacular Christmas present this year. If not for her maid's help, she could never have gotten her gown off so quickly and Clara's plain brown one on. Even Clara had winced at its plainness.

"I save that gown for when I'm helping the other maids clean right before one of your mother's big balls. I'd never wear that dress in public," she'd said, wrinkling her nose.

"I know, and I'm sorry I'm such a poor representative of your profession," Katherine said with a cheeky grin as she yanked her hair out of the complicated style that Clara had worked so hard on.

"Here," Clara said, grabbing a silk pink sash and securing it about her waist. She eyed Katherine critically. "There's no helping it, but it will have to do."

Katherine quickly put her hair into a simple bun, gave herself a cursory look in the mirror, and rushed to the door. "Goodness, it's already past midnight."

"He'll wait. The cad."

"He's not a cad," Katherine said. "He's smitten." With that, she closed the door, laughing at Clara's expression of amused disgust.

Now here she was, rushing down Brighton Beach, getting drizzled upon and praying she wasn't too late. Praying he was smitten, even though it was all meaningless. All for nothing. *I'll save my kisses for tonight.* She pushed that thought away as she squinted her eyes to see if she could spy him standing by the pier. There he was, pacing, head down, no doubt thinking he was a fool for waiting for a girl in the rain. He stopped when he saw her, straightening, and took the four broad steps toward her, closing the distance between them before stopping up short.

"Good evening," he said.

"Good evening," Katherine said. "Or rather, not. Unless one likes rain." From the look of him, he'd been out in the drizzle for quite some time. His coat was shiny from the rain and his hat dripped.

"I thought perhaps the rain would keep you away." He smiled down at her, seeming as happy to see her as she was to see him. "I'm glad it did not."

"This is not rain. This is mist. Heavy mist. And I rather like it. Not sugar, remember?"

"If you like this weather, you would fare well in London, where this is quite the daily event."

They stood three feet apart, not close enough to touch, but Katherine felt the terrible urge to lessen that gap, to embrace him. To touch his rain-dampened face as if she were truly his girl, as if they could have a future. As if he was simply a man courting a woman. But they were not, and a sharp needle of guilt stabbed into her heart. This was so wrong of her. This man had stood in the rain, likely for several long minutes, waiting for her, a woman he thought was a lady's maid. Waiting for a girl he perhaps thought might possibly be convinced to stay in England. A girl who liked the rain, and who liked him enough to sneak out at midnight to see him.

"I've a surprise," he said, taking another step toward her, then stopping as if encountering a low fence.

Katherine pushed the guilt away. "Oh? I adore surprises."

"We're going dancing. Come on."

With that, he grabbed her arm and pulled her toward the main thoroughfare, his grip firm and warm. She had to run to keep up with his long strides, and she started laughing, becoming breathless. "Is the dancing almost over?" she said between laughs.

"No," he said, stopping so abruptly she stumbled a bit. "But if we're dancing, I'll be able to hold you in my arms."

She was a drug. She was a fine brandy that burned his gut but drove away his demons. He remembered his friend, John Atwell, how he had been so obviously in love with Melissa before he'd admitted to that fact. And now, here he was all these lonely years later, finally, finally feeling a hint of what had driven John quite mad with longing. He could not have Katy. And yet, by God, he did want her. After *two days*.

He couldn't explain it any more than he could explain the universe. It simply was. He had only two more nights with her, and then she'd be gone. He would go back to his life, such as it was. He would marry Miss Von Haupt because she was rich and pretty and would give him rich, pretty children. He had to save Avonleigh, had to help his people. He would not be one of those peers who let their land rot and their people starve in run-down hovels while he went to balls and horse races. People depended upon him for their lives, and he would not put himself before their needs.

But tonight, this moment? He would live, he would dance with a lovely girl, and he might even allow himself to fall in love just a little, just to prove that he had that emotion in him—even if it was only a tiny bit and even if it was only for a brief time.

She'd arrived without a hat, her hair glistening from the rain, as if she wore a gossamer thin veil of diamonds. The small strands that framed her face curled becomingly, making her look even prettier. No one had ever looked up at him so guilelessly, so obviously happy to see him. It was heady. It *was* like taking that long drink of brandy.

As they got closer to the Brighton Arms, the music spilled out like the people, loud and raucous and not at all the kind of place a marquess would bring a lady—which was precisely why he pulled her inside. Pulled, because Katy did hesitate.

"It's so loud," she said, moving closer to his ear, pressing nearly the entire length of her body against his. Yes, he decided, this was the place they should be. It was loud and crowded with what Brighton could claim was a "better sort" of middle class—and not at all the sort of place Graham would normally be found. Brighton was not only famous for its bathing; it was also famous for its pubs and gin houses. Every street had several, and they were all filled to brimming nearly every night of the week. It was astounding, really. People here on holiday would go to a pub every night of the week and never dream of stepping through the threshold of a similar place back home.

A sea of people, men and women, sat and stood and laughed, while others danced raucously near the back. Though it was decorated as if for the aristocracy with its ornate carvings and gold-leaf paint, there wasn't a stiff upper lip in this crowd. There were no lords or ladies, just people having a grand time. Graham wasn't the sort who frequented even his own clubs in London, never mind a middle-class pub. He found himself smiling broadly as he realized no one was giving them a second look. Mr. Chase might not approve of his sneaking out at night to see Katy, but he'd been surprisingly accommodating when he requested his valet buy him clothing that would not stand out amongst the pub-goers.

He looked down at Katy, taking in her lively expression, one tinged with excitement and perhaps a bit of fear. Certainly she was not used to frequenting such a gin joint. It was smoky and loud, and the air was filled with the sour smell of spilt liquor and human bodies, and yet when he looked down at her, she smiled up at him as if he'd just brought her to Almacks in its heyday.

The music—a reel—was stridently played by a pianist, who banged out notes rapidly and expertly, and a fiddler, a toothless old man whose bow flew joyfully over his worn instrument. On the stage, a small raised section of the pub, four couples danced, swinging each other recklessly, yet somehow managing to avoid smashing into the other couples.

"Will you do me the honor of this dance?" he said, giving her his most proper bow. She laughed aloud, then curtsied like a true lady, giving her his hand. Then he pulled her rather roughly onto the stage and began whirling her around. Graham had always prided himself on his dancing skill, but it had been years since he'd danced with such abandon. And it was immediately obvious to him that

Katy never had. It took her at least three turns around the stage before she gave up and just let him spin and turn until they were both dizzy and out of breath.

Katherine had never had such fun. She didn't worry about what someone would think, that prying eyes were staring at her, that people were whispering frantically in one another's ears. No one here knew her or cared to know her. It didn't matter that her hair had come mostly undone from her loose bun or that her cheeks were flushed and dewy. She hardly cared that she liked the taste of the dark ale Gray bought for her, and she cared even less that the mug was water-stained and chipped near the handle. This is what is it like, she thought, to be ordinary. To not worry that your back isn't straight or that your dress isn't the latest style. Freedom. That's what she was tasting—and it was far headier than the ale she drank.

But most heady of all was the way this man was looking at her—as if she were the most beautiful girl in the world. As if everything she said was delightful and interesting—with no pretense. Was this what women did all the time? Did they go for walks along the beach and dance in pubs and drink ale?

"Thank you," she said close to his ear. "This is the most fun I've had in some time."

"Then I'm afraid you've led a rather sedate life, Katy."

"Oh, I have. Perfectly dreary. I've never been in a pub before. At least not as lively as this one."

Something passed over his face, and Katy was afraid it was regret, but it was gone before she could figure out what it was.

"Do you see the fiddler?" he asked.

Katherine leaned to watch the old man play. He was shorter than she, with a head as bald as a potato and a beard that made up for that empty pate. "He's very good," she said. And just then, he played a run that even the most accomplished virtuoso would have been impressed with—or threatened by. The room grew silent, as if they knew what was coming, and goose bumps formed on Katherine's arms as he began.

Within a few moments, Katherine's eyes filled with unshed tears as the music flowed over her and the rest of the silent crowd. "Brahms," she said softly, staring at this crooked little man, his eyes screwed shut as he played. Katherine looked up at Gray to find him studying her with a strange intensity, and warmth spread through her that had little to do with the incredible violinist in their midst. When he'd finished, those who were sitting jumped to their feet, clapping, shouting, and stomping their feet. The man smiled and took a bow, and then played a jig that soon filled the dance floor.

"Let's go," Gray said, taking her hand.

When they got outside, she breathed in deeply. The fresh sea air was wonderful after the myriad smells of the pub. The mist was gone, and the moon was actually shining through a break in the heavily clouded sky. "Did you know he could play?"

"Not as well as he did. But he had a technique that most fiddlers don't have. I knew he was classically trained."

"Oh?"

"The marquess is a bit of a music connoisseur, and I have learned much over the years," Gray said with a shrug.

With unspoken consent, they walked arm-in-arm to the seaside. As they left the lights and noise of the street behind them, Katherine became more aware of how dark it was, how late. And yet, she felt curiously safe. She shouldn't. How many of her friends would be doing what she was doing at this moment? Walking with a man she hardly knew, a valet, a member of the serving class. None of them. Not one. And if she told them, they would think she was making a joke. Her mother would be horrified, her father—incensed. She would most certainly be ruined. Then why was she taking such a horrid chance?

"You are quiet," he said.

She bit her lip. "I'm not who you think I am," she said in a rush, closing her eyes, willing herself to tell him the truth.

"I know," he said softly.

She stopped and looked up at him, surprised. "You do?"

"I know you are not the kind of girl to walk out by yourself with a virtual stranger. And I know you have never danced in a pub or drunk ale."

Katherine looked out to the blackness of the sea. What did it matter if he never learned who she was? She was leaving in two days—one now, for it was long past midnight. Why couldn't she have this one memory of a man who desired her?

"That is true. I have not. And I have never—" She stopped abruptly, willing herself to say what she truly wanted to say. When would she ever have this chance again, to feel this magic, this strange pull she felt for Gray? Gray the *valet*. Oh goodness. "—been kissed. Not really."

He grew still next to her, and she thought she heard a sharp intake of breath. "Not really? I'm not certain what that means."

Her cheeks flushed, not from her own boldness, but the memory she had of seeing the newly married Harringtons. She'd been just sixteen years old and visiting her grandparents in upstate New York and she'd come across the couple in a meadow having a picnic. Except, they hadn't been eating, they'd been kissing. Passionately. As if the world had disappeared, as if they could gain sustenance from each other. It had been been . . . riveting. Watching them had made her feel strange, a feeling she now better recognized as arousal.

"Of course I've been kissed."

"Of course." There was a smile in his tone. He came to stand in front of her, blocking the view of the sea. "But not truly kissed. Not like this."

And then his lips were on hers, pressing softly, insistently, creating an instant warmth that was most startling. Katherine pulled back. "Oh," she breathed. "Very nice."

"My God, Katy, *that* was not a kiss. Not a real one."

"It wasn't?" she asked weakly.

He shook his head, his eyes glittering from the gaslight on the boardwalk. "No. This is a kiss."

He drew her against him, pressing her full-length against him, so her breasts flattened against his solid chest. Then he took possession of her mouth in a way she could not have imagined. His hands enveloped her head and he moved his thumb on her chin, opening her mouth so he could gain access. His tongue was inside, touching hers, causing a rush of heat between her legs so unexpected, she moaned aloud. It was intoxicating, heady, and real. A real kiss. A kiss you would give your lover.

She pressed herself closer, feeling for the first time the hard ridge of his arousal—and froze.

"No," he muttered against her lips. "Don't pull away, my Katy. Don't."

His hands drifted down, skimming her sides, and moving to her backside, molding her curves and pressing her to him. He moved against her, an erotic pressing that sent her blood singing through her veins. It was as if another woman took over her body at that moment. She let out a sound of relief just as her arms wrapped around his neck and she opened her mouth fully to him, meeting his thrusting tongue with hers. He grunted in approval, one hand moving up between them to cup her breast. No man had ever touched her in this way. No man had pressed himself against her, had let her feel his arousal, had touched her breast. No man had ever moved his thumb over her nipple, making it come erect, making her want more. And though every sensation was new, it felt right, as if finally, finally her body was doing what it was meant to do.

Graham pulled his head away, his breathing harsh, and he rested his chin atop her head, fighting the fierce arousal she had evoked. Her hair smelled of lemon and was soft beneath his chin. He wanted her, wanted to lay her down in the sand and enter her. Taste her. Make her scream for him. It was pure insanity that he should even contemplate such things with her. Guilt pressed against this insanity, and he slowly pulled away from her.

"That certainly was a real kiss, wasn't it?" she asked, her voice slightly shaking.

"It was something even a bit more than that," he said with a soft chuckle. He grabbed her hand and dragged her laughing behind him as he ran along the hard-packed sand away from the Grand Hotel.

"Where are you going?" she said, laughing.

"Nowhere," he called back as she struggled to keep up. "Anywhere. To the moon." This last was a joyful shout, and Katherine smiled as she struggled to keep up with his long strides.

A shadow loomed in front of them, and Katherine realized it was one of the bathing machines. He let go of her hand and ran ahead, then jumped inside and turned to hold out his hand to her.

She stopped, suddenly wary. Kissing a man on a beach was bad enough, but to go into this vehicle—this extremely *private* vehicle—would not be a very smart thing to do. And Katherine might be a bit reckless, but she wasn't stupid.

He tilted his head and shook his hand. "No kissing. Promise."

She gave him a skeptical look.

"Promise."

"Isn't it trespassing?" she asked, looking warily past him to the sparse interior. He sighed, then sat on the edge, his legs dangling near the sand, and patted the wagon next to him. She supposed sitting next to him wouldn't get her into too much trouble. Goodness, she'd already snuck out at midnight to meet him, gone to a pub, danced, and drunk ale. Certainly sitting on the edge of a bathing machine couldn't do her any more harm than she'd already done. She hopped up and looked out to the sea, molten and silver beneath the moon.

"Tell me about your marquess," she said, wanting to know more about his life. "Is he a very demanding employer?"

"He is driven. Loyal." There was a long pause. "And lonely, I think."

Katherine turned to look at him. "Why do you say that?"

Graham shrugged, disliking where this conversation was going, but carrying on anyway. If he stopped talking, she might decide to end their evening, and he wasn't ready for that. Not yet. "He hasn't a lot of friends. Not close friends, at any rate. He takes his title very seriously, and his responsibilities."

"His father must have died quite young to have left him the title," Katy said, unknowingly causing a sharp pain in his breast.

"He did. The marquess was only twenty-one."

"How did his father die?"

Graham tensed, and then the strangest feeling of calm stole over him. No one knew how his father had died, except his personal physician and Mr. Chase. It had become such a heavy burden to carry. "He shot himself."

He heard her gasp and could feel her eyes on him. "Oh, how horrible. The poor man. And son. I cannot imagine."

"Only three people know the truth, and I am one of them."

"And you've told me. You needn't worry it will go further. I promise. What a terrible burden for you—and him—to hold all these years." She sat silently for a long moment and finally asked what he prayed she would not. "Who found him? Please tell me it was not his son."

Graham swallowed. "It was, as a matter of fact. He had just left to go back to school for his final semester. Cambridge. He was looking forward to completing the term and returning home. He was very close to his father, you see. But he forgot something. He got all the way to the train station and had to go back to get his pen.

A fountain pen his father had given him. It was a new design. Very special. He went back for it. He opened the door and heard the shot.

"I found him there. The son. He was holding his father's head as if . . . as if he might fix him somehow. I can still see it. Them." It had been Mr. Chase, of course, who had come upon Graham holding his father, rocking, back and forth. It had taken his old valet many long minutes to pry him away. He'd helped him to wash, taken his blood-soaked clothes and thrown them away. Burned them, as if he could burn away the pain of finding his own father that way.

Katy's only reaction was to grab his forearm and squeeze, as if somehow transmitting her strength to him. Finally, she said, "How awful for the poor marquess, to carry such a burden. If his father were alive, I'd slap him."

Graham looked over to her, surprised by her words. "I think he never would have done it if he thought for even a moment it would be his own son who found him. I believe that wholly."

"Yes, you are probably right. Did the marquess ever learn why his father took his life?"

"No," Graham lied. "He didn't."

They sat in silence for a long time. Katy had moved her hand down and he grabbed it, holding it there on the rough wood of the bathing machine. The night sky was still dark, now that the clouds had once again claimed the moon, but it was very late and Graham knew he would have to say good-bye. No doubt she would have to get up early to take care of her spoiled little heiress and would have little time to rest.

"It is very late," she said.

"Yes. And you leave the day after next. Or rather tomorrow. I'd forgotten how late it is."

She nodded and squeezed his hand.

"I wish you didn't have to leave," he said, before better sense could stop him. Hell, even if she didn't leave, he could never have her. He couldn't marry her, and he'd be damned if he'd shame her by taking her innocence and leaving her open to the possibility of having a bastard to raise alone. It was for the best that she go. He knew it, but damn if his ridiculous heart wasn't protesting.

"I will always remember you. Gray the valet. When I am back

home with all those awful American boys. I will remember my not-so-proper English beau."

He leaned over and kissed her cheek, lingering, closing his eyes. "Will I see you tomorrow before we say good-bye?"

She did not hesitate. "Yes," she said. "At midnight." And then she pressed a bit of cloth—his own handkerchief—into his hand.

Graham returned to his hotel room and sat down heavily on his bed and stared at his image in the mirror opposite. He almost laughed aloud at the man who stared back at him, that lovesick, rumple-haired commoner.

"Good morning, my lord." Mr. Chase entered the room, his white hair standing straight on end, wearing his nightshirt. It was rare, indeed, to see Chase not impeccably dressed, and the sight of him so unkempt tugged a bit at Graham's heart.

"I didn't mean to wake you," Graham said.

"I couldn't sleep, sir." Mr. Chase smoothed his rooster top down. Now, guilt tugged at Graham's heart.

"Pray tell me your insomnia wasn't caused by me," Graham said, pulling off his simple tie with a snap and crumpling it up in his palm. When he heard Chase let out a sharp breath, he tried, unsuccessfully, to iron out the wrinkles with his hand.

The older man stood in silence, studying him, making Graham feel like a boy who'd been out and up to no good. "I don't know what it is about her that fascinates me," Graham said finally, angrily. "I've known prettier girls. More sophisticated, certainly."

"Perhaps it is because she is out of reach," Chase offered.

Graham shook his head. "No. I could have her, you see. I could have had her this very night." Just thinking about how her body molded to his made him ache.

"Perhaps, then, you should examine why you didn't."

Graham raised his head and looked at his old friend. "I can't fathom why." He'd wanted to. God above knew he had. Never before had he felt that heavy ache and willingly withdrawn. Why? Why Katy? Because she'd been so unexpectedly willing even though he knew she was innocent? Because he had a deep suspicion that he had been the first to awaken her carnal yearnings?

Because she made him laugh?

Graham clenched one fist and pounded it against his thigh. He stood up and began pacing about the room, keenly aware of Mr. Chase's eyes following his progress curiously. He didn't like feeling out of sorts. He didn't like feeling as if he'd lost a part of him when she'd walked into that hotel. She was a maid, for God's sake, and an American maid at that. There wasn't a proper English lady who would even think of hiring her. He felt like a young boy with spots lusting after the chambermaid. It was abominable. He was a marquess, and marquesses—at least those with any scruples at all—did not bed servants. Ever.

"I'll make an offer," he said, thinking aloud. "I'll need a mistress once I marry." Yes, that was it. She could be his mistress. He could buy her a lovely home with a pretty garden. Filled with dahlias. She would have a small staff of servants and would want for nothing. He would be with her nearly always, returning to London and Avonleigh only when he must. He would have his heir and spare and then he would live out the rest of the days with Katy. She would balk at first, of course. Those American girls weren't used to such things. But he could convince her, he knew he could. It was the only answer. The only way to be truly happy and also gain the necessary funds by marrying that Von Haupt girl. He felt himself recoil inwardly at the thought of bedding that blank-faced doll-of-a-girl. Her expression rarely varied—it was always the same stare, mouth slightly agape, that made it entirely clear there was nothing going on behind those soulless eyes of hers.

"May I speak candidly, sir?"

Graham snapped his head. "Can I stop you from doing so?"

"Probably not," Chase said grimly. "I don't think it wise to arrange for a mistress during your betrothal negotiations. If word got out, it could end badly."

"Word would not get out," he said quickly. Ah, but it would. It always did. He would have to purchase clothes and jewelry for a mistress, and if those same items were not later seen on his new fiancée, there would be whispers. One could not let a house or purchase furniture without someone speaking of it. And unless they never left their home or he put Katy up in some remote Scottish manor house, he would eventually be seen with her by someone he knew.

Graham sat down heavily on his bed and leaned his head upon his hands. "It's just that I'm so damned lonely, Chase, and I don't see how marriage to Miss Von Haupt is going to change that." He looked up. "She's leaving tomorrow. I need to settle things with her. I can't let her leave."

Mr. Chase gently took the crumpled tie from his hand, and the older man studied him as if he'd gone quite mad. "If she agrees, then I would make the arrangements for you," he said finally.

"Thank you, Mr. Chase." It was not the best solution, but it was the only one in which he could know she would be his forever.

Chapter 5

"The Wrights are gone? What do you mean, they've left?" Graham demanded. He knew what he looked like, his hair windblown, his cheeks ruddy, his eyes no doubt flashing with anger. Graham was frightening the poor clerk, who was still young enough to have spots on his face but who was trying mightily to retain his dignity in the face of some commoner demanding to know where one of his wealthiest clients had gone.

"I do not need to explain what I mean. Not to you," the clerk said, his cheeks flushing.

In his most proper and clipped tones, Graham said, "I am Lord Avonleigh, and the Wrights are particular friends of mine. I was to meet with Mrs. Wright and her daughter this very evening for a late dinner, and when they did not arrive, I became alarmed. Now, if this hotel has done something to offend the Wrights, then I'm afraid I will have to—"

"No, no, my lord," the clerk stuttered. "I do apologize." He gave Graham's clothes a curious look.

"I'm on holiday," Graham ground out, as if that explained his middle-class garb.

The clerk brought out a heavy register and flipped through some pages, his eyes scanning the pages. "Yes, here we are," he muttered. "They were originally planning to check out tomorrow, yes indeed, but left unexpectedly this morning." The clerk looked up as if pleased with this announcement.

"And where did they go?" Graham asked with forced pleasantness.

The clerk's hand fluttered over the open register. "Oh. I really cannot say." At Graham's dark look, the clerk clarified quickly. "That is, they did not inform us of their plans. One moment." He disappeared through a door and returned a few moments later. "No, my lord. I do apologize, but they did not leave a forwarding address for us."

Graham stood there dumbly for a few moments, disbelieving that she was gone, that he would never see her again. Even if he found the Wrights, it would be nearly impossible to reach Katy to even have a conversation, never mind take the time to convince her to be his mistress. "Thank you, sir, for your help," Graham said, before turning slowly away from the counter. He reached into his pocket and withdrew the handkerchief she had returned to him the previous night. He brought it to his nose, praying it would still retain some of her scent, but not even a hint of her remained. She had disappeared.

"For goodness' sake, Katherine, stop moping," Elizabeth said, exasperated and entirely too cheerful.

"I'm not moping, Mother," Katherine said on a sigh. But she was. And it was more than mere moping. She wanted to cry, great sobbing gulps that she'd never be able to explain. What would she tell her mother? That she missed the sea so much she was distraught?

She loved her mother dearly, but she hated being subject to her whims. She never had a say in anything they did, and her mother would brook no argument. What could she have said? Please, Mother, we cannot go because I think I'm falling in love with a valet? She could hardly say that! Clara gave her a look of commiseration, but even she didn't know how purely devastated she was—and how foolish she felt to feel so purely devastated. She'd hardly known him. She'd shared but one kiss. Oh, certainly it was a magnificent kiss. The kiss she would no doubt measure all kisses in the future against. And he was so very handsome and lively and fun and . . . wonderful.

Perhaps what made this worse was knowing she would never see him again. Even if, by some coincidence, she ended up in the same room as the marquess, she could hardly approach that man and ask after his valet.

"It's for the best," Clara had said. "You know nothing could have come of it."

She'd swallowed past the lump in her throat—the lump that now seemed to be a permanent fixture there—and nodded her head, saying, "Perhaps you are right."

But Clara wasn't right. Katherine was twenty-one years old and had met scores of men and not one had made her feel even a smidgeon of what she felt with Gray. She'd never even gotten the chance to ask him if his mother had named him because of his remarkable eyes. She'd never gotten the chance to ask him all sorts of questions, such as whether he liked museums or if he'd read Dickens. Or if he liked children and ever thought of marrying.

And now she was going to have to spend one week at a house party with people she didn't know and be charming and pretend to be happy and suffer her mother's obvious matchmaking efforts. It was all so wretchedly tedious, and Katherine just wanted to go home.

"How much longer will it be?" she asked no one in particular. They'd taken the rail from Brighton to north of London and were now in a coach provided by Lord and Lady Haversly. She was exhausted from getting little sleep while in Brighton, as well as the trip north to Essex.

"I think we're very nearly there. I thought I saw us pass through a gate quite a bit ago," Elizabeth said. She was strangely cheerful and excited about this house party, which made Katherine nervous. Her mother was always scheming to get her in the same vicinity as anyone with a title. That was what their trip to Brighton had been all about, after all.

Thankfully, her mother hadn't gotten wind of the fact that the Marquess of Avonleigh was not four blocks from their hotel. She would have no doubt made a cake of herself trying to get an invitation. Part of Katherine felt sorry for men like Avonleigh, lords who were no doubt ill equipped for a modern world that required that men make their fortune themselves. Then to have women hounding them and coveting their titles had to be a bit distasteful. And no man, no matter how desperate, should be sentenced to a life with

Claudia Von Haupt. Still, how could she feel sorry for a man who was willing to marry a girl like Claudia just to get at her millions? She'd heard from a very good source—Clara—that the family was actually considering offering the marquess a dowry of one million pounds plus a ridiculous fifty-thousand-dollar-a-year allowance. He would probably sprint down the aisle for that sum. What man wouldn't?

Gray would live in better conditions with the marquess doing so well for himself. He would probably get more income, perhaps have more luxurious quarters. But he would still be a valet, and she would still be an heiress with a title-hunting mother. Katherine looked out the window and saw in the distance Briarbrook, the Haverslys' country estate. She shook her head at the size of it. "There's Briarbrook. It certainly is impressive."

Clara craned her neck to see the sprawling mansion, and she let out a long "oh" when she saw it. The home was a stately structure three stories high with windows on each floor that looked as if they went floor to ceiling. The grounds were impeccable, with a large expanse of green lawn stretching from the home to a small pond, where two swans, as if strategically placed, calmly drifted.

Her mother leaned forward to take a peek, then sighed. "Their son is married. Happily," she said, as if that were a tragedy.

"Mother," Katherine said. "You don't truly think I'm going to find a husband on this trip, do you? I thought it was a bit of a lark for you, but lately I've gotten the feeling that you seriously believe someone will make an offer."

Her mother looked at her as if she were a simpleton. "Why on earth do you think your father and I would have gone to such expense unless we were serious about finding you a title?"

Katherine sat back, stunned. Her mother was serious. How stupid of her not to have realized it, and yet she hadn't. This trip, while tedious but for Brighton, had seemed only to be something to get through; once it was over, she could go back to her life. Her mother had been quite clear what this trip was about, but Katherine hadn't thought her mother was so determined. She'd thought it was wishful thinking, a hope, not an all-out campaign to win a title.

"Will you be very disappointed if I don't find a titled man?" she asked. "Because I truly do not think it will happen. No one has shown any interest in me at all."

Her mother lifted one eyebrow. "That's simply not true," Elizabeth said enigmatically, and Katherine's stomach clenched.

"What are you talking about?"

Her mother laughed. "Oh, don't be so dramatic, dear. No one has made an *official* offer."

"How can anyone have made any offer at all? I haven't met a single man I would even consider courting, never mind marrying." Next to her, Clara let out a choking sound and Katherine gave her a subtle nudge.

The coach stopped. "Ah, here we are," Elizabeth said, ending the conversation and leaving Katherine frustrated. Her mother and her maid left the coach first, helped down by an impressive-looking footman in blue- and gold-trimmed livery, and Katherine turned to Clara, whispering, "Do you know what she is talking about? Has anyone made any kind of offer?"

Clara seemed just as baffled as she, but that did little to ease Katherine's mind.

In Katherine's experience, a house party lasted one day, perhaps even over an entire weekend (a term she had discovered marked her as an uncouth American). These English trekked about from party to party for the entire months of August and September. Her mother had said there were several more such parties on their schedule before the start of the Little Season, and the thought made Katherine's stomach twist.

After they'd been shown to their rooms—hers a sunny, yellow and white space overlooking the expansive gardens—her mother gleefully showed her a schedule that was mind-numbing. And also a bit frightening. It seemed reasonable to assume that the Marquess of Avonleigh would be found at one of these parties. The thought of being so close to Gray and being unable to talk to him was nearly unbearable. Would he see her and know she'd been lying? He would be humiliated, and no doubt think terrible things about her. And she'd deserve every awful thought.

"An infatuation," Clara had said with a knowing nod. "You'll forget him in no time."

Katherine wasn't so certain. She'd gone her entire life never becoming infatuated with a single man. Had she opened some sort of chamber in her heart that now allowed infatuations in more easily?

And, now this was truly silly, she felt it was more than an infatuation. That if they had been two different people in another time, they could have fallen in love. That was a thought she pushed firmly away.

She stood at the window, idly watching a gardener pluck dead leaves and flowers from the multitude of plants placed in a precise diamond-shape, and fiddled with the mermaid necklace.

What was it about Gray that had so captivated her? Was it the way he looked at her, those gray eyes that seemed to touch her? His lips that curved up slightly, as if he were constantly fighting a smile? The way she felt when he touched her? Oh goodness, she could still feel his lips on her neck, grazing the fine hairs at her nape, making her entire body feel as if it were melting into a pool of pure desire. She smiled at that thought—and then realized she was smiling at a young woman below her who thought she was smiling a hullo.

"Hello," she called down. The woman looked like a picture from a fashion plate, and Katherine grimaced inwardly. How would she ever attract a titled gentleman when her competition was someone like the woman standing below her? Her mother ought to take a good look at the lovely girl and book the first ship back to New York. The girl's dark curls and pale skin gave her that wonderful, soft complexion that English men seemed so enamored with. A cascade of silk ribbons flowed down the front of her champagne-colored gown, defining her trim figure.

"Do come down and join me," the girl called, then added, "You are the first person to arrive who isn't ancient."

Not wanting to shout, Katherine smiled and held out her index finger, indicating she'd come down to the garden in a moment. She quickly grabbed a straw hat and a light pair of gloves and hurried from her room. When she arrived, the girl was near the door, inspecting a late summer rose.

"Marjorie Penwhistle," she said with a nod.

"Katherine Wright. And as I'm new to England, should I be putting a 'lady' in front of your name?"

"Oh, an American. Wonderful. And yes, a lady will do nicely but only in front of my mother. I'll be certain to point her out to you. She has a perpetually sour expression and she loathes Americans. Which means you, darling, are my new favorite friend."

Katherine laughed, completely charmed by her forthright manner. "That would be wonderful. I haven't any friends in England as yet. At least none who will be at this party."

"What brings you to our fair isle?" Marjorie asked.

"My mother, God bless her, hopes to find me a husband. I do believe she is sure to be disappointed. If I cannot find a husband in New York, I've little hope of finding one here."

"A husband with a title perhaps?"

Katherine winced, but she found Marjorie's candor refreshing and not at all rude. She couldn't say for certain why she wasn't offended; perhaps it was the way Marjorie talked, as if she didn't care a fig what anyone did. "Yes. I'm one of those Americans. At least my mother is. Dreadful, isn't it?"

Marjorie waved a dismissive hand at her. "As far as I'm concerned, you can have the lot of them. I've been through three seasons and found not a single man with whom I could have an engaging conversation. My mother insists conversation between a man and a woman is not important, but I will not spend the rest of my days staring at the back of the *Times* at the breakfast table and listening to my husband grunt in answer to my questions until he dies unceremoniously in the bed of a housemaid." She said all this calmly, but she punctuated her sentence by swatting at a gnat with a resounding slap to her arm. Katherine looked at that little black corpse before Marjorie flicked it away and imagined it represented all those men who sat at the breakfast table reading the *Times*.

"You haven't found a single man you liked even a little?" Katherine asked.

"I like all of them a bit. But none of them in particular. And I imagine one would strive to like one in particular if marriage was in the offing." She looked directly into Katherine's eyes and asked, "And what of you? Have you found anyone in particular?"

Katherine hesitated just enough to make Marjorie smile knowingly. "You have, haven't you?"

"He was the most handsome man I've ever met. His name was Gray," Katherine said impulsively. It felt wonderful to talk about him with someone who didn't know the entire story as Clara did. "We met in Brighton. On the beach."

Marjorie grinned. "Do tell me more."

"My mother was ill much of the time we were there and I was dreadfully bored. I wandered down the beach one day. Unchaperoned."

"No," she gasped with satisfying horror and admiration. "Here, this sounds like a very good story. Let's sit," Marjorie said, and led Katherine to a small bench.

"It is a good story. A wonderful one," Katherine said. Once she was seated, she turned slightly toward her new friend and related the story of how Gray had rescued her from near drowning. She did like to embellish a bit when she told a story. She also knew enough about the British aristocracy not to divulge the fact that Gray was a member of the servant class, knowing that would be frowned upon even by the most tolerant. So she invented a man who was very much like the Gray she'd met, but made him simply a gentleman who'd happened to be in Brighton on holiday.

"I knew nothing could come of it, but the more I got to know him, the more I wished there wasn't such a divide in our stations," she said wistfully. "He is my Heathcliff, but with slightly less tragedy and drama."

Marjorie laughed. "Oh, I adore anything by the Brontë sisters. My mother dislikes such romantic fluff, but I must confess *Jane Eyre* is one of my favorite books. *Wuthering Heights* was a bit dark for me. All that palpable longing and such a dreary ending."

"It's never good when the important characters die, is it?" Katherine said, grinning.

Marjorie was thoughtful for a moment. "Do you really care for this man?" she asked tentatively.

Katherine examined her gloved hands for a moment before nodding. "If he'd been someone different, if *I'd* been someone different, I think we might have fallen in love," she said softly.

"Oh dear."

That "oh dear" didn't sound judgmental, but it occurred to her that she didn't know Marjorie at all and had just divulged her greatest secret. The cat was out of the proverbial bag, and she suddenly regretted saying a word about Gray to her. She knew from experience how spiteful other girls could get. Just thinking about what Claudia Von Haupt and her mother had done should have been enough to make her more cautious about whom she considered a friend.

"If you're worried I will tell anyone your story, you needn't be," Marjorie said, and Katherine looked at her with surprise.

"I was worried, actually. This has been bubbling up inside of me all day and I felt I needed to tell someone."

"But you don't know me."

Katherine shook her head, feeling foolish. "No, I don't."

Marjorie smiled. "You needn't worry. Everyone is entitled to one secret, aren't they?"

"Yes. One. Do you have one?"

Marjorie gave her an impish smile. "Of course, but I'm not foolish enough to tell a complete stranger." She laughed, and Katherine joined her. "Your secret is safe with me," she said once she'd gained control of herself. "You'll learn soon enough I don't have a spiteful bone in my body."

"I do," Katherine said feelingly, then laughed. She eyed the other woman's dress, hoping to turn the conversation to something less personal. "Is that a Worth?"

Marjorie looked down as if she'd forgotten which dress she wore. "Yes. Nothing but the best for me," she said brightly, but something about her tone made Katherine think Marjorie somehow resented that fact.

"My mother hopes to get me in to see Mr. Worth, but I truly don't care what's on my back as long as it covers me. I don't think we'll have time to go to Paris at any rate. Thank goodness Mother has an eye for current fashion because I am truly hopeless."

"You haven't an appointment?"

"I've told my mother he turns people away, but she's determined. One of our acquaintances has a daughter with a closet full of Worth, which she manages to insert into every conversation, I might add, and I think it drives my mother a bit mad at the thought that her own daughter doesn't have a single Worth gown."

Marjorie narrowed her eyes. "I think I may know this acquaintance."

"Truly?" Katherine asked, giving her a curious look.

"Perhaps a Miss Von Haupt?"

Katherine looked at her incredulously. "How on earth could you possibly know . . ." Then it dawned on her. "You've met them. Obviously." She tried to determine what Marjorie thought of Claudia, but couldn't read her. It wouldn't do to disparage Claudia if Marjorie considered her a friend.

"They are an interesting family," Marjorie said with obvious caution.

"Yes," Katherine said, just as cautious. "Very . . ."

"Ambitious."

The two girls grinned at each other. "She is the bane of my existence," Katherine said finally.

"I find her completely objectionable," the other girl said, seeming proud to have found just the right word. "I'm so glad you're not like her."

"Claudia and I have a bit of bad blood between us, I'm afraid, so I cannot be at all impartial."

"Oh?"

"Her mother—and I really cannot blame Claudia for this, even though she likely delighted in it at the time—prevented nearly everyone in New York from attending my coming-out ball."

Even now, four years later, it made her sick to her stomach to think about her mother's disappointment that night when only a handful of the people she'd invited—most of them elderly—walked through their doors. Her mother had spent weeks—and a great deal of money—planning the ball. At first, it had been as baffling as it was devastating when only a few of their guests planned to attend. Katherine had wondered if she were truly that disliked by all her friends. It soon became quite clear, however, that Suzanna Von Haupt had threatened and cajoled everyone on their guest list into not attending. Katherine had been stunned and hurt; she'd considered Claudia somewhat of a friend and had been completely unaware of the history between Claudia's mother and her own. Her mother told her soon after her coming-out disaster.

Her mother had referred to Mrs. Von Haupt as "that woman" for years. Katherine had naïvely assumed it was simply that the two women didn't get along. But there was far more to their story. It turned out Mrs. Von Haupt had married a man who'd been desperately in love with Katherine's mother and had made no secret of his desire over the years. Her mother had always insisted she'd never reciprocated Mr. Von Haupt's feelings, but the animosity between the two women was apparently legendary in New York society. Mrs.

Von Haupt lived in a perpetual state of humiliation, and over the years had made it her life's work to prove to the world—or at least to New York's elite—that she was better than Katherine's mother.

Katherine gave Marjorie the basic outline of the feud between her mother and Mrs. Von Haupt. "I'm afraid Claudia is a victim of her mother's ambition and resentment."

Marjorie sat stunned during the telling of the story, then she grasped Katherine's wrist and let out a small squeal. "The Von Haupts are coming to this party," she said.

Katherine closed her eyes. She and her mother would have to spend an entire week with a false smile plastered on their faces, pretending that they weren't bothered by the presence of the vicious pair. Pretending to be friends. It would be excruciating. "I knew they were in England, but I had no idea they were planning to attend this particular party. I suppose we'll just have to grin and bear it. We get along quite well publically, you see. Even though it's fairly well-known my mother and Mrs. Von Haupt are not friends, they do their best to hide that fact."

Katherine let out a sigh. This week was going to be torturous.

Joseph Winn and his family had lived on Avonleigh land for three generations. He was seventy-two and his sons were gone—one in Yorkshire working the coal mines, the other in Boston. Mr. Winn had lost his right thumb and index finger last winter, and though he'd been trying hard to make his rent, it was clear he could not.

And his wife, Minnie, was outside Graham's study wearing her Sunday best. He knew some of his contemporaries would have told the old couple to go live with one of their children, to leave the land for someone who could work it and pay their rent. He knew most would. But he had a soft heart as his father had, and he knew he wouldn't be able to.

"Please send Mrs. Winn in, Roger," he said to his secretary, who lifted his head up as if it were weighted down. The old chap had probably been asleep. Another inheritance from his father. He watched with fondness as Roger creaked his way over to the door, shuffling steadily but excruciatingly slowly. Hell, he couldn't fire Roger because he couldn't afford what the younger secretaries were now demanding for salaries.

"Mrs. Winn," he heard Roger call in his fragile voice. It sounded as if at any moment his voice box would break permanently, leaving him with a mere whisper.

He waited only a brief moment for Mrs. Winn to appear, fear and determination in her brown eyes. Standing, he directed her to a chair in front of his desk, where she sat, clutching her carpet bag fiercely, not even looking around.

"How may I help you?" he asked.

"Rent's due, my lord. Can't pay it."

"That's four months now, is it not, Mrs. Winn?"

"Five."

"Ah." He pretended to look in his ledger. "Yes, I see it is." He gave the carpet bag a long look, wondering what delights it held for him. Last time it was eight pair of itchy woolen socks. The time before that a rather handsome scarf—he planned to wear it this winter. Twenty jars of honey, ten jars of preserved strawberry jam, all given to him over the months in lieu of rent.

She reached into her bag and pulled out a wooden object with holes in it. "It's for yer pipes, my lord. A pipe holder. Rosewood, Mr. Winn used. Very nice indeed and very precious."

Graham stood and walked over to where Mrs. Winn sat clutching the pipe holder in her ruddy hands. He took it from her, examining it closely. It was really quite lovely, with a finely carved hunting scene across the front. "Very well. It'll do nicely to hold my pipes. Consider your rent paid, Mrs. Winn."

She relaxed slightly, as if in a thousand years he would not accept her gift for rent. Lifting her chin and meeting his eyes—hers softening just slightly—she stood. "Thank you, my lord. We'll make rent next month, I'm sure."

"I have no doubt, Mrs. Winn."

She gave a small curtsy, then turned and left. Graham placed the pipe holder carefully on his desk, letting one finger drift around one of the holes created for a pipe. It would hold five pipes. Too bad he didn't smoke.

"Sir, Lord Willington is here," Roger said.

"Alone?" Graham asked, with a small amount of mock fear.

"Very, sir. Shall I send him in?"

"Yes, thank you, Roger."

Moments later, John Atwell, Viscount Willington, stepped through the doors, smiling as if he were about to encounter a roomful of willing women—not Graham. Graham frowned.

"Cheerful as always, I take it?" the viscount said, throwing himself down into the chair Mrs. Winn had just vacated.

"I'm faint with relief that you don't have your brood with you. How many do you have now? Twelve?"

"Four," his friend said happily.

John's giddiness at his happy life was nauseating at times, but as Graham had few friends, he tolerated the man's incessant smile.

"What brings you to my home?" Graham asked, moving back behind his desk.

"Just passing through," John said idly, glancing around the room with measured nonchalance.

"Passing through Northumberland. No one passes through Northumberland." Graham pointed this out with a weary sigh.

"Well, Avon, my wife has put me on a mission. I'd like to apologize in advance for what I'm about to say. I do have business in London, which I know is in the opposite direction, but even so I don't want you to think I took this trip solely to badger you."

"I am beside myself to hear what you have to say," Graham said dryly, and John grinned.

"We've heard you're planning to marry. Congratulations."

"Oh, good God."

John leaned forward. "Hear me out, Avon. Do you really know what marriage involves? You have to spend *time* with them. A lot of it. And not just in the bedroom." Graham nearly rolled his eyes at the silly grin that appeared on John's face. Hell, the man had been married for nearly ten years. "Parties, balls. And when you have children, well, you're bonded together with a permanence that's difficult to comprehend. I cannot imagine spending all that time with someone I disliked."

Graham gave his friend a level look. "I adore my soon-to-be fiancée."

John laughed aloud. "Perhaps you didn't know, but my mother has met her, Avon."

"I see. Then let me clarify. I adore my soon-to-be fiancée's money. She has quite a lot of it, apparently. I would like to put the record straight, however. I have made no offer. I haven't said the word *wedding* or *marriage* or *bride*. But the girl's mother is in a mad frenzy to get us down the aisle. And to be honest, at least financially, the sooner the better. If I can stomach it all."

John became serious. "Is it really so bad?" he asked.

Graham gave a short nod. "Did you see that woman who just left? She's one of my tenants. Lovely woman. She makes wonderful jam. Which she uses at times to pay rent. This month it was this pipe holder."

"I didn't know that you smoked a pipe."

"I don't. I have one tenant who gave me a pig. His only boar, mind you. Makes it a bit difficult to breed pigs when you don't have a male. So I nicked the thing's ear and put him back where he belonged. They think it's a strange pig—and a miracle at that—that wandered into their garden. They think this, because I made a big show of saying how delicious their pig tasted when I roasted it." Graham shook his head. "These people are old and poor and their children are leaving their farms to make real money elsewhere. Their homes are in disrepair, their equipment outdated, and I cannot afford to replace it, so it's no wonder their children leave. If I have to marry a disagreeable woman to help them, I will. But I haven't decided on which disagreeable woman, so you may relax."

John slapped his hands on his knees. "All right then. I did what I set out to do. Melissa will have to be satisfied with that. I could use a brandy."

"I could use two. Tomorrow I'm headed to Briarbrook for a week of torture. Care to join me?" Graham stood and walked over to a half-full decanter and poured two glasses.

"I'd love to, but cannot. Once I've concluded business in London, it's back home for me. Melissa's expecting again, and, well, I'd like to be home."

A jab of something that might have been envy struck Graham hard but he resolutely pushed it down. "Then home you should go," he said, handing him his snifter.

Graham felt John's eyes on him and tried to ignore him as the sharp smell of the liquor filled his nostrils and he took a long drink. He knew John was about to begin some sort of speech on how wonderful it was to find a woman to love, a woman who when you left her, all you could think about was the next time you would hold her in your arms. He'd felt that way, briefly, just last week. He still couldn't believe how he'd acted, felt. Stupid to fall for anyone, but particularly stupid to find oneself infatuated with a servant.

"You know, Avon, the right woman can make you happy. I thought you and Laura might end up together."

"Truly? She's happy with Brewster, isn't she?"

John shrugged, and that told Graham all he needed to know. "Have you ever found anyone who even vaguely made you happy?"

"Good Lord, you've turned into a woman."

John laughed and raised his glass as if admitting this flaw. "No, I'm worse. I'm a converted man."

"It just so happens I did meet someone. Recently. But she wasn't suitable to marry."

"Oh? Tell me more."

Graham shrugged. "I met her in Brighton. She was lively. Lovely. And I wanted to make her my mistress. But before I could ask her, she left. I don't know where the devil she is. And even if I did, I don't think I'd pursue her. I don't think she'd agree." He took another long drink. "It was foolish," he said softly.

He refused to look at his friend's eyes, because he feared what he might see—pity.

Chapter 6

Katherine stood with her new friend, Marjorie, punch glasses in gloved hands as they surveyed the room they'd just entered. It was the reception, the evening set aside for old friends to meet and new friends to be introduced. The Haverslys were gracious hosts, known for their fun and elaborate house parties, which were always well-attended affairs. Marjorie, as Katherine was quickly learning, had a closet full of exquisite gowns. This evening she wore a dress with intricate, gold embroidery on the bodice and a robin's-egg blue skirt. Katherine had never seen anything like it. The small bustle in the back of the gown was of the same rich embroidery as the bodice.

Katherine's own dress was much plainer, a simple peach-colored gown with delicate brown lace along the neckline and sleeves that reached just past her elbow.

"Let's see who we have here this evening," Marjorie said. "Ah, there is the gouty Lord Mandeville. He's a widower and a baron. I crossed him off my list years ago. Too old and his breath is foul enough to curl your toes. Sir Robert Browne. He's the tall one talking to Lady Wellsworth in the horrible green gown. He's rather nice, but, alas, no title. And . . ." Marjorie let out a small gasp. "It's Lord Avonleigh."

Katherine was suddenly more alert. If Lord Avonleigh were

here, that meant Gray was also somewhere in this house. She felt her entire body flush. "Where?" she managed.

"That beautiful brooding man in the corner. The tall one. His waistcoat is deep burgundy. Every girl I know, including me, has tried to get his interest but to no avail. Apparently our pockets aren't deep enough."

Katherine followed where her friend was looking and stared with disbelief. "But that's . . ." she said, her breath leaving her. *Gray*.

"That's who?"

"The one Claudia Von Haupt has set her sights on," she said, recovering quickly. That devil! She simply could not believe her eyes. There he was, Gray, the man who'd kissed her senseless, who made her act so recklessly, the man who'd said he was Lord Avonleigh's valet. He stood looking bored, almost angry, among a group of men, while her heart pounded painfully in her chest.

"From what I've heard, they merely need to sign the contract. Her father is on his way from New York to do just that. And do you know from whom I learned this tidbit?" she asked with a gleam in her eyes. "From Miss Von Haupt herself. She was quite giddy with the news when I saw her earlier. Certainly you've heard of him if you've been in England more than a day."

"I have. Of course. The famous Miserable Marquess."

"And you know the story?"

"That he will marry the first girl he smiles at? Yes, I've heard it. I don't put a bit of stock in it, however," she finished darkly. She narrowed her eyes, remembering the easy way he'd smiled at her when he thought she was a maid. She wondered if he would have smiled as broadly had he known she was one of the title-hungry heiresses he held in such contempt. Or perhaps he had known and was simply having a bit of fun with her.

Then, as if he were truly feeling the daggers that were flying from her eyes, he looked up and froze. His beautiful eyes narrowed, then widened, before he turned fully toward her, shock registering in his face.

And that's when Katherine knew. He hadn't known who she was. Just as she hadn't known who he was. They began walking toward each other, leaving behind curious companions, until they met nearly in the center of the room, completely oblivious to anyone else at the gathering.

Katherine lifted her head and smiled. "Lord Avonleigh. What a surprise."

He seemed slightly confused, until she saw realization appear on his face. "Miss Wright, I presume?" He lifted one elegant eyebrow.

And then in unison: "Did you know?"

And again: "No, I didn't."

Katherine burst out laughing and grasped his extended hands in hers, looking up at him, completely delighted by the turn of events. Gray—no, it was Graham, wasn't it?—threw back his head and laughed, then smiled down at her as if unable to believe his good fortune.

"You truly didn't know who I was?" he asked.

"No, of course not. What a pair we are. Why did you pretend to be your own valet?"

"Probably for much the same reason you pretended to be your own maid. Anonymity." He smiled again, completely unaware that every eye in the room was watching this exchange with rabid interest.

Among those staring were Suzanna and Claudia Von Haupt, the former pushing the latter with near violence toward the smiling pair in the center of the room.

"It's so good to—" Katherine was cut off by the sudden appearance of Claudia Von Haupt, who wrapped her hands around Graham's forearm in a painfully obvious attempt to stake her claim.

"Hello, Katherine," Claudia gushed, seemingly happy to see her. "I see you've met my—" She put one gloved hand to her lips, as if the slip were just that. "I see you've met Lord Avonleigh."

"Yes, we met in Brighton," Katherine said, feeling her stomach twist as all the implications of who Gray—no, Graham—was finally seeped into her mind. He'd told her himself that Lord Avonleigh was being pursued by Claudia. Obviously that pursuit had been successful. It was almost as if all her blood drained away from her head. He was going to marry Claudia Von Haupt even though he didn't love her.

"How lovely," Claudia said. "It's so nice to see a familiar face. What brings you to England?"

"A ship," Katherine said, and she was gratified to see not only confusion on Claudia's face, but a quickly stifled smile on Graham's.

"I meant, *why* are you here?"

"Why, I imagine for the same reason you are. To nab a lofty title to hang on my name." Katherine's voice was as brittle and bright as fine crystal. "I see you've found yours."

Claudia gave her a confused smile, obviously uncertain whether Katherine was joking with her or not. "Yes, I have." She looked up at Graham like a woman looks at a new frock that all her other friends have been eying. "It's not official, yet, of course, so let's keep this between us," she said in a whisper.

"Of course." Katherine smiled, and no one in the room would have guessed it was not genuine. She embraced Claudia, congratulating her warmly. "Are there any titled gentlemen left for me?" She looked from Claudia to Graham, seeing something momentarily dark flicker in his eyes.

Claudia, her face shining brightly, made a great show of looking about the room at the gathering. "Lord Mandeville is looking for a wife," Claudia said with a nod toward the gouty old man Marjorie had pointed out earlier. "Isn't he, Graham?" She blushed prettily. "Oh, pardon, Lord Avonleigh."

"I wouldn't know. However, I suppose one title is as good as another to you Americans." He said the words drolly, with a dry wit, as if the entire conversation was so *boring* to him.

Katherine nearly gasped at his words, his derisive tone. She felt a sharp pain as she realized this was the true Lord Avonleigh—jaded and slightly cruel. The man she had met in Brighton, the one who'd dragged her into a pub, who ran down the beach on a misty night, didn't exist.

"You are probably right, my lord. It was good to see you both again," she said gaily. "Please enjoy the evening. I'm certain my mother is wondering where I am. Oh, and Claudia, I promise not to tell anyone the *wonderful* news." She flashed a brilliant smile to Graham, then turned away, blind to all the stares that followed her from the room. She felt unaccountably like crying, as if she'd just learned Gray had tragically died. She felt foolish even to have such thoughts. Oh God, was he laughing at her right now? Sharing their ridiculous story with Claudia?

She walked into a vacant hall and pressed her hand against her stomach, thankful to find herself alone.

"Katy."

Oh God. She steeled herself. "My name is Katherine." She turned toward him and tried not to be affected by the look in his eyes. She would not be foolish enough to believe it was longing she saw. "And you are Graham Spencer, Lord Avonleigh, the marquess who is in desperate straits and in need of a wealthy heiress. I'm afraid not even we can afford you, my lord."

He hardened his jaw, whether in pain or anger, Katherine was unsure. "Please don't speak to me that way."

"What way should I speak? As a maid does to a valet? I'm not that Brighton girl. And you are certainly not that man."

Graham let her go, watched her walk stiffly away, knowing there was nothing he could say. He could hardly ask an heiress to become his mistress. But seeing her again was like having the sun come out after a long bout of cold rain. He heard footsteps behind him and closed his eyes wearily. If it was Claudia, he didn't know whether he could pretend to be pleasant. She was presuming things she shouldn't, probably encouraged by her ambitious mother.

"Lord Avonleigh."

He nearly visibly winced. It was worse than Claudia; it was her mother. He schooled his features and turned, offering a polite countenance.

"Mrs. Von Haupt. I trust you are enjoying your evening?"

"Of course." Her eyes darted behind him, but Katherine was no longer in sight. Not that he cared whether she'd seen them together or not. He would marry her daughter; she need not have a worry. The Wrights were wealthy, and no doubt Katherine came with an impressive dowry, but it could be no match for the million dollars the Von Haupts had hinted at. As sick as it made him feel inside, he knew he would do just about anything to give the people who depended upon him a better life. John thought he was being foolish, but he'd never seen his tenants go hungry, their roofs letting in rain, the snow blowing through ill-fitted windows. They were proud people who rarely asked for anything, who did their best to pay their rents and keep their homes neat and clean. They did not deserve the poverty they now faced thanks to three generations of tragically shortsighted investments.

"Your daughter looks very charming this evening," he said to put the woman at ease. She gave him an assessing look, and Graham realized the mother was far more intelligent than her daughter.

"I picked out her dress, so thank you. Claudia is a biddable girl, Lord Avonleigh. I'm sure there are times when Mr. Von Haupt wishes he had married a similar girl." She searched his face for any reaction. "I couldn't help but notice you spoke with Miss Wright."

"Yes. We met in Brighton."

Mrs. Von Haupt let out a musical little laugh. "I know *of* the girl. Her family doesn't really run in our circles, you see. I think her mother was the daughter of a butcher. That's the beauty of America, don't you think?"

"Americans are very clever," he said blandly, looking over her shoulder in hopes of seeing some acquaintance waving to him.

"Your estate is not far from here, is it?"

He silently cursed his great-grandfather for leaving the estate to his father. His father, of course, had been delighted to have such a grand country home so close to London, but Graham had always preferred their country seat, Avonleigh, even though it was in the wilderness of Northumberland. "Bryant Park is not one hour on horseback."

"Perhaps we can all make a visit. Claudia isn't much for the hunt, though she sits a horse well enough. I understand the Haverslys are planning a hunt the day after tomorrow. If it is a pleasant day, we should visit your home."

It was not a question. "An excellent idea. I'm certain there will be others who are also not interested in chasing a fox about. I'll be sure to extend the invitation." He gazed down at her, and she pursed her lips but remained silent. She would learn soon enough that he could not be manipulated.

Katherine dreaded going back into the large sitting room. She knew all eyes would be on her—the girl who'd managed to draw a smile from the Marquess of Avonleigh. She stepped in quietly and was almost immediately accosted by first Marjorie, then her mother, then Marjorie's mother, who all converged upon her with varying degrees of urgency.

"Do you know what you've done?" Marjorie asked, seemingly delighted to finally have something exciting to talk about.

"Pray tell, what." No inflection, no curiosity.

"My dear, you are the talk of the party," Katherine's mother gushed. "Lady Summerfield has just informed me of the great importance of the marquess giving you special attention."

"Shall I inform the *Times*?" Marjorie said, earning an exasperated look from Katherine.

"My dear, you don't seem to understand the importance of this evening's events," Lady Summerfield said. Katherine looked at Marjorie's mother and wondered briefly if she had actually borne her own daughter. She was a squarish woman, the kind one might call handsome if one were very drunk. Her hair was a nondescript gray, her eyes dull brown, and she sported a rather thick mustache. She was, in a word, formidable, and Katherine found herself standing a bit straighter. "I've known Lord Avonleigh since he was a boy. I'd held out some small hope that Marjorie would catch his eye, but she did not. His great loss, not ours, I assure you. In fact, no one has caught his eye—not even that Von Haupt girl." It was almost as if Lady Summerfield suppressed a shudder. "He has chosen you."

Katherine would have laughed if it weren't so obvious that this woman was dead serious. She was wrong, but convincing her of that fact would be difficult. "You misunderstand. We were laughing at our own folly. He wasn't smiling at me as much as he was the predicament we'd found ourselves in." Unbidden, all those other smiles that had been so freely given while they were in Brighton flashed in her mind like a zoetrope.

"And what predicament is that?" Elizabeth said, half-alarmed.

Katherine quickly came up with an ingenious lie that was so close to the truth, it was believable. "You remember how sick you were in Brighton. Always abed."

"Of course," Elizabeth said, her cheeks flushing as if she were embarrassed to have other people know she'd been ill.

"Clara and I—Clara is my maid, you see—went for a walk along the beach. I was wearing my simplest frock and Lord Avonleigh mistook us for two servants. I had a letter from Lucy, Mother, and part of it blew into the water. Lord Avonleigh rescued it and we spoke for a bit. I suppose he was curious because we were Americans. It was clear to me he thought I was a maid, and I didn't want to embarrass him by correcting him. And that's all it was."

Three sets of female eyes narrowed. She'd thought it was a logical explanation, but perhaps not.

"How long was your conversation?" her mother asked.

"Oh, five minutes. Less. Or more. I can't recall."

"And he remembered you from Brighton, from that brief meeting?"

"Apparently so. I remembered him."

"But you knew he was Lord Avonleigh. Of course you would remember him," Lady Summerfield pointed out reasonably.

"I cannot say why. Perhaps we should ask Lord Avonleigh why he has such a good memory." Katherine pretended to look about the room.

"Not necessary," Lady Summerfield said. She gave Katherine another assessing look, and Katherine smiled weakly at her. "Mrs. Wright, let me introduce you about."

As soon as the two older women were gone, Marjorie grabbed her arm and pulled her to the side of the room. "Now tell me what actually happened. And do please tell me that Lord Avonleigh is not the man you met in Brighton. Tell me, please. Because if he is, it would be simply too delicious."

Katherine grimaced.

"Oh, he *is* the man! I knew it. How tragic and wonderful and . . ." She paused, apparently having run out of descriptive words to paint a proper picture. "You love him," she finally said softly.

Katherine shook her head. "I could hardly love a man I've only spent a few hours with. But I suppose I *could* have loved him had circumstances been different."

Marjorie made a face. "The man you described to me wasn't Lord Avonleigh. I cannot imagine having any warm feelings toward him at all. Don't forget, I've been out for three years, and I've had the privilege of watching him—and watching myriad women make a cake of themselves over him. I simply do not understand his attraction."

"He is handsome," Katherine said, feeling the need to defend him. "And the man I knew in Brighton likely wasn't at all like the man you know. He was carefree and happy. You see, both of us for our own reasons pretended to be servants. He introduced himself as a valet and I thought if I told him who I was, he would go away. And he was handsome and charming and I suppose I thought it would do no harm to let a handsome, charming valet believe I was a lady's maid."

Marjorie clapped her hands together. "This is wonderful."

"This is not wonderful," Katherine said darkly.

"No, no. You misunderstand. Mrs. Von Haupt is already in a tizzy over that smile. You should have seen the look on her face when her daughter approached the two of you. It was *priceless*."

Katherine shook her head, still not understanding what could be wonderful about the situation.

"I daresay you'll soon see the silver lining in this very dark cloud," Marjorie said mysteriously. And no amount of prodding could make her explain herself.

Chapter 7

He needed a new textile mill. Better irrigation, certainly. The roads were rutted, the trees diseased, the storage buildings dilapidated. New wells needed to be dug, new fencing erected, new equipment purchased. He did have some rather nice horseflesh and a stable built in the last half century, so there was that. But other than the stable, their lands hadn't been improved upon in more than seventy-five years. How could they ever compete against American farmers who were using innovative, modern techniques to produce better and bigger crops when his tenants were still using an ox and single-blade cast-iron plows? It was mind-numbing, the amount that needed to be done thanks to decades of neglect.

Graham had loved his father, but thinking about what needed to be done made him slightly ill. His father had been a lover of the arts. He'd collected violins, even though he hadn't played. No, he'd attracted the finest musicians to their home so that they could see— and perhaps play—some of the finest instruments ever created. Those violins were long gone—the proceeds used to build a sturdy bridge over the river that ran through Avonleigh. It was difficult to think of his father as being unkind, but wasn't this neglect a form of cruelty? He could not imagine buying a rare violin when a tenant's well was dry. And yet his father had done such things over and over again.

He put his pen in the ink pot and sat back, his head aching. A knock on the door was a welcome distraction.

"Enter." A footman appeared.

"The picnic is about to begin, Lord Avonleigh. Shall I tell the party to wait?"

Graham pulled out his watch, stunned that it could be time for luncheon. "Indeed it is. Thank you. I'll be right down so there's no need to tell anyone to wait. I can catch up, no doubt."

He gave himself a cursory look in the mirror, adjusting his cravat and pulling on his jacket, and headed toward the door.

"My lord, your sleeve," Mr. Chase said in the same way one might say, "My lord, your arm fell off."

Graham looked down and frowned at an ink stain.

"I have another shirt pressed and ready," Mr. Chase said, with slightly less panic in his tone. Graham knew it would be extremely difficult for Mr. Chase to let him walk out the door with that stain, so he stripped off his jacket, vest, collar, and shirt. Looking pleased, Mr. Chase took the discarded items and headed toward the wardrobe. Now Graham truly would be late, though he didn't mind. The fewer minutes spent with the Von Haupts, the better.

When he finally did reach the outside, he saw a few stragglers behind a larger group of people heading down a footpath that wound its way around a small lake. Two young ladies walked in front of him, with two older ones in the lead. He stopped dead when he heard one of the young ladies laugh, then resolutely stepped forward, his eyes on the back of Katherine Wright's head.

It was, perhaps, inevitable that they would hear him behind them and turn to see who was there. And perhaps it was just as inevitable that when Lady Marjorie saw him, she would quickly speak to Katherine then hurry to catch up with their mothers, opening her parasol as she went. Katherine waited for him to catch up, an enigmatic smile on her lovely face.

Odd, he hadn't thought her beautiful in Brighton, but the girl standing in front of him took his breath away. She wore a forest green dress with froths of creamy lace at her neck and sleeves, and a jaunty little hat with a large green ribbon tied beneath her chin. Her eyes today were green—and at the moment slightly narrowed.

"Miss Wright," he said with a bit of irony, dipping his head in a polite bow.

"Lord Avonleigh," she returned, just as ironic, and with a nearly infinitesimal curtsy.

"Was that a curtsy or did you just have a spasm?" he asked dryly. She laughed, delighted, and any ice between them melted.

"I'm glad you are straggling behind. I did want to talk to you." She began walking toward the lake and he fell into step beside her.

"Oh?" He studied her profile and felt a now-familiar longing.

"Our discussions in Brighton. I assume everything you told me was the truth, and that it was really about you. And your father."

Graham walked a few steps in silence before saying simply, "Yes."

"Oh Graham, I am so sorry," she said, grasping his hand. "You cannot know how horrid I felt last night after I realized everything you'd told me, all those awful things, were really about you. And I knew you might worry about me, worry that I would repeat your stories. I want you to know I have not and I never will."

He squeezed her small hand before letting it go, because he knew if he maintained even that small contact, it would be difficult not to haul her into his arms. "Thank you."

Ahead of them, the group had turned off the footpath to gather near the lake. Servants had already been there, laying out pristine white cloths and putting a matching basket upon each blanket.

"At some point I would like to discuss your mendacity, sir." He laughed, causing nearly every head to turn toward them. "Good grief, is your reputation as the Miserable Marquess truly that widely known? Every time you smile or laugh, it's as if a momentous event has occurred," she said just above a whisper.

"It is only because until recently, no one in the ton had ever seen me laugh," he said, and watched as a becoming flush bloomed on her cheeks.

"That cannot be so."

"It is. You do have the oddest effect on me, Miss Wright. And now, I cannot blame it on the sea air."

Katherine walked over to her mother, feeling the eyes of nearly everyone on her—and rather enjoying it. She got a particularly icy glare from Mrs. Von Haupt, though Claudia gave her a little wave and smile. Claudia had seemed genuinely happy to see her the previous evening, almost as if she were completely oblivious to the harm her mother had done to her. At the time, she'd thought Claudia simply a very good actress, but now she was starting to think that perhaps the girl was rather simpleminded.

"I do not understand at all how you can still be standing there breathing when so many daggers are being sent your way," Marjorie said, taking a bite of an apple. "If looks could kill and all that. One might call Mrs. Von Haupt's fury a silver lining."

"Marjorie, you are awful," Katherine said, not meaning one syllable. Katherine looked over to Mrs. Von Haupt and smiled a greeting. The older woman didn't change her expression, but said something to Claudia, and the girl jumped up to greet Lord Avonleigh.

"Katherine, something has just occurred to me," Elizabeth said, and the way she said it told Katherine it was something her mother had been thinking about for some time.

"Yes, Mother?" she asked, gracefully sitting on the blanket and opening her parasol after her mother eyed it sternly.

"Each time Lord Avonleigh shows you even the smallest bit of attention, Mrs. Von Haupt looks like she's about to have a seizure."

"I hadn't noticed," Katherine said, laughter in her tone.

"I fear I can be rather petty," Elizabeth said aloud to no one in particular. "But I find it's rather satisfying to see those looks of venom. A bit of retribution for what she has done to us. I would not discourage you from spending time with Lord Avonleigh."

Katherine was a bit confused. She lowered her voice so that only those at their blanket could hear her. "Mother, if you have any delusions about Lord Avonleigh, I would like you to set them aside now." Katherine looked for support from Marjorie and Lady Summerfield. "I'm afraid Lord Avonleigh feels compelled to marry Miss Von Haupt and the contract is all but signed. She is bringing a rather sizeable dowry to the marriage."

Her mother narrowed her eyes. "How sizeable?"

"One million pounds."

Her mother gasped, then frowned. "Oh," she said, that one word filled with disappointment, disgust, and envy. "Really."

"It's difficult to overcome such a significant obstacle, but I believe it can be done," Lady Summerfield said with a sharp nod.

"I wouldn't want to stop Lord Avonleigh from marrying Claudia," Katherine said sternly. "Lord Avonleigh wants to help his people, and to do that he needs a large amount of money. I'm afraid we cannot compete with the Von Haupts. I think they would sell their souls for a title as prestigious as Avonleigh's."

Her mother popped a grape in her mouth and chewed thoughtfully. "Then we'll simply have to settle on torturing the Von Haupts," she said with a wicked smile.

"That's just what I was thinking, Mrs. Wright," Marjorie said, clapping her hands together.

Katherine's mother quickly explained to Lady Summerfield all that had passed between the families. The lady's response was not surprising. "Then we have even more reason to make certain Katherine and Lord Avonleigh marry."

Katherine suppressed a frustrated groan, but remained silent. If the older women wanted to dream a bit about a wedding between Graham and her, she would let them. They couldn't know she knew Graham far better than she should; far better than Claudia did, certainly. And it would be gauche to mention that her own dowry was only one-tenth of Claudia's.

She heard Claudia's giggle and turned to look at the small group. Graham sat, one leg stretched out, the other bent, a hand dangling casually over his knee. He had opened his jacket and was the picture of an elegant aristocrat. Whatever was tickling Claudia, apparently wasn't as amusing to Graham, whose smile—if it could be called such—was tolerant at best. She almost felt sorry for Claudia at that moment. Graham would never love her, and Claudia was just silly enough to fall in love with him. Graham looked over to her at that moment, his gaze steady, and Katherine saw a subtle change in his smile. Then Claudia touched his arm with her hand, just a brief gesture, and Graham looked away. That small touch felt like a fist to Katherine's stomach. It was a jarring reminder that she would never be allowed to touch Graham so publically, that their kisses must remain a secret. *He is hers*, she told herself forcefully. She had the terrible feeling she would not be able to be as blasé about Graham marrying Claudia as she'd thought.

Katherine looked away, only to find Marjorie gazing at her with concern. "What did Cook provide?" Katherine asked with false cheer.

"Chicken sprinkled with envy," Marjorie quipped, and Katherine wrinkled her nose at her.

Lady Summerfield let out a strong laugh, apparently delighted with her daughter's wit. Katherine had never seen a mother take such delight in a daughter. The woman, who was as attractive as the stern of a ship, lit up whenever Marjorie was about. Then, in a matter of a few moments, Lady Summerfield frowned heavily. "Your brother is here. Goodness, what is he wearing?"

Katherine followed Lady Summerfield's gaze to find a tall, thin young man with a mop of bright red hair walking toward them. He wore a dark red jacket that clashed rather awfully with his hair.

"I'll have to speak with his valet. Again," Lady Summerfield said. "Does he have to be late for everything?"

Marjorie leapt up and greeted her brother with an enthusiastic hug, which he seemed to accept reluctantly, then drew him to their blanket. "George, let me introduce you to Miss Wright and Mrs. Wright. They're Americans. Ladies, please meet my brother, George Penwhistle, Lord Summerfield."

"Pleased to meet you," George said hesitantly, nodding his head in time to his words. "It takes eight days on a steamship to go from New York to London."

"Yes, I know," Katherine said, slightly confused at his pronouncement.

"George, they took a steamship here, so they already know how long it takes. You need a haircut," Lady Summerfield said, and immediately George's hand swept up to his unruly mop.

"Oh. Yes, Mother."

"Sit down, George. There's plenty here," Marjorie said, sitting and dragging her brother down with her. He let out a laugh as he nearly lost his balance.

It was obvious to Katherine that Marjorie and her brother were close, and it made her miss her sister, Lucy. It was also obvious that something was a bit off about George. Little things, like the way he spoke, bobbing his head nearly continuously. He never quite met Katherine in the eye, as if she were a Medusa who could turn him to stone. And yet he seemed to be an intelligent man; perhaps he was just socially awkward. Throughout the luncheon, Marjorie encouraged him to talk as much as her mother discouraged him. The poor young man was quite at odds with whom to please. He would turn to Marjorie and enthusiastically start to tell her about some prank a boy at school had perpetrated, only to be silenced by his mother. It was almost as if Lady Summerfield disliked her own son.

"Do you enjoy school?" Katherine asked.

"Oh yes, indeed I do," George said, darting a look first to his mother then to Marjorie. "I have six professors. One is from Sussex, two from London, one from—"

"I'm certain Miss Wright doesn't need to know where your professors were born, George," Lady Summerfield said.

He looked momentarily stunned that Katherine wouldn't be interested, then nodded his head.

"Where are the other two from? I'm interested," Marjorie said, looking not at her brother but at her mother.

"One is from Sussex, two from London, one from Glasgow, one from Leeds, and one from York."

"George was born breech," Lady Summerfield said succinctly.

Marjorie squeezed her brother's hand. "Shall I make you a plate, George?"

He nodded, staring at his hands as Lady Summerfield sat stoically, gazing at the lake, her lips pressed tightly together. Clearly, her son was a Disappointment.

Katherine chatted as they ate, but it seemed as if a pall had come over the day. Though Marjorie laughed at the stories about carefree summers in upstate New York, her laughter seemed forced, especially in light of the fact that Lady Summerfield continued to act as if she had a burr in her drawers.

"Shall we all go for a walk?" Katherine said when they'd finished eating.

"You young people go on," Lady Summerfield said, and Katherine could tell her mother was a tad disappointed to be left behind with the taciturn woman.

When they were well away from the picnic, Marjorie said, "She is so horrid to George that I want to scream."

"She just thinks I'm an idiot," George said without inflection.

"But she's wrong," Marjorie said with force.

George shrugged. "It doesn't matter what she thinks. I have the best reports at Cambridge, so I know I'm not an idiot."

"Of course you're not."

"I want to go to university," Katherine said in a rush. She rarely admitted that ambition out loud.

"Truly? And what would you study?"

"I don't really know. My parents are both opposed, of course. They want me to marry."

"Don't you want to get married?"

"I don't see why I can't do both. Men do."

"That's true," Marjorie said, but it was clear she was skeptical. "But it might be difficult being a scholar and a marchioness at the same time."

Katherine gave her friend a look of pure exasperation. "I do wish you and your mother would stop this nonsense."

"I'll stop when he stops smiling brilliantly every time he sees you."

Yes, there was that. Katherine was frankly amazed at how seriously these folks took their legends. She had no doubt they already were envisioning the wedding. Too bad they couldn't envision a way for Graham to obtain a million pounds on his own so he didn't have to marry Claudia.

"When do you go back to school?" Katherine asked George, desperate to change the subject.

"September ten. Next Tuesday."

"He's studying law. He has a brain for facts and figures and really is a genius at remembering case study."

George bobbed his head in agreement. "My father studied law," he said. "He was the second son and I am the first and only son. He died January fourteenth in 1865 and that made me heir. His older brother died when he was thirty-five, October sixth, 1854, and my father was Viscount of Summerfield for ten years and three months before he died and I became a viscount. I've been viscount for nine years and nine months."

Marjorie gave a light laugh. "George adores being very specific about nearly everything."

George smiled sheepishly and nodded, his pale cheeks flushing with the compliment.

"Hello," a female voice called—an American female voice.

Katherine turned to see Claudia leading Graham toward them.

"Isn't it a glorious day?" she asked. "I'd heard that England was nothing but dreary rain and cold mists."

Despite herself, Katherine laughed, keeping her eyes carefully averted from Graham's steady gaze. She did wish he would stop looking at her with such . . . intensity. "I'd heard the same. But I do believe we're seeing England at its best. I've heard that August and September can be far less wet than other months. Isn't that so, Marjorie?"

"July and August are the driest months—" Marjorie stayed her brother, who was no doubt about to go into a lengthy and detailed account of England's weather, with a gentle touch to his wrist. Katherine wondered if this was some sort of signal the two had contrived to keep George from rattling off facts and figures.

"Miss Von Haupt, if you don't mind, I'd like to show Miss Wright the lake," Graham said. "We were there yesterday and I'd hate to bore you with the same speech."

Claudia's smile was just a bit hesitant, but she nodded and released his arm. Katherine had no choice but to follow Graham a bit farther down the path, especially when Marjorie gave her a small nudge in his direction.

When they were away from the others, Katherine said, "What are you thinking? It's bad enough that you smile at me constantly, fueling rumors that you have been enchanted by me and our wedding is inevitable, but to drag me off alone is really too much."

Graham raised one eyebrow and looked at the small party, not thirty yards from where they stood. Huffing, Katherine crossed her arms and turned toward the lake. "This lake smells odd," she said.

"The Haverslys perfume it."

Katherine turned to him, startled. "They what?"

"They perfume it. It usually has a rather unpleasant odor. Perhaps because of the dragon arum that grows along the shore."

"Dragon arum?"

"A plant that smells like a corpse."

Katherine wrinkled her nose.

"You look lovely," he said.

"And you should not say such things to me when your fiancée is a mere few feet away."

"You have been misinformed. Miss Von Haupt is not my fiancée. I am aware that it is her mother's grandest wish that there be a marriage between us, and thus far I have not gainsaid her. However, we are not engaged."

Katherine looked up at him, slightly surprised, and an unexpected and unwanted feeling of hope bloomed in her heart.

"Claudia has been rather free with information about the betrothal negotiations."

"In which I have had no part. I'm aware that the father is willing to pay an outrageous dowry, but only because Claudia let that information slip," he said, stressing the word *slip*.

"One million pounds is an awful lot of money," Katherine said.

"Yes, it is," he said shortly. "And I will probably take it. But I see no reason to suffer unnecessarily by depriving myself of your pleasant company in the meantime. I should like to take you over there"—he nodded with his head to a secluded, shadowy glade—"and kiss you silly."

Katherine's eyes widened with horror, tinged by delight. "Graham," she whispered harshly, desperately trying not to smile. "You are insane."

"I am aware of that fact." He then made a big show of pointing to the glade as if he'd seen something fascinating, then began walking toward the secluded spot.

"Graham, no," Katherine said, even as she took a step to follow him. She felt that same pull she'd felt in Brighton, that nearly overwhelming need to be with him, to have an adventure, to do something she would never, ever do under normal circumstances. Had he truly enchanted her with his smile?

It was a lovely spot, sun-drenched and surrounded by trees and brush, and completely cut off from the rest of their group. She tried to look through the trees, but she could see nothing but the blue waters of the lake. Then she turned toward him. He stood five paces away, staring at her with a look of pure relief—which was much the same way she felt. Before she could even think of protesting, she was in his arms and he was kissing her with a hunger that was stunning. Goodness, it felt wonderful to be in his arms.

His mouth was warm and firm and tasted slightly of mint. She opened her mouth and welcomed his tongue with a moan, feeling as if she never wanted to stop this madness that had come over her. His hands moved down her back, stopping when he reached her buttocks, then pulling her tightly against him so that she felt his arousal. A now-familiar liquid heat melted through her, settling with a surge between her legs. This was so dangerous. So wonderful. He felt so good in her arms, solid and warm and strong. Like Gray, only better.

"God, I missed you," he said between kisses. He brought his hands up to either side of her face and peered down at her, smiling. Of course, he would smile. "I hear them coming, so I only have time for one more ravishing kiss. Then we shall pretend we saw a fawn and its mother."

He kissed her again, deeply and with frightening need, leaving her stunned.

"You look like you've just been kissed," he said gruffly.

"So do you."

He grinned and wiped a thumb across her bottom lip. Then he stepped back, leaving a more-than-proper distance between them as Marjorie and Claudia, trailed by George, came crashing through the woods and into the small glade.

"We just saw the most precious fawn," Katherine gushed. "It still had its spots. We should have called you over, but I was afraid if we shouted, it would run away."

Claudia looked quite disappointed that she'd missed such a sight, but Marjorie gave Katherine a look of pure skepticism. "Oh? What type of deer was it?"

Katherine shrugged. "I haven't the slightest notion. But it was a bit larger than the deer back home and the mother's coat was a bit red. Wasn't it, Lord Avonleigh?"

"Quite so, Miss Wright. It was a red deer."

Marjorie seemed slightly disappointed by their answers, and Katherine was thrilled she'd taken the time to read up on England's natural history. Katherine waved a gnat away from her face. "I think I've had enough traipsing about the woods, however. Shall we return to the picnic?"

She led the way, the small party trailing behind her, and Katherine overheard Claudia say, "I do wish I'd seen the fawn, too, my lord. Perhaps we can return tomorrow and they'll be back."

Katherine didn't overhear Graham's answer, but she did wonder if the girl were as oblivious as she seemed. When they returned to the picnic, Katherine was rewarded with an answer.

"Mother," Claudia called excitedly. "Miss Wright and Lord Avonleigh saw a fawn in the woods. How lucky!"

Mrs. Von Haupt immediately became alert and glared first at her daughter and then at Katherine. "Why didn't you see the fawn?" she asked.

"Lord Avonleigh was showing me the lake and we saw the fawn and its mother in a small clearing and decided to investigate," Katherine said evenly. She shouldn't delight in Mrs. Von Haupt's outrage, but she did.

"Really." She gave Lord Avonleigh a sharp look.

"They really were a charming pair," he said, sounding bored.

Mrs. Von Haupt seemed to relax, and Katherine and Marjorie excused themselves to return to their own blanket. Their mothers were nowhere in sight, and Katherine assumed they'd gone back to the house. Katherine was just beginning to think she'd gotten away with her adventure when Marjorie said, "If you'd been caught, it would have been disastrous for him."

"What do you mean?"

"You would have been compromised, and Lord Avonleigh would be forced to marry you," Marjorie whispered. "It's all fun until something horrid like that happens."

"Perhaps I shall make it happen, then," Katherine said, laughing. "Being married to Lord Avonleigh wouldn't be so horrible, would it?"

Marjorie looked shocked, and Katherine laughed again. "My goodness, Marjorie, I am only jesting. I would never do something so rash. I want Lord Avonleigh to marry whomever he pleases. And since I fully plan to return to America, he is safe from me. Truly." That "truly" was a bit of a lie, but Katherine could not let Marjorie know she might be falling in love with him.

"I do like you, Katherine, but you have no idea what it is like to have that kind of responsibility, to have a title under your care, people who depend upon you. To come from a prestigious family and need to uphold that name and its honor. I think I may have given you the wrong impression when I supported your plan to worry the Von Haupts. I never thought you would . . ." She paused and looked uncomfortable, and Katherine realized Marjorie was truly horrified by the thought they might have been kissing. And Katherine *should* be horrified by her actions, but strangely found she was not. "It is bad enough Lord Avonleigh is being forced to consider marrying out of his class because of finances, but to be forced into such a marriage because of scandal would be purely awful."

Katherine was slightly stunned by her friend's speech. "I think you've just insulted me," she said, trying to push down the familiar hurt of not being accepted. Her family was on the fringes of New York society, something she knew her mother was trying to fix by garnering a title for her daughter.

"Please don't misunderstand, Katherine. I think you're a wonderful girl. But you're not English. You weren't born here."

"Ah. My blood isn't quite blue enough."

Marjorie looked miserable. "That's not what I meant. Oh, perhaps it *is* what I meant. But I certainly didn't mean to hurt you, merely to explain why such an event would be considered a tragedy. I don't think you truly understand the consequences of being compromised. Just being alone with him was scandalous. And if you were . . . doing something . . . then he would have no choice but to offer for you." She stopped, flushing even redder.

"Would it still be a tragedy if Lord Avonleigh decided of his own will to marry me?"

Marjorie giggled. "Not nearly so awful." Then she added, "Please don't be angry with me."

Katherine sighed. "I'm not." Marjorie gave her a look of skepticism. "Perhaps a small bit, but I shall endeavor to forgive you for your cruel honesty."

Marjorie pouted a bit, which made Katherine laugh. But it still bothered her that Marjorie would think her capable of trapping Graham—and that such an event would be considered a "tragedy."

Chapter 8

Breakfast that morning was a simple affair. The Haverslys' excellent staff had put out various dishes on a large, elaborate buffet, and replenished them with fresh food whenever something became depleted.

"General Lawton is staring at you again, Mother," Katherine said beneath her breath. "Perhaps you should remind the gentleman you are married. He seems to have attached himself to you ever since Brighton."

Her mother waved a hand at her, then smiled at the general. "He's harmless enough. And I do enjoy his company. He has such a wonderful way of telling a story. I haven't laughed so much in years."

Katherine eyed the general skeptically. She'd thought him rather loud and boisterous, but she supposed he was good company.

They carried their plates to the large dining table, her mother sitting next to the general and Katherine beside her. Within moments, the Von Haupts had gotten their food and seated themselves across from their party.

"Good morning, Miss Von Haupt, Mrs. Von Haupt," Katherine said politely. She looked at the door, hoping to see Marjorie and Lady Summerfield enter but was disappointed.

"Good morning, Miss Wright," Claudia said brightly, and

Katherine swore Mrs. Von Haupt cringed. "Are you excited about today's hunt?"

Katherine wrinkled her nose. "I know it's not quite the thing to disdain the hunt while in England, but I do believe I'll stay here and catch up with my correspondence today."

"Or you could come with us," Claudia said, causing Mrs. Von Haupt's head to turn so quickly, Katherine thought the older woman might have harmed her neck. "Lord Avonleigh's estate is less than an hour's ride and we're going to visit it."

"I'm sure the Wrights have other things they'd rather do," Mrs. Von Haupt said with such false politeness, Katherine felt her temperature rise.

"Actually," Katherine's mother said, "that would be lovely."

This time it was Katherine's turn to snap her head around. She widened her eyes, trying to tell her mother it was not a good idea to tag along, but she could see any protest would be in vain. Her mother was having entirely too much fun trying to torture Mrs. Von Haupt.

"Thank you so much for inviting us," Elizabeth said, before turning to the general and inviting him to join their small party.

"I've heard enough gunshots in my lifetime," he said, his tone edged with a bit of poignancy. "And I'd like to see Bryant Park again. I remember visiting the place when the old marquess was alive. Grand old building."

"That's wonderful," Claudia gushed. "The more the merrier." And Katherine began to wonder if Claudia was afraid to be alone with Lord Avonleigh. She thought back to all those stories she'd heard about him, how gruff and serious he was, how caustic and jaded. Was that the man Claudia saw?

Katherine did not want to go, for she knew if she did, Graham would no doubt try to maneuver her to be alone with him, and she wasn't sure she could resist him. Even now, she felt that odd tug. She'd thought a great deal about what Marjorie had told her at the picnic and she'd decided she would not put him in danger of being forced to marry her—or herself in danger of ruining her reputation. She knew she should not have gone into that glade alone with him. She'd been taught better than that. She believed wholeheartedly in having good morals, in keeping oneself pure before marriage. The problem with having these high moral beliefs was dealing with them once they were tested. She was afraid if he asked for another kiss, she'd quickly forget about everything else and fall into his arms. What kind of girl did that make her?

Graham knew God had not answered his most fervent prayers when he woke up to see the sun shining brightly. Where was the bloody rotten weather when you needed it? He would have much preferred attending the hunt than dragging Miss Von Haupt and her mother to Bryant Park. He had no idea who would make up their party, but he did know Katherine would not be among them. She'd been studiously avoiding him since their kiss, and he could find no fault in her doing so. He'd been rash, foolishly so, but he could not honestly say he regretted it. Perhaps that was not completely honest. He did regret kissing her, if only because it had made him mad for more.

Bryant Park was relatively small, by aristocratic standards. The house itself had been built in the late seventeenth century on three hundred acres, a relatively diminutive plot. Graham knew he should sell it—as his solicitor had suggested—but the old place wouldn't bring much, and he felt if he did let it go, he would be selling the last memories of his father off to a stranger. It was the only bit of unentailed property he owned, and he was probably every kind of fool not to sell it, but just the thought of strangers living in it, renovating it, made him physically ill. Once, it had held a large bevy of servants. Now, the rich golden exterior held only a skeleton crew of aging staff who could barely keep the old place livable. As he had in Avonleigh, he hadn't let a single person go at Bryant Park, but he hadn't replaced anyone in ten years—whether they left for more lucrative employment elsewhere or died. Even a small house like Bryant Park should have nearly two times the staff he had on hand, and the thought that he would someday soon be able to run the old place the way it should be run was gratifying.

It was embarrassing to bring the Americans to see it. He knew Mrs. Von Haupt in particular would be assessing the place with greedy eyes, likely redecorating each room to suit her own lavish taste. The main living areas of the home were well-maintained, if a bit worn. But the upper floors were all but empty, furniture that was worth selling long gone. Halls empty of paintings, sitting rooms with no furniture to sit upon. He'd sold every bit of unentailed property his father had owned except for Bryant Park, then put nearly every dime of it into a growing American brokerage house, Jay Cooke & Company. Graham had been assured that his money would not only be safe, but would grow tenfold. He'd personally spoken to several investors who swore by the man, who'd made a fortune with Cooke. Cooke was a genius at investing, he'd been assured, but only two years after his investment, he'd received word of the company's full collapse. All his money was gone, and he had absolutely no hope of regaining it for he had no more funds to invest. Just the thought of the telegram he'd received not six months earlier made his heart pound sickeningly in his chest. He'd been so damned certain all his financial woes had been solved, only to find out he was in far worse shape than he'd ever been. His meetings in Brighton had proved fruitless and humiliating. There was no way to earn back the money he'd lost with Cooke.

It had taken him two months to come to grips with this new reality; the only way for him to quickly gain enough money to save his estate and help his tenants at Avonleigh was through marriage. And the only marriageable women with that kind of money were Americans.

His man of business, Menders, had made a list of American heiresses, and Katherine Wright wasn't even on it as a potential bride—whether because of their finances or her parents' rather humble beginnings, he did not know. He did know Menders found the list slightly distasteful, handing it to him with obvious reluctance. It was nearly unheard of for a member of the peerage to even consider marrying a commoner (worse still, an American commoner)—unless she was a great heiress, which Katherine was not.

Just that brief thought of her filled him with uncomfortable longing. He knew they were playing a dangerous game, but he found he could not stop himself. This feeling was so beyond his experience, it was more than disturbing. He knew he could not marry her, he knew he could not have her, and yet he felt compelled to be with her, touch her. God above knew he didn't *want* to feel this way. It was a completely foreign notion—a woman who fascinated him.

Graham walked from the house and stopped abruptly when he saw Katherine and Claudia standing side-by-side, both looking charming in their riding habits. Their mothers sat in a carriage—

Mrs. Von Haupt looking stone-faced and Mrs. Wright appearing relaxed and happy. General Lawton, in full regalia, sat across from the ladies, animatedly telling a story.

"What an unexpected surprise," Graham said, gazing levelly at Katherine.

"I do hope you don't mind," Claudia gushed. "This morning at breakfast Miss Wright mentioned she was not attending the hunt, and I invited her along with us."

Graham raised one eyebrow. "Really. How thoughtful of you, Miss Von Haupt."

"Mrs. Von Haupt was thrilled to have company in the carriage," Katherine said blandly, but her eyes sparkled in mirth.

While the groomsmen assisted the ladies onto their horses, he mounted his own horse, patting its neck affectionately. His rooms might be empty at Bryant Park, but he hadn't yet had the heart to empty his stable. He had some of the finest cattle in England, including the fine Arabian he now sat upon.

"A beautiful animal," Katherine said. "My father has a few Arabians back home at his parents' farm. He's the envy of the neighborhood."

"I imagine he is."

"We don't have Arabians," Claudia said. "Just regular horses. A matching black pair for our carriage. But mother wants to replace one because it has a small white spot on its nose and the other hasn't any. She says it's easier to find a horse without a spot than one with a spot just like the one he has. Or is it a she?" She giggled. "I'm not really certain."

"You can tell by looking beneath," Katherine said. "If it has male parts, it's male."

Claudia blushed crimson. "Oh, I could never do *that*."

Graham had to use all his will not to smile at the exchange, but he could not stop himself from darting a glance at Katherine, who gave him a look of pure innocence that he didn't believe for a moment.

Claudia and Katherine led the way, with Graham behind them and the carriage trailing a bit. The two women sat their horses beautifully, but his eyes were drawn to Katherine, to the way she held her head so proudly, to the large lavender plume that bobbed in time to her horse's steps. He'd never met a woman so enamored with silly hats. Nature had not created a feather that color, he was fairly certain.

"I say, Miss Wright, what type of bird did your feather come from?"

She turned her head so he could see the sharp definition of her jaw. "American ostrich." No hesitation. No hint that she had just made up a species of bird. "They run wild about Central Park."

And poor Claudia, bless her, looked aghast at Katherine as if learning something absolutely amazing. "I've never seen a wild ostrich. Why, when I get home I'll have to have Papa take me looking for one."

Katherine looked over to her companion, and felt instantly sorry for making up such a tale. "I was teasing, Claudia. It's a dyed African ostrich feather."

"Oh." She was clearly disappointed.

"You won't be back home for quite a while at any rate, will you?"

Claudia looked instantly alarmed, as if she'd quite forgotten what she was doing in England. "No, I don't suppose I will," she said slowly.

They rode in silence for perhaps five paces before Claudia recovered and began talking. Claudia chatted on—and on—about parties she'd gone to in New York, about people Katherine knew of but hardly counted in her circle of friends. She could feel Graham behind her, silent and no doubt staring at her. It was almost as if his gaze could physically manifest itself and caress her spine. She felt the nearly overwhelming urge to turn around and tell him to stop, and only the realization of how stupid she would look to everyone in their party halted her.

Finally, Claudia's prattling was too much for him to bear, and he retreated to the carriage two dozen yards back to talk to the general.

"Do you shop on Fifth Avenue?" Claudia asked, then continued on as if Katherine's answer had no bearing whatsoever to whether she'd tell her next tale. "There was this lovely necklace in Carlyle's window. Stunning sapphire and diamond with a charming little floret, and I wanted it so badly. I'd walk by almost every day." She turned to Katherine and laughed. "I do love to shop. My friends and I, mostly Barbara Knight, would stare and stare at it. She wanted it nearly as badly as I. Of course, I asked Mama and then Papa, but it was very dear, you see. Quite beyond anything I had in my collection of jewels. But I pestered them endlessly. I nearly made myself sick with the wanting of it. Have you ever felt that way about anything?"

A bit startled that she was actually being asked to participate in this conversation, Katherine said, "A bit."

"I get that way about nearly everything I truly want," Claudia confessed. "One day, the necklace was gone. I was quite upset, as you can imagine. Wouldn't you know it? At my birthday, my father presented me with that sapphire and diamond necklace."

"My goodness, you must have been thrilled," Katherine said, now fully engaged in the story.

"That's just it, I wasn't. The day the necklace disappeared from the window, I was disappointed certainly, but there was another pretty necklace in its place and I rather liked that one, too. Not as much as the first, mind you, but it was still lovely and not nearly so expensive. And when I finally had the necklace, I realized I didn't really want it after all. It's heavy and uncomfortable and doesn't go with a thing I have."

"Ah," Katherine said. "Be careful what you wish for."

Claudia brightened upon hearing that adage. "Yes." Then she frowned. "I fear I feel about Lord Avonleigh the same as I felt about that necklace," she said in a rush, looking as if she might be ill.

"Oh no, I'm sure you do not. He is a person, not a necklace. He's going to be your husband."

Claudia stared ahead, clearly distressed. "Can I tell you something?"

"Of course," Katherine said.

"Yesterday, when you were in the woods with Lord Avonleigh and we came upon you, I . . ." Claudia pressed her lips together.

"Yes?" Katherine urged, even though she was filled with sudden trepidation. What if Claudia suspected they'd been kissing? She truly wasn't certain what she could say.

"I was hoping we'd catch you in a compromising position," Claudia said in a giddy rush.

"What?" Too loud. Then, "What can you possibly mean?"

"Oh, I know it was awful of me even to think such a thing, but I thought if you were compromised, I wouldn't have to marry him." She closed her eyes briefly and let out a small sound, as if she were in pain. "Is that horrid?"

"Yes, it is. Very," Katherine said fervently. She thought back upon what Marjorie had told her. She'd always known on some level how scandalous such an occurrence would be, but she now had a much better understanding. "It would hurt everyone. You and Lord Avonleigh most of all."

"I suppose it would," Claudia said, sounding disappointed.

"Don't you want to marry Lord Avonleigh?"

"Yes, no. I don't know. He frightens me. He's always scowling and growling things at me. And he does truly seem to like you. He smiled at you. He *laughed* with you."

For just an instant, Katherine wished she had been caught in that glade, wished it fervently. Then Marjorie's outrage rang in her ears.

"He isn't an entirely unpleasant man," Katherine said. "I think once you get to know him, you'll agree."

Claudia wrung her hands, and her mount, as if sensing her distress, shied a bit before straightening. "I'm certain you are right. Father will be here soon. We expect him any day now and then everything will be settled."

"And just imagine, you'll be a marchioness."

"And I'll live there," Claudia said, pointing ahead as her face brightened like a little girl who'd just seen her first pony.

Bryant Park was made from golden stone, a home as grand as the title it housed. Two wings of the building reached out as if to embrace Katherine. Its copper roof was streaked with age, its chimneys blackened from centuries of use. It looked as if it would stand there forever, waiting for her to come to it.

As they drew closer, Graham caught up with them. "What do you think?" he asked.

"Can we paint it?" Claudia asked. "I mean to say, have you ever thought about painting it?"

Graham looked as if he'd just swallowed a large walnut, shell and all. "Paint?"

"Think how grand it would look white."

Katherine stared at the stone structure and tried to picture it whitewashed. "But, Claudia, the paint would chip so close to the sea. You'd constantly be having to paint it. And the smell. Awful. I think you're much better off keeping it this lovely yellow stone."

"You think it lovely?" Graham asked, his voice low.

Katherine looked at him and tried to brace herself for the impact of his eyes on her—and failed miserably. Why was it whenever she looked upon him, she felt as if her lungs ceased to work properly? "I think it's the loveliest home I've ever seen."

"Truly?" Claudia asked, looking at the house a bit skeptically. "Have you seen Blenheim Palace? It's quite grander than this. The Duke of Marble lives there."

"Marlborough," Graham corrected.

Claudia waved a dismissive hand, as if it didn't matter what the duke's title was. "Yes. Marlborough. He has quite a lovely home."

Behind them, the carriage pulled up, and Graham dismounted gracefully and handed his reins to a waiting groom. He waved a rather elderly looking footman away and helped the two older women down from the carriage.

"Oh." Mrs. Von Haupt looked upon the manor house as if it were a grave disappointment. "The photographs I've seen made it seem quite a bit bigger." She looked down at the rutted drive, her eyes taking in the stained stones, the cracked steps that led up to a door that perhaps needed some refinishing to bring it back to grandeur. "And in better condition."

Katherine saw Graham clench his jaw, but he remained rigidly polite. "Yes, she has seen better days."

"Everything in England is so very old, isn't it," Claudia said, sounding slightly dismayed.

"The inside is far worse," Graham said grimly, and almost in a tone that sounded as though he was rather enjoying their disappointment. "If you think Bryant Park is run-down, you should see Avonleigh Manor in Northumberland. Last time I was there it had bats."

Claudia looked horrified, which Katherine suspected was his intent. "Bats? I shouldn't like that."

"I rather like the old place. And the bats."

Now Katherine *knew* he was being contrary. "Bats are one thing, of course, but bat guano quite another," Katherine said, feeling the strangest need to protect Claudia.

Graham turned his gaze to her, his eyes bright with humor. "Of course. Shall we have the grand tour? After you, ladies."

Katherine walked by him, again feeling that stare, and vowed to ignore him completely from now on.

Graham stared after them, his mind in turmoil. Here he was,

showing his potential bride her new home, and he felt nothing but depressed at the thought that her money could bring it back to grandeur.

"Which girl is it you have your sights on?"

Graham started at the sound of the general's voice in his ear.

"Leave off, General," Graham said irritably. He'd known Hortence Lawton for years and normally liked the older man's candor. He was in no mood for it at the moment. "And if I'm not mistaken, it's a bit of the pot calling the kettle black. I do believe Mrs. Wright is a married woman."

If he thought the general would feel put in his place, he was sorely mistaken. The old codger simply threw back his head after he'd let Graham's jibe settle in and had himself a good laugh. "Married women," the general muttered. "Indeed, they are the most gratifying."

"There is no gas?" Mrs. Von Haupt looked with horror at the candles gracing the walls of the entry. She might have been looking up and seeing blue sky and saying: There is no roof? "Surely you have a gas works nearby."

Graham swallowed down his retort. "The house does have gas in the private quarters and kitchen," he said. "At the time, that seemed sufficient." And less costly, if he remembered the reason his father had forgone lighting the entire house.

"The ballroom? Surely that is laid."

"No."

Graham looked at the old house through their eyes. It was grand, certainly, but obviously neglected. His small staff of mostly elderly servants simply couldn't maintain the house as it should be maintained. Directly above his head, he noticed a long string of dust wafting in the breeze coming in through the open door. And below his feet, the marble was decidedly gritty, as if it had been some time since the entrance had seen a broom.

Just then a woman, her mobcap askew, entered the hall and stopped in her tracks, her hand fluttering to her chest as if she were experiencing palpitations.

"Oh my lord," she said, giving a quick curtsy, and Graham wasn't certain whether she was greeting him or using the Lord's name in vain. "We hadn't realized you'd be visitin' today with *guests*, my lord. I'm afraid there's only meself and Jones here right now."

A thirty-thousand-square-foot home and two servants in residence. Lovely.

"Pray tell, Mrs. Porter, where are the other members of the staff?" Graham asked. All five of them. He suppressed a sigh.

"Why, to the christening, of course. Mrs. Berkley's granddaughter, sir. She had a boy not two weeks ago. I couldn't go. My joints, you see, my lord."

"I see. Please give Mrs. Berkley my congratulations. It is her first great-grandchild, is it not?"

"Oh yes, my lord." Mrs. Porter beamed at him.

"Thank you, Mrs. Porter, that will be all," he said, dismissing the elderly woman. She, if he wasn't mistaken, was also a great-grandmother. The old lady limped off whence she came, and Graham made a mental note to buy the woman a cane.

"One of the younger members of my staff," Graham said dryly. The two Von Haupts looked horrified, but behind him, he heard what sounded like a stifled laugh, and he knew immediately it was Katherine. "Would you like to begin your tour in the gallery or the ballroom?"

"The ballroom, I think," Claudia said. No doubt she was imagining grand balls and entertainments. As ballrooms went, his was not very impressive, and he knew Claudia would be sorely disappointed.

"I've no idea of its condition as it hasn't been used in nearly fifteen years."

Claudia seemed shocked. "Fifteen years? Why that's nearly as long as I've been alive."

He walked them down a long, dusty corridor at the end of which was a set of French doors leading to Bryant Park's ballroom. "Lift your skirts," he heard Mrs. Von Haupt hiss. "You'll ruin your hem."

When he turned to open the doors, Katherine sneezed into her handkerchief, then gave him a cheeky grin. She was enjoying his discomfort, he was certain of it.

"Why, this can't be it," Claudia said, gazing around the dark and rather dreary room. "It's no bigger than my sitting room at home.

This will never do. Surely, this cannot be your home's only ball-room."

"At the present, I'm afraid so. My father converted our former ballroom into a theater, you see."

"A theater?" Mrs. Von Haupt said, clearly scandalized. "Why on earth would he do such a thing?"

"He enjoyed the theater," Graham said, barely loosening up his jaw enough to sound civil. "He imported acts from France and Germany and invited his London friends. Once, we hosted the Liverpool Philharmonic Orchestra. I shudder to think what that cost."

"I liked those French shows, myself," the general said, waggling his brows at Katherine's mother, who giggled shamelessly. Katherine frowned at her mother, and Graham wondered if she suspected what he did—that her mother was carrying on an affair.

"Certainly the theater could be converted back to a ballroom," Mrs. Von Haupt said.

"I'm certain it could be, Mrs. Von Haupt, but it shall never happen. At least not while I'm the master of this home. I'm rather fond of the theater. It was my father's passion and holds many happy memories."

Mrs. Von Haupt pressed her mouth into a straight line, clearly unhappy with this. "We shall see," she said, and it was all Graham could do not to usher her out of his home forever. It was only the thought of all the people who depended upon him for their livelihood that stopped him. No doubt she'd add a stipulation into the marriage contract about the blasted ballroom.

"May we see the theater?" Katherine asked, uttering her first words since entering his home.

"I'd rather not," huffed Mrs. Von Haupt. "Surely you have a gallery that might be of interest."

"Certainly I do," Graham said. "Why don't I escort you there before I take the others to the theater."

"Excellent idea, Avonleigh. I have many fond memories of that theater. And your father. I've never known anyone before or since who could keep his guests so well entertained."

"Yes, I'm certain while his estate was crumbling around him he had a very grand time," Mrs. Von Haupt said, her gaze going to the moth-eaten curtains and stained wall coverings.

Katherine looked at Graham, fearing he actually might do violence to Mrs. Von Haupt. How could she be so completely oblivious to the needles she was thrusting into him? Katherine was well aware Mrs. Von Haupt enjoyed wielding her power over people, but surely it did not extend to her daughter's future husband.

"If you'll follow me, ladies and General, I'll show you to the gallery. It's on the second floor, as is the theater," Graham said, and Katherine wanted to applaud his control.

They all walked up the stairs, one of the few places Katherine had seen that was actually clean—or at the very least where they hadn't left footprints in their wake. At the top of the landing was a large door, which led to the gallery. It was well-lit and spotless, no doubt cared for by a servant who had great pride working for the Spencer family.

"I hope you ladies will be fine while I show the others the theater."

"Yes, of course," Claudia said. "Oh, there you are, my lord."

Katherine, unable to stop herself, walked into the gallery to view Graham's portrait—and burst out laughing.

She could feel Graham come up next to her. "You find it not a good likeness?" he asked.

She stared up at the man in the picture, the arrogant, angry man, and shook her head. "It looks like the artist just insulted you," she said, trying to hide her mirth. "You look so very annoyed."

"I think it looks just like him. Handsome and yet serious," Claudia said, apparently defending him. Her eyes were on the empty space next to his portrait, no doubt imagining her own lovely likeness there.

"Oh, it does very much look like Lord Avonleigh," Katherine said. "I suppose that's what I find so amusing."

She heard him huff out a breath behind her. "Those of you who would like to see the theater may follow me."

Katherine had much more interest in the theater than the gallery, and knowing her mother and the general would be there, followed the small group down a maze of halls until they stopped at two of the largest doors she'd ever seen inside a home.

"And here we have Philip's Folly," Graham said fondly. Above the door, it indeed said, "Philip's Folly" in gold leaf, each side adorned by outlandish cupids bearing the requisite bow and arrow and lavish wings. She wondered how a man who could be so ridiculously whimsical could have ended his own life.

Graham opened the doors with a flourish, revealing a darkened interior. He hurried first down one side, then the other, slowly bringing the exquisite theater to light. She had but one thought: It must have cost a fortune to build. While it was a small theater, it was as richly appointed as anything she'd seen in London or New York. The gilding, the moldings, the thick carpeting beneath her feet, the well-appointed private boxes one level above the orchestra seats—all spoke of affluence that went beyond anything Katherine had seen in a private home. Folly, indeed.

"I say, I'm going to show Mrs. Wright the box I used when I was here last," the general said, and before Katherine could utter a word, the two were gone.

When Graham returned from turning on the lights, he looked around, obviously curious to find Katherine standing there by herself.

"Where are your mother and the general?"

Katherine took a step back, even though he was still some distance from her. "He said something about exploring one of the boxes he was familiar with."

"Ah."

She looked almost frantically around, straining her ears to hear them. Where on earth had they gone, and had her mother gone quite mad to leave her alone with Graham?

"It's a lovely theater. I'm glad you have happy memories of your father here."

Graham looked around, a small smile on his lips. "The arts were his passion. His greatest wish was to discover some talent that hadn't yet been discovered. The house was always filled with interesting people from nearly every country. It was a very lively place."

Katherine turned to walk down the right aisle, and Graham, mirroring her actions, turned and walked down the left side. They were separated by a row of fourteen seats, and Katherine relaxed just slightly. Above her, she thought she heard her mother's voice, but she didn't see the other couple. "It's very grand."

"I know what you're thinking, that Philip's Folly is aptly named, that if my father hadn't been so foolish with his money I wouldn't be in the position I'm in today."

Katherine felt herself blush guiltily, for that was very close to what she had been thinking. "It does seem a bit extravagant."

"It made my father happy," he said simply. "He was not a happy man, and yet when he was here, planning a concert, filling this house with friends, he was happy."

"Then it was worth it, I suppose." She turned the corner just as he did, and they walked to the front of the theater, where the orchestra pit lay empty of even chairs. It was so silent, it was difficult to imagine the room filled with people, the stage alight and crowded with performers.

A movement above her caught her eye, and she saw her mother on the opposite side of the theater sitting in a box next to the general. "Isn't this fabulous?" her mother called down.

"It is," Katherine said. Then to Graham, "It truly is the most wonderful place. You must never allow Claudia to change it into a ballroom."

"I want to kiss you."

She swallowed, ignoring the instant heat those low words sent spiraling through her body. "Don't."

"I won't," he said casually, but his eyes said something far, far different. "But I do want to."

"Why must you say such things?" Katherine said, whispering harshly, her eyes darting to where her mother and the general sat, even though they were far too distant for them to hear. "When you know that I want you to." She pressed her lips together as if the action would stop her from saying anything else so foolish. His nostrils flared at her words, and he took a small step toward her.

"I want to do more than kiss you. I want to hold you, touch you. I want to taste you. I want to feel your skin against mine."

Katherine closed her eyes briefly. "You know that's impossible."

"The thought that I might never even kiss you again . . . it's driving me a bit mad."

Katherine's breath was becoming shallow as she stared at him, every part of her being wanting exactly what he wanted. But it was wrong. They would never marry. And she would never give herself to a man who was not her husband. But a kiss? What harm could one kiss do? He wasn't officially engaged; Claudia didn't truly care for him. A kiss would hurt no one. It amazed Katherine, who'd lived her life in shades of black and white, that she could make kissing Graham seem perfectly fine, almost good and right.

He must have seen her decision in her eyes, for he immediately walked beneath the boxes where her mother sat with the general. She followed, smiling brilliantly up at her mother and waving, trying desperately not to run directly into his arms. In the end, it was hopeless. As soon as she reached the overhang, he pulled on her wrist and she fell into his arms. They were silent, though God above knew that was perhaps the most difficult thing to manage. For the minute Graham's lips touched hers, she wanted to scream out from the joy of it, from the exquisite relief of finally having him kiss her. He turned her so that her back was to the wall and leaned into her so she could feel his arousal. She wasn't surprised this time and felt no fear. Instead, she welcomed his maleness, moving against him, relishing the feeling of him against her center. He was familiar to her and even that thought was thrilling.

His mouth found her neck, and she tilted her head, loving the way his hot tongue felt against her sensitive skin. One hand cupped her breast, and then his thumb moved against her nipple, shooting lightning through her. She had never been so aroused in her life, never felt such a heavy fullness, never wanted to strip herself of her clothing and press her body against another's flesh. What was wrong with her? What was he doing to her? What sort of madness had taken over her that had her pressing against him to find some relief from the beautiful torture happening between her legs?

Katherine couldn't believe she was able to feel all these things and remain silent. He moved his hand from her breast, trailing downward along her side, then slowly placing it between her legs. She should be mortified, but she wasn't. Instead she pulled his head away, put her lips near his ear, and said, "Yes." *Yes.* He let out a breath that sounded like, "Oh God." He moved his hand on her, pressing, and she could feel the wetness between her legs.

"Katherine?" Her mother.

Graham pressed a hard kiss to her mouth and removed his hand from between her legs, stepping back slightly with a pained expression on his handsome face. "Answer her," he whispered.

"Yes, Mother. We're heading back to the gallery now. Are you coming?" She moved from beneath the overhang to look up at her mother.

"There you are. Yes, we'll meet you at the theater entrance."

Her mother disappeared from view, and Katherine slumped in relief.

"I'm sorry," she whispered miserably. "I don't know what comes over me when you are near me. I'm not myself. I'm never myself when you're around. I don't understand it. I am not a woman who does these things."

"You are, Katherine," Graham said, his gray eyes still blazing. "And I'm damned glad for it."

She shook her head miserably, but still managed to let out a chuckle. "Let's go meet my mother and the general. I would like to see your gallery and gaze upon all your dour ancestors."

By the time they all returned to Briarbrook, the hunting party was back and had, for the most part, retired to their rooms until supper. Lady Haversly greeted their small group, pulling Graham aside.

"Mr. Norris is here," she said, shifting her eyes toward the others. "I understand he is a particular friend of yours?"

Indeed, Charles Norris, the second son of Viscount Melbourne, could be considered a friend, Graham supposed. At least they had been chums during school, though Charles was a bit younger. Graham had seen little of Charles of late, something about his going to India— or was it Africa—after his failed courtship of Melissa Stanhope, now the Countess of Willington. It would be good to see him, he realized. "Yes, I've known Charles since Cambridge," Graham said.

Lady Haversly seemed markedly glad to hear of it, which struck Graham as a bit odd. He'd always thought of Charles as a cheerful, if not bland fellow. "He's just come back from Africa," she said, as if that explained her behavior. "I've put him two doors down from you, on the left."

Graham turned to his party and excused himself, making an effort not to allow his gaze to linger too long on Katherine, then headed to his room to change out of his dusty clothes. He was about to open his room when he heard a man bellow, "Goddamn and bloody hell, are you trying to kill me?"

A low murmur was the response, and then another word that

Graham hadn't heard in polite company in quite some time. Grinning, he stopped two doors down from his own and knocked politely on the door. More cursing, this time in a much more subdued voice, and the door was opened by an Indian fellow, dressed in gold, a yellow turban on his head.

"How can I help you, sir?" he asked, his brown eyes challenging, as if he were protecting Charles, not simply making an inquiry.

"Would you please tell Mr. Norris that Lord Avonleigh is here and would like to welcome him home." Graham said this loudly enough that Charles could hear him. He was quite certain Charles cursed beneath his breath before calling out, "Let him in, Prajit, he's an old friend."

If Graham didn't know he was looking at Charles Norris, he would not have recognized the man. The Charles he remembered was slim and elegant. This man looked as if he could tear a house down with his bared hands. He'd always been tall, very nearly as tall as Graham, but his elegance had made him appear smaller. His skin was now darker than the typical Englishman's, his hair longer, his face less shaved, his dress negligent.

"What the deuce happened to you?" Avonleigh asked without preamble.

"India," Charles said, glaring at Prajit as if it were somehow his servant's fault. "And a bit of Africa thrown in for good measure."

"India is kind to those who are kind to India," Prajit said calmly as he returned to unpacking Charles's trunk.

Charles glared at the man, but Graham had the distinct feeling he wasn't truly angry. It was then Graham realized Charles was still sitting, and sitting rather awkwardly, with one leg stretched out. Charles apparently noticed his curiosity and rubbed his leg. "I got caught in the middle of a skirmish," he said.

"I was led to believe relations with India were quite good," Graham said, searching his mind for any news of discontent in India.

"Ah, but our relations with some in the African continent are not so good. I was in the Gold Coast." Prajit mumbled something under his breath in Hindu, gaining a dark look from Charles. "I wouldn't let them take the leg. Or rather, Prajit didn't let them take it. Still hurts like a devil, though." As if to prove his point, Charles suddenly tensed, his face contorting. "Bloody fucking hell," he said, grasping his leg. Prajit immediately came to his side, holding a vial out to Charles, who batted his hand away.

"How long has it been?" Graham asked.

"Ten hellish months. But the leg's much better," Charles said, laughing at the dichotomy of such a statement. "The ride here wasn't good for it, but I'll be fine in an hour or two. How have you been, Avonleigh?"

"Better than you, apparently," Graham said dryly. "I'm getting married."

"Married. I haven't been looking out the windows much of late, but I haven't heard of pigs flying. Or hell freezing over."

Despite himself, Graham chuckled. "She's a lovely American girl."

Charles narrowed his eyes. "Ah, then it's true," he said.

"What is true?"

"An heiress. I'd heard rumors." Charles shrugged, and Graham was flabbergasted.

"How long have you been back in England?" Graham asked, rather shocked that his friend could have possibly heard such a thing so quickly. Perhaps he was naïve, but he truly hadn't known it was common knowledge that he was in financial straits. Good God, the creditors would come pounding on his door at any moment.

"I've been home two weeks."

"And the rumor mill was able to reach your ears?"

Charles grinned. "I saw Willington, you idiot. He was giddy about his wife's pregnancy and mentioned you were seriously looking for a bride. I suppose it slipped out."

"I think she's had ten brats by now," Graham said.

"This is number five," Charles said, his cheeks beneath his tanned skin turning slightly ruddy.

"They are happy," Graham said, rather shocked to see that Charles was still sensitive about the subject of Melissa. Then again, he had made quite a cake of himself all those years ago by falling for a woman who was already in love with their good friend John Atwell, Lord Willington. Now that he thought about it, Charles had a habit of falling in love quickly—and with the wrong woman. "Makes one rather ill to watch the two of them together. And what of you? Do you have a wife?"

Charles smiled. "That's why I'm here. To find myself one."

* * *

That night, the group played charades—men against the women—and it was great fun for Katherine watching a stone-faced Graham try to entertain. Honestly, the man looked like he was attending a funeral, not playing an amusing parlor game. He'd been joined by a man Katherine didn't recognize, a striking gentlemen who reminded her of the frontiersmen who lived in the wilderness of America. He was rugged, with too-long hair and a square jaw that looked like it had been shaped by an ax rather than a blade. His eyes were strangely intense—and often on her—which was rather disconcerting, if not a tiny bit thrilling.

The two teams wrote various subjects on small bits of paper and placed them in a hat that the other team would have to pick from. Each member of the team—there were conveniently eight men and eight women—would get the chance to draw out a piece of paper and act out whatever was on the card. It had been Claudia who'd come up the game's theme: happy things. She'd said this and clapped her hands, charming everyone in the room with her childlike enthusiasm. The minute the words came from her mouth, Graham frowned. Likely, it would be difficult for him to come up with something happy, Katherine thought. She caught his eye and raised one eyebrow, acknowledging this fact, and he very nearly smiled. She thought she detected the slight glint of amusement in his eyes.

The first charade, acted out expertly by Mrs. Von Haupt—who strangely enough seemed to be enjoying herself—was *Christmas pudding*. The men's first charade was *new ball gown* (this submitted by Claudia), and General Lawton had the party in stitches as he acted it out. Next to her, Katherine's mother wiped tears of mirth from her eyes as the general dipped a curtsy after the men had guessed correctly.

An hour later, Lady Haversly stood, grabbed a piece of paper, and smiled. The score was tied, and this was the very last clue. The women all leaned forward, ferocious in their desire to best the men. She held up her hand, showing two fingers. "Two words," the women said in unison.

Then, Lady Haversly held her hands in front of her face and squinted her eyes. "Fear," shouted one lady. "Monster." "Light."

"Oh, bright," Claudia said triumphantly as Lady Haversly touched her nose, indicating that was, indeed, the right answer.

Then the lady put one fist atop the other. "On," her mother shouted.

Katherine scanned the men, who were enjoying the scene being acted out by Lady Haversly, and stopped dead at Graham. From the look on his face, she knew he was the one who'd put this piece of paper in the hat. He was staring at her in a way that made her entire body flush. She quickly looked away, her heart thudding heavily in her chest, as Lady Haversly made a great show of thrashing her arms about. "Beach," Katherine murmured. "Brighton Beach."

"What? What did you say, Miss Wright?"

Katherine lifted her head and studiously avoided looking at Graham, feeling unaccountably angry. "Brighton Beach," she repeated.

The women clapped, ecstatic that they had won the game, and Katherine forced a smile. Brighton Beach came under the list of "happy things" for Graham. Of all the things he could have chosen—a fine cigar, French brandy, a new horse—he had chosen Brighton. It was a private declaration made publicly that Katherine had to hold secret in her heart. And that simply reminded her of what they had done together that morning. Katherine felt Claudia look at her, and Katherine turned, forcing a smile.

"Isn't it wonderful we won?" Katherine asked.

Claudia nodded, but a little furrow was showing between her brows, as she no doubt remembered that Brighton Beach was where she'd met Graham.

After the game, the guests dispersed to follow their own entertainments. Mrs. Von Haupt dragged poor Claudia over to the pianoforte, admonishing her to play, which she did adequately. Those who had not retired for the evening sat around the room in small groups. Her mother and the general had bidden Katherine a good night, and Katherine got an anxious feeling in her stomach at the easy way the two of them had departed the room. As if they were a couple, as if they were a *married* couple headed off to sleep—together.

"They may not be," Graham said in a low voice next to her.

It truly hadn't occurred to Katherine that her mother might be carrying on an affair right under her nose until that very moment. It was unthinkable. Her mother was married to her father. Such a thing was so far beyond Katherine's imagination, having it bloom in her mind suddenly was disorienting.

She looked up at Graham, the horror of the situation clear in her eyes.

"Take care, Katherine, every thought in your head is clearly showing on your face."

Katherine schooled her features with great effort. "Do you think they might be . . ."

Graham sighed. "I would be surprised if they were not," he said gently.

"But . . . she's my mother. And they're so . . . *old*. And she's married to my father!"

Graham shrugged and she wanted to punch him in the arm for his casual response. "There are far more shocking things you can discover about a parent. But please remember, Katherine, her decisions, while they may not be something you agree with or can even stomach, have nothing to do with you or how she feels about you. Unless she is discovered," he added sardonically. "Then I suppose it would affect you rather greatly."

"How can you be so blasé? Is this how you feel? Will you have an affair after your marriage?"

Graham's eyes shifted momentarily to Claudia, who continued to struggle through a Chopin piece. "I have no plans to, but I am only human."

"That is a ridiculous answer," Katherine said, hating that his eyes had flickered to Claudia. She knew what she was feeling— jealousy. She'd known all along that Graham would marry Claudia, but it did nothing to stop her heart from screaming. She wanted to throttle him—and herself for wanting even now to press her lips to his. "Do vows mean nothing?"

"Life is long, Katherine, and marriage is forever." He sounded weary.

"I think now I understand."

"What do you understand?"

"Why you can act this way with me. You are, for all intents and purposes, an engaged man. Yet at every turn, you pay me attention. No doubt this is how men in your world are. No doubt I'm simply a silly girl, a diversion from your insipid life."

"You're angry," he said, sounding just enough surprised that Katherine momentarily was blinded by her anger.

The man who'd been staring at her all night walked up to Graham's side, and Katherine immediately schooled her features into something more pleasant.

"Ah, Norris. Let me introduce you to Miss Katherine Wright. Mr. Charles Norris," Graham said with an ease that made Katherine even angrier. How could he be so calm when she wanted to throttle him?

Katherine knew her cheeks were flushed, and no doubt her smile didn't seem as genuine as it might, but she *did* smile as she held out her hand.

"A pleasure, Miss Wright," Charles said, taking her hand and bowing gracefully, a movement that seemed slightly at odds with his rough appearance. "How are you enjoying England so far?"

"I suppose it depends on the day, Mr. Norris," Katherine said. "And with whom I am keeping company."

Graham stiffened slightly, and Katherine's smile widened. "Then I shall have to rescue you the next time you find yourself in onerous company," Charles said.

Katherine laughed, surprised that the gentleman was so charming. And since her laughter seemed to bother Graham, she laughed a bit louder and a tad longer than she might have otherwise.

"Mr. Norris has been living in India," Graham said. "Returning there soon, are you?"

"I've no plans to, no," Charles said easily. "I've missed England and its dreary, cool weather. In India it's either raining incessantly or brutally hot. Or at least that's how it seemed to me."

Katherine looked coolly at Graham. "My lord, have you introduced Mr. Norris to your fiancée?"

"She is not my fiancée," he ground out.

Katherine waved a dismissive hand. "A mere technicality." Then, turning to Mr. Norris, she asked, "Where is your wife, Mr. Norris?"

Charles smiled, and Graham clamped a hand on his shoulder in what seemed a friendly gesture. "As a matter of fact, I find myself in need of a wife," Charles said, ignoring the hand on his shoulder.

"There are many delightful young women in England. I'm sure someone will catch your eye," Katherine said, giving him what she knew was her best and most charming smile. She hoped Graham would feel one small bit of what she felt when he looked at Claudia.

"I think someone already has," Charles said, then winced. Graham dropped his hand.

"Leg bothering you?" Graham asked, all solicitous innocence.

Charles gave his friend the oddest look just then, almost as if he couldn't believe Graham had asked that question. "Yes, my leg," he said as he rolled the shoulder Graham had just been touching.

Claudia came up to their group and put her arm around Katherine's waist, giving it a quick squeeze. "We're playing whist and I need a partner. Come on."

"If you could spare a moment, Miss Von Haupt. I'd like to introduce you to my friend, Mr. Charles Norris."

Claudia looked up at him with her China-blue eyes and smiled politely. "A pleasure, Mr. Norris," she said, and Katherine thought she heard just the slightest emphasis on "mister."

Graham watched the woman he likely loved being dragged away by the woman he would likely marry, until a soft chuckle distracted him.

"I cannot believe my bad luck," Charles said. "I finally meet a woman I would like to court, only to find out yet another of my friends has staked a claim."

"You are mistaken," Graham said with calm finality. "I have no claim on Miss Wright."

Chapter 9

What in God's name had he done? He'd practically given Charles carte blanche to court Katherine, something both of them seemed to be enjoying. Charles might not be the vacant boy he'd once been, but the chap still knew how to flirt and capture a girl's attention. From the looks of it, he had Katherine's full attention.

Disgusted, Graham sought out Claudia and wished her a good night, but not before she happily noted Charles's interest in Katherine.

"I think they look charming together, don't you, my lord?"

Graham forced himself to look at the pair, who chatted amiably with Lady Haversly. The older woman and Charles seemed completely enraptured in whatever it was Katherine was saying, damn them both. And not once did she look to see if he were still in the room. Apparently Charles had her complete attention. And why shouldn't he? He was a good man from a wealthy family. Amiable. Available.

"How unfortunate for both of them that he hasn't a title," she said mournfully.

Graham's brows furrowed. "I daresay that's not important to Miss Wright."

Claudia laughed as if that were the greatest of jokes. "Of course it's important to her. Why, it's all she can talk about. What title is this and what title is that. Of course, she hasn't the dowry to attract a grand title, but surely she can do better than a *mister*."

"His father is a viscount, Miss Von Haupt. His blood is as blue as that of anyone else in this room."

Claudia pursed her lips. "But he still hasn't got a title, and I'm certain Miss Wright would never consider him."

"No, and it's unlikely he'll obtain one anytime soon as his brother, who is next in line, already has three sons. I bid you good evening, Miss Von Haupt. Perhaps I'll see you in the morning. I hear an outing is planned to some nearby ruins."

"Good night, Lord Avonleigh."

He knew he should have corrected her and given her license to call him by his given name; they were having a private conversation, after all. But he simply couldn't bring himself to do it.

Graham entered his room and went directly to a decanter of brandy, poured a hefty amount, and took a long drink.

"Pleasant evening, sir?" Mr. Chase asked.

"As always, Chase," Graham said, turning his back so the valet could remove his jacket.

"A new guest has arrived," Mr. Chase said in a way that Graham knew this new guest was someone important.

"Do you mean Charles Norris? Yes, I know."

"No, sir. Mr. Von Haupt has arrived, sir."

Graham was about to take another sip of brandy, but paused momentarily before downing the rest of it. He would have sworn loudly, but he knew how much Chase hated curse words.

"I imagine there will be an announcement soon, sir?"

Was Chase purposely trying to grate on his nerves? Or was he genuinely excited about the news of his engagement?

"I imagine so," Graham said, as if the pending announcement was his own date for the gallows. He wished at that moment he'd never met Katherine Wright, that he'd never gone to Brighton Beach, that he'd never known what it was like to finally feel something other than mild interest in a woman. She was angry with him and he supposed she had a right to be. He acted like a besotted idiot when he was around her, fully aware that nothing could ever come of it. Good God, it was a wonder she hadn't slapped him. He deserved it.

"I ought to be horsewhipped," he said, sitting down upon his bed.

"I do think that's a bit harsh, sir. Perhaps a caning would do."

Graham let out a chuckle. "You always were soft, Everett."

Mr. Chase busied himself about the room, brushing Graham's jacket and putting his collar aside for cleaning later, while Graham brooded and looked at his empty glass.

"Sir," Mr. Chase said, breaking the silence. "If I may be . . ."

"Yes, be frank. You have infinite permission to speak frankly," Graham snapped, then instantly felt badly about it.

The valet simply raised an eyebrow and continued. "What do you truly know about this Miss Wright other than the fact she lied outright to you when you met?"

Graham straightened. The audacity of the man! How dare he disparage Miss Wright's character? "If you remember correctly," he said, his voice hard, "I lied, as well."

"Yes, you lied and told the young lady you were a valet. But I find it difficult to believe that anyone—even an American—could possibly mistake you for a valet."

That did give him pause, Graham had to admit. Then again, he'd thought she, an American heiress, was a maid. Of course, she had been dressed as a maid would dress.

"Sir, I hesitate to ask this final question. Please know that I mean no insult to you or to the lady if I'm wrong."

Graham felt a small amount of trepidation at Mr. Chase's tone. "Go on."

Seemingly reluctant, Mr. Chase finally asked, "How many times has the young lady allowed you to be alone with her unchaper-oned?"

Graham immediately knew what he was suggesting, that Katherine was a scheming girl bent on forcing his hand. But that could not be true. She seemed so genuine. And if that were the truth, it could only mean he was the biggest of fools. Because the answer to Mr. Chase's question was many times—far too many to completely disregard his valet's suspicions.

As if reading his mind, Mr. Chase said gently, "Sir, what kind of girl would allow that?"

Graham looked up at the valet, feeling very much like a little boy having done something interminably stupid. And yet, he still clung to the idea that they had simply fallen for one another, that what she felt for him was just as strong as what he felt for her. Yes, she might have allowed them to be alone, but in each case *he* had been the one to instigate it. Still . . .

"I shall be more cautious in the future, Mr. Chase. There is much at stake."

The older man relaxed, likely relieved he hadn't gotten angry. "Very good, sir. And I nearly forgot whilst basking in the light of your good humor that a letter came from your estate."

"But I was just there," Graham said, slightly baffled that whatever had been important enough to send a letter couldn't have been discussed a week ago. "Damn," he said as he read the short note.

"Sir?"

"Apparently, there was a kitchen fire at the Blackshires' and their home was all but destroyed. They're staying with a relative right now, but the cottage will have to be rebuilt." It was just one more thing to remind Graham that marrying Miss Von Haupt was the right thing to do. He felt as if someone had poured a warm, thick batter of gloom over his head, and he realized it was because some small, unrecognized part of him had still hoped that he wouldn't have to marry her. That he could choose his own bride. Hell, he'd been pursuing Katherine as if it were a possibility. He was acting as if he were still on holiday, still sneaking out to meet a maid and knowing it was wrong all along. It had to stop.

Katherine stood at the base of the hill, looking up at what had once been a castle, but was now the remains of a single tower, her mother and the general standing next to her. Her mother was glowing with happiness, which Katherine found extremely irritating.

"I was thinking of writing to Father to have him join us," Katherine said. "He could be here in less than two weeks, and I know he would enjoy such outings as these."

Her mother looked annoyed. "Your father is entirely too busy to visit us here. He hinted at some large doings with Mr. Rockefeller in his last letter. And he despises history."

Katherine sighed, because her mother was right. Her father would have looked at the tower and declared it an old pile of stones. He had absolutely no imagination and would have thought Katherine's romantic musings about what the castle had once looked like and how its people had lived a waste of time.

"It was built in the thirteen hundreds," Marjorie said. "Can you imagine? I can just picture the knights riding their white steeds, carrying the castle's banner. By the way, who is that man with Lord Avonleigh? The one who scowls all the time?"

Katherine turned to see Graham walking beside Mr. Norris. "Mr. Charles Norris. Apparently, he's been in India for years and has only recently returned home."

Marjorie furrowed her brow as if trying to remember the family. "Oh yes," she said after a time. "He's the second son of Viscount Melbourne. Pity."

Katherine gave her a look of pure exasperation. "I simply do not understand everyone's fascination with titles."

Marjorie grinned. "It's not my fascination, it's my mother's. She's been trying to get me married off for four years now and she won't even consider an untitled gentleman. Besides, if I get married, who will take care of George?"

She said the words breezily, but Katherine sensed she was completely serious—and now she had a better understanding of the sacrifice Marjorie was making to protect her younger brother.

Katherine gave Graham another sidelong glance before focusing on the ruins in front of her. Though much of the castle was gone, the tower that was left standing was enormous. She imagined if one could fly, one would be able to see the original size, as here and there were small remnants of walls.

Graham had been decidedly cool today, she thought. Each time she looked his way, he was otherwise engaged, a distinct change from the previous days. She hated that they were angry with one another. The futility of her feelings for Graham was not lost on her, but she simply could not stop the longing she felt in her heart. Was it her imagination or had he seemed more solicitous to Claudia and her mother?

At that very moment, Claudia went up to him, like an eager puppy, and he smiled down at her. It was not the smile he'd given to Katherine, that carefree, open one that made her heart sing, but it was a smile nonetheless. And it felt like a knife stabbed at her heart when she saw it.

"Cow eyes are so unbecoming," Marjorie said next to her.

Katherine turned away and wrinkled her nose at her friend.

"Who's to say I wasn't looking at Mr. Norris? He's quite good look-ing. And he must be wealthy enough if he's the son of a viscount."

"Oh, I daresay he is," Marjorie said with a frown. "Wealthy, that is. I don't care for a man who looks like a lumberjack. I prefer a man of more grace and refinement. Have you heard him laugh? It's actually frightening."

Katherine giggled. "He did rather remind me of one of those wild mountain men from my country. Perhaps Daniel Boone. Have you heard of him?"

"Oh yes, the famous frontiersman. My brother adores stories about him."

Katherine realized just then that she and Marjorie were walking in a convergent path with Graham and his small party. Graham ap-parently noticed this, too, and Katherine watched, with a small amount of dismay, as he steered his group in the opposite direction. Ridiculous tears burned in her eyes and she forced them away, dis-gusted with herself. This was for the better. They never should have had any sort of relationship, and now that it was severed, she should be dancing the jig, not fighting back tears.

"Mr. Norris would be a good catch for you," Marjorie said, oblivious for once to what was going on in Katherine's head. "That is, if your mother could ever get over not nabbing a title for her daughter. I know my mother would not."

"No, that would never do for Mother. She must have a title or nothing," Katherine said with no small amount of bitterness. The two women stood at the top of the small knoll, looking down at those who had joined the expedition to the ruins. A man she hadn't noticed before stood by Mrs. Von Haupt, and Katherine squinted her eyes trying to put him into focus. "Oh," she said, pulling back a bit. "Mr. Von Haupt is here." Katherine smiled, as if the sun had broken through the clouds after a long bout of rain. His presence certainly explained Graham's attentiveness to Claudia. Perhaps he was not angry with her after all. And then she frowned. If Mr. Von Haupt was here, it could only mean an announcement was immi-nent. As if on a spring, her heart plunged once again.

"I think all this marriage business is just so tiring," she said. "Why can't we be like men? They don't have to worry about find-ing a bride unless they require an heir. It seems so unfair."

Marjorie laughed. "When men can have children, then I suppose we'll truly be equal."

Katherine grinned, and just that made her feel a bit better. "Can you imagine Lord Wrentham over there large with child?" Lord Wrentham was tall and extremely thin, though Katherine had watched with some fascination the vast amount of food he ate.

"I cannot even imagine *myself* large with child," Marjorie said. "In fact, if I don't have a child, it will be perfectly fine with me."

"Truly? While I don't want a husband, I do rather like children." Katherine slapped her hand over her mouth, her eyes sparkling in mirth. "I didn't mean that quite the way it came out. Of course I'd want a husband if I had children."

"I suppose they are necessary," Marjorie said. "A bit like a sturdy plow horse is necessary to a farmer."

Katherine laughed aloud, glad to have a friend who could bring her out of her gloomy mood.

Would Katherine not stop laughing? And smiling? And . . . walking where he could see her?

Graham studiously avoided looking her way, but he was as aware of her as he was of the boots that were painfully pinching his feet. He stared at the ruins, but he could see her from the corner of his eye, all frothy green gown and shining red-gold hair only partially covered by yet another outrageous hat with a large green plume. And he could hear her, laughing with Lady Marjorie, having such a grand time when he was wishing he had ear plugs so he wouldn't have to listen to Claudia's endless stories about people he didn't know and would never want to know.

Chase had to be wrong. He could not be so fooled by her. He thought back on every moment they'd spent together—and yes, it was wrong of her and wrong of him for them to be alone so often. He'd come far too close to ruining her. Anyone walking into the theater and finding them pressed up against the wall would have sealed his fate.

But would that be so bad?

Yes. Yes and yes and yes. His estate and his people's salvation were walking next to him, twittering like a happy bird in the spring. At least Claudia wasn't a shrew like her mother. He supposed it took a certain amount of intelligence to be a shrew.

"Oh, there is Miss Wright and Lady Marjorie," Claudia said.

"Yes, indeed. But I find I would rather walk only with you, Miss Von Haupt." Claudia beamed, then gave a confused look to Charles, who was standing just apart from them. Graham explained: "I'd rather walk with only one lovely girl today. And Charles, as you can see, is hardly a lovely girl." She giggled, as was his intent, and he forced a smile.

One might have thought he'd handed her the Hope Diamond instead of a false smile. She clasped her hands together beneath her chin and looked up at him as if he were some sort of god. His stomach actually felt a bit sick and he suffered from more than a little guilt. And, of course, he was distinctly aware that Katherine was looking their way.

"Oh look," Claudia said. "Mama and Papa have finally arrived. I was beginning to think they'd gotten lost. Shall we join them?"

Good God, no. "Of course. I can think of nothing I'd like more." She missed his sarcasm, as he suspected she would, and felt even more depressed.

As they walked over to her parents, every step he took brought him figuratively and literally away from Katherine. This was it, the deciding moment. He'd formally met Von Haupt at the breakfast table that morning, but he'd avoided being alone with the man because he'd known the subject of the marriage contract would be raised. It was for the best, he told himself. At least with Claudia, he knew exactly what he was getting, while with Katherine, he wasn't quite certain. Mr. Chase's words kept ringing in his head, and no matter how many times he told himself Katherine was not a mercenary title-hunter, she had allowed herself to be alone with him—and more than once. Her actions in Brighton alone were shocking, considering she was a well-bred heiress.

And yet, every time he looked at her, heard her speak, got a hint of her wonderful scent, his heart felt as if it were expanding painfully in his chest. He'd never been a man to follow his heart—or listen overmuch to another insistent organ, either. For some reason he could not fathom, she drew him. It was clear his valet disapproved of her, and Graham couldn't blame the man. Mr. Chase loved Avonleigh nearly as much as he did, and he knew the estate's salvation was with Claudia. With Graham's marriage to her, he could make much needed repairs to Bryant Park, he could set about helping his tenants at Avonleigh. As much as he enjoyed Bryant Park and its proximity to London, Northumberland was where he'd spent his youth and it held a special place in his heart. No doubt, if Claudia was horrified by the condition of Bryant Park, she'd faint dead away if she saw Avonleigh.

He walked toward his financial salvation, pushing harshly down what he was feeling inside for a certain woman in a silly hat. Mr. Von Haupt was an imposing figure, tall with muttonchops that lent him an air of command. This entire process went against what Graham had always believed would happen. Wasn't it up to him to approach the father and beg for his daughter's hand? Instead, it was Von Haupt pursuing him with a piece of paper in hand. It was nothing more than a business contract, and everyone seemed to understand that but Claudia. He almost felt sorrier for her than he did for himself.

"Lord Avonleigh," Von Haupt said in greeting, pulling out his pocket watch. "I've arranged to meet in the Haversly library at three so we can discuss some details of the marriage contract. I expect you'll be there?"

Here it was. He could say no, he could beg pardon and run away down the path to his horse and ride home—to his crumbling estate and his needy tenants. He felt as if a steel ball were lodged in his throat. He felt Claudia clutching his arm in rabid anticipation, but he was more aware of the girl behind him, that ridiculous feather no doubt swaying back and forth in the soft breeze.

"Three o'clock," he said, and he saw Mrs. Von Haupt smile for the first time—at least at him. It was not a pleasant sight.

That evening, there was a concert with a string quartet from London. They played a fugue so hauntingly beautiful, Katherine had to fight back tears for fear of embarrassing herself. It was either that or the realization that following the concert, a formal announcement would be made.

Claudia had been walking on air all afternoon, and it was obvious to all why this was. Mr. Von Haupt had met with Lord Avonleigh that very afternoon to hash out the financial details of the marriage contract. Katherine's chest hurt all day, a squeezing in her heart that persisted no matter how she tried not to think about Graham truly marrying Claudia. And to see Claudia so happy when she was so very miserable made her feel even worse. She wanted to remain in her rooms, but her mother had insisted she participate in the evening's events. No doubt there was some new title in the room that her mother had her eye on.

Graham was sitting with the Von Haupts in the front row. His hair was neatly combed, his clothing impeccable, his back straight. He looked neither left nor right, but stared with unrelenting concentration on the musicians in front of him. He'd moved once, when Claudia leaned over to say something to him, and he'd nodded, once, sharp and definitive, and Katherine agonized over what Claudia had said.

Once the concert was over, Lord Haversly immediately stood, still clapping and thanking the quartet for their fine performance. Then he gestured that all should remain seated.

"We have a bit of an exciting announcement to make. Actually, Lord Avonleigh does."

Was it Katherine's imagination, or had several in the audience just looked her way? She sat, her heart slowly dissolving in her chest, and gave Lord Haversly a careful and pleasant smile of mild anticipation. *Oh, what on earth could the announcement be?* her smile said.

Graham stood, and goodness, he looked handsome. His gray eyes scanned the audience politely, skimming over her, as if she were simply another member of the crowd. Katherine's throat ached to the point of physical pain, but she would not let anyone know what was happening. Oh God, her heart was breaking. It was, and she must not let a soul even have a hint of what was happening inside her.

"Miss Von Haupt and I are engaged," he said, holding out his hand for Claudia to join him. Just as their hands touched, his eyes met Katherine's, just briefly, and with no emotion in them. For that instant, Katherine felt as if she might faint, and she looked down and did not see the small step he took toward her. It was all so subtle, no one else in the room could guess at the drama unfolding.

Katherine wasn't certain how she got through the rest of the evening. It was shocking, really, the effect that announcement had on her. It wasn't as if she hadn't known all along that he would marry Claudia. Still, hearing it, seeing it, seemed to tear a small part of herself away.

Nearly everyone else in the room was giddy with the news. An engagement was almost always a happy event, and it was unlikely that everyone in the room knew Graham had been forced into it due to finances. Those who expressed any disappointment did so softly, and if they did it was because Graham was marrying an American girl and not one of their own.

"Oh well, my dear. There are other titles," Elizabeth said. "And his house really was a shambles. Certainly he needs the kind of money the Von Haupts have, but it does go up my craw that Mrs. Von Haupt will be so smug about it all. Just look at her over there. You might think she was the queen herself, the way she's acting."

Mrs. Von Haupt, indeed, was acting like the cat who'd caught the canary. She basked in the glow of knowing her daughter would be a marchioness. Katherine couldn't help wondering if Claudia, now that she had the prize, wished she hadn't won him. That small, bitter part of her wished it with all her heart.

"I'm happy for them," Katherine said.

"Then I am, too," Elizabeth said cheerfully, completely oblivious to the fact her daughter's heart was breaking. "Oh look, Lord Avonleigh is making the rounds and we are next. It is a shame. When he smiled at you, I did have such high hopes."

When Graham saw who was next, he paused for a fraction of a second before continuing on. Katherine wanted to applaud his performance.

"Congratulations, Lord Avonleigh," her mother gushed. "Have you set a date?"

He bowed and Katherine clenched her teeth so tightly, her jaw ached. She could not do it. She could not congratulate him on his engagement when every part of her wanted to scream and shake him and kiss him. Oh God, how could she think such things, even now?

"Thank you, Mrs. Wright, and no, we have not set a date." He glanced at Katherine, who had plastered a pleasant smile on her face. She wondered if this particular smile would be permanently affixed to her, as it was taking such a grand effort to make it.

"Congratulations," she said, and was horrified when her throat closed up slightly at the last syllable. She prayed he would not notice. She needn't worry about her mother, who was again distracted by the general, who was waving her over.

When she was gone, Graham said, his voice low, "I need to speak with you."

"We have nothing to say, Lord Avonleigh."

"I need to know if you, if your heart, was at all engaged."

Her eyes filled immediately, and Katherine desperately looked for an escape. She turned then walked through the doors to the hallway, knowing he would follow and uncertain whether she wanted him to or not. By the time she turned to him, she had gained control of herself, and it was as if she'd never felt any emotion other than annoyance.

"My heart was as engaged as yours. Obviously."

"What is that supposed to mean? You cannot know how difficult this has been."

Katherine looked at him incredulously. "You just announced your engagement to another woman. And you say it has been difficult for *you*?"

Just then, Claudia, no doubt pushed out the door by her mother, rushed into the hall, pulling up sharply when she found them standing within a few feet of her.

"My, I do hope you're not trying to steal away Graham," she said, her laughter as false as her smile. She darted a look to her mother, who was just visible through the door. Katherine nearly laughed at the look on her face. Poor Claudia was likely sent out here posthaste and told to claim her fiancé.

"Your marquess is quite safe from me, Miss Von Haupt. I'm afraid I haven't the funds to purchase him."

That little crease appeared again between Claudia's eyes, as if she was confused by Katherine's hostility. She turned toward Graham, laying a gloved hand on his arm. Katherine felt like vomiting. "I do apologize for Katherine's remarks, for it is clear she will not," Claudia said.

Katherine glanced from one to the other. Claudia looked slightly angry, but Graham, he looked completely unaffected, as if they were standing there chatting about the price of livestock.

She turned and started to walk away, then stopped and turned slowly. "There is no need for you to apologize for me, Miss Von Haupt. I'll apologize for myself when it's warranted."

Katherine heard Claudia's slight gasp, the low murmur of Graham's voice, no doubt consoling his fiancée, and made it as far as the top of the stairs before the first tear fell. Then she ran the rest of the way down the hall to her room, flew through the door, and threw herself onto her bed, sobbing. Clara was there in an instant, holding her and muttering all kinds of nonsense to her in an effort to calm her down.

"It was dreadful," Katherine said, her voice watery from tears. "He stood there and announced their engagement as if . . . as if I were nothing and then . . ." She sniffed loudly, then blew her nose into the handkerchief Clara proffered. "Then he actually asked if my heart had been engaged. My *heart*," she said, clutching her hands above that very organ.

"A cad," Clara said definitively.

Katherine nodded, but was soon shaking her head in denial. "He's not a cad. He's just stupid. Stupid and blind and I hope he's miserable with her." She blew her nose again.

"He will be."

"No, I don't hope that. That's an awful thing to hope. I hope he's happy. I hope . . ." And she dissolved into tears again. Once she'd regained control, she sat there forlornly, clutching the soggy handkerchief in her fist. "Would you like to know the worst part of all of this?"

"Of course."

"The worst part is that no one knew. No one will ever know how much I loved him—not even him. I can't tell anyone. Even Marjorie doesn't know. I had to pretend that everything was fine, that I was just as happy to marry someone else, when"—she stopped and swallowed heavily—"when I truly wanted to marry him. I couldn't even admit it to myself until just now."

"I know, miss."

Katherine hugged Clara again. "Thank goodness for you, Clara. I think I might have drowned in tears if you hadn't been here."

"What a silly goose you are," Clara said fondly. "There'll be no drowning, and we'll try not to have too many more tears. They make your complexion all blotchy."

Katherine let out a watery laugh. "I just know I'll wake up with swollen eyes in the morning."

"If you do, I'll make your excuses. Don't you worry about a thing."

Katherine spent the next day writing letters to friends back home. She knew they were mostly envious of her trip and would never believe that she only wanted to return home to her old life. Everything was going wrong. She'd fallen in love with the wrong man, her mother was probably having an affair, and her eyes were still red and puffy even at eleven in the morning.

Her mother hadn't even checked in on her. No doubt she was gallivanting about with the general doing God knew what. Katherine didn't want to think about it. She didn't want to think about anything. So she wrote letter after letter describing a party that would probably make her friends sick with envy and never once even hinted that she was miserable. She kept all tears at bay until she wrote to her sister, but the feeling of homesickness was nearly overwhelming and she let out a few tears before angrily dashing them away.

She was quite certain Graham was not wallowing in self-pity. He was probably living it up downstairs, playing billiards or cards or perhaps taking a walk with Claudia. He probably hadn't spared her a single thought. Her letter was ruined, for a tear had landed directly on a bit of ink that had yet to dry and expanded and obliterated the word *home*. It was almost an evil omen, that word marred and distorted, so she crumpled up the paper and decided to write to her sister later when she wasn't quite so upset.

Looking in the mirror, Katherine decided she didn't look as if she'd been crying, and smiled. Funny, how simply the act of smiling made her feel better. She would not wallow in self-pity one minute more. As Clara had said so correctly the night before, if this was the worst thing ever to happen in her life, then she would have a very happy one.

Of course, she hadn't counted on her stomach dropping to her slippers when she heard Graham's voice as she descended the stairs. She wasn't quite ready to face him, but face him she would, for he stood there talking with that Norris fellow. At least Claudia was nowhere in sight. She was probably already off to Paris to order her wedding gown.

"Good morning, gentlemen," Katherine said, proud that her voice sounded pleasant.

They both turned, and Katherine got a small bit of gratification from the admiration in Norris's eyes—and perhaps even more gratification from the scowl on Graham's face.

"Ah, Miss Wright," Mr. Norris said. "A few of us are going to watch the All-England Eleven play against the North. You should join us."

"Should I?" Katherine asked on a laugh. "What is the All-England Eleven? You can't expect me to make a decision if I haven't an idea what you are talking about."

Mr. Norris looked shocked. "Cricket."

"You're watching *insects*?" she asked with a furrowed brow.

"Insects!"

Katherine pressed her lips together to stop from smiling. "She's joking with you, Norris," Graham said with no small amount of impatience. My, he seemed in a rare ill temper this day.

"I hate to disappoint you, sir, but I have seen cricket matches and I have to admit I find the game quite difficult to follow as compared to American baseball."

"Quite understood, but you should go. Or rather, will you? Avonleigh used to be quite the cricket player back in our school days. He is a fan of the North, you see. I was hoping to persuade you to my side."

Katherine smiled, wondering if he meant the double entendre. "I believe I'll have to stay neutral, sir, if you don't mind. One mustn't get emotional about something that will have absolutely no consequence to one's future."

Charles laughed and Graham remained stone-faced, for Katherine had no doubt he *did* understand her double entendre.

"Quite true, Miss Wright."

"You don't have to go if you don't want to," Graham said. "The carriage is full as it is."

"Then she'll simply have to ride with me," Charles said cheerfully. "Lady and Lord Haversly are sharing, and there's room for one more."

"She doesn't like cricket," Graham said, very nearly sounding petulant, and Katherine smiled.

"Perhaps I shall have to learn to like it," she said, noticing with no small amount of pleasure that Graham's nostrils flared ever so slightly in displeasure. He didn't like her flirting with Norris, it was obvious. How dare he! He'd announced his engagement to another woman the night before and he had the audacity to be miffed with a bit of innocent flirtation?

"I'll only go if you promise to explain the intricacies of the game," she said, all charm. Katherine could flirt with the best of them when she put her mind to it. "I daresay if everyone in England is so mad about the sport, it must have some positive attributes."

Graham shoved his hands into his pockets and turned slightly away, his jaw tense, and Katherine felt a small slice of pain at the gesture. She was hurting him. She hadn't truly known she could.

"Will your mother and the general be joining us, or will they find their own entertainments?" Graham asked, so blasé, so carelessly, that Katherine had to stifle a gasp. All tender feelings were immediately wiped away. She couldn't even bring herself to respond. And when he turned to look at her, a slow movement of his head as if he were completely unaware of the dagger he'd just thrown, Katherine didn't have the fortitude to hide the hurt.

He had the good grace to look down, and she wondered if there was a small, tender part of him that felt slightly ashamed. Probably not.

"Ah, there are Lord and Lady Haversly now," Charles said, moving toward the couple, leaving Katherine standing awkwardly near Graham.

"Sometimes," Graham said, his voice low, "when a thing, an animal or perhaps . . . a man, is experiencing terrible pain, it lashes out unthinkingly. And cruelly."

There it was, back in full force, that awful pain in her throat. All she could manage was a quick shake of her head, a silent plea for him to stop. She suddenly wished he would be mean to her; it was far easier to take.

He took a step closer, so that he was by her side, but facing opposite her. "Don't think for one minute that I am not suffering. I am." And then he stepped away, greeting the older couple, leaving Katherine swaying slightly from the devastation he'd left in his wake.

*   *   *

Mr. Norris had been all patience trying to explain the game of cricket, and by the end of the interminable match won by the All-England Eleven, Katherine had a slightly better understanding of cricket. But she continued to be baffled by the excitement it generated in the crowd—that was until Mr. Norris pointed out that the game was made far more interesting when there were bets on the table.

During the entire match, Graham sat stone-faced and silent, and Katherine wasn't certain whether it was because of her or because his team was being badly beaten. Mr. Norris, of course, fully believed Graham's sour mood was due to the North Eleven's poor showing. Katherine did learn one thing, however. She didn't believe she could marry Mr. Norris. He was too raucous, too rough around the edges. Each time he turned to speak with her, he bumped her, as if unaware of how large he was. She noticed he'd jostled Graham several times, as well. He was like a six-month-old puppy, appearing to be a grown dog but frolicking about, crashing into things in its enthusiasm.

Halfway through the match, she excused herself to sit next to Marjorie and her friend's mother and brother, leaving Graham and Charles alone.

"You're in a foul mood for a man who's just announced his engagement to a lovely heiress," Charles said when Katherine had gone.

"I have much on my mind of late," Graham said, forcing himself not to follow Katherine with his eyes as Charles was doing.

"What do you think of Miss Wright?"

"I don't."

"Good. Because I *have* been doing quite a bit of thinking about her. My mother would likely skin me alive if I married an American girl, but she just might be worth it."

Graham was so tense, his muscles began to ache. "She wants a title," he said.

"Don't they all? But perhaps I can persuade her that a mister would do just as well. I'm not a pauper, after all. No offense."

Most men would have quaked under the look Graham gave Charles, but the fool simply smiled.

"Leave off," Graham snapped.

Charles gave him a look of mock confusion. "Leave off talking about finances? Or Miss Wright?"

Graham could feel his blood nearly come to a boil, and he fought it, fought it with every part of his being. He could feel Charles staring at him, studying him. Almost as if his eyes had a will of their own, he sought out Katherine. Hell, how could he let her go? "Just leave off."

Even Graham could hear the hostility in his tone. He might as well put a sign on Katherine that said "Property of Graham Spencer."

Charles narrowed his eyes. "That's just it, Avon, I wasn't asking permission. But I'll be damned if I give my heart to another girl whose heart is engaged elsewhere. Once in a lifetime is enough, thank you very much."

"Still smarting over the countess, are you?"

"Only my pride at this point," Charles said easily.

Graham stared at the back of Katherine's head. "If you plan to court Miss Wright in earnest, please do so out of my sight, will you?"

"I find that an odd request for a man who is about to marry a very beautiful and very wealthy woman." Then Charles looked at Graham, surprise in his expression. He leaned in closer before saying, "Is *your* heart engaged, as well?"

It took Graham a long moment before he could answer. "It is."

Charles drew back in surprise. "Well, I'll be damned. The mighty Avonleigh has finally fallen."

Graham let out a puff of impatience. "Perhaps you don't remember; you were so gone over Miss Stanhope, you were oblivious to what was happening under your very nose. But I remember Willington was sick with it. I remember thinking what a fool he was, not only to fall in love, but more to let a woman he loved marry another."

Charles shook his head slightly. "Holy hell, Avon. Why marry someone else, then? Why not succumb like Willington did?"

"Why do you think?" he snapped. "Do you think I would allow another man even to look at her if I had a choice? My estate is in a shambles and I've no way out. Five generations. I will *not* be the one who allows it to fall to ruin."

"You always took your duties too seriously," Charles said, then drew sharply back at the look Graham shot him.

"It is easy for a second son to say such a thing. You have no responsibilities. No one depends upon you for their livelihood. If you fail, hundreds of families will not suffer. If you fail, a legacy of more than two hundred years will not crumble."

Charles looked close to murder; then his features softened. "I apologize, Avon. I just hope to hell she understands your sacrifice. And I hope Miss Von Haupt never does."

Chapter 10

"Well, that was a marvelous house party," Elizabeth said shortly after they'd entered the carriage. "One can only hope Lord and Lady Wrentham are as gracious. I'm certain they will be. Everyone has been so welcoming."

"Especially General Lawton," Katherine said, unable to help herself. She was miserable, the house party a pure disaster, and her mother's cheerfulness was more than grating. Next to her, her mother stiffened, but remained silent, all but confirming to Katherine that she was, indeed, carrying on with the general. The entire thing made her angry, for she loved her mother and actually liked the general. But she loathed what they were doing. If anything, it only made her more resolved never to marry.

They rode in silence for nearly an hour, Katherine looking morosely out the window, her mother trying unsuccessfully to read a book in the jostling carriage.

"Your father and I never loved one another."

"I don't want to hear it."

"Nevertheless, you're going to listen. I was sixteen when we married. Sixteen. A child. I vowed I would never do that to my daughter and I will not. Which is why you are nearly twenty-one and still unmarried. I was excited, yes, and felt so very grown up."

Katherine let out a beleaguered sigh but remained silent.

"Your father was older than I, of course. And very much in love with another girl. But she was engaged to be married, and did marry in the end. That did not stop them from loving one another." Her mother looked at her. "Do you understand what I'm saying?"

Katherine felt as if her entire world were spinning backward. "Why are you telling me this?"

"Because you are judging me and you should not. For the first time in my life, I feel loved. I'm forty-three years old, Katherine, and in love for the first time."

Katherine swallowed down the lump that had been growing in her throat for the past few days.

"Over the years, my resentment and anger have disappeared, but when I was young I still held hope for us." She shook her head. "I think I understand now more than ever what your father went through, and I feel sorry for him. He is a good man. He simply had the misfortune of loving the wrong woman. I think he did try. I know he did. He's been a good father, a good provider. He sent us on this trip to secure your future and raise our status in society. I do love your father. We are great friends, Katherine."

Katherine twisted her gloves in her hand. "I thought you were happy. I aspired to have a marriage like yours, but it was all a lie."

"We *have* a good marriage. Better than most. You must get romantic notions of marriage out of your head, my dear. Just look at Lord Avonleigh and that silly Claudia. Do you think for one minute they will be happy together?"

Katherine shook her head, hating that the mere mention of his name caused such an ache in her heart. "No, I don't."

"Yet they are both getting precisely what they want, aren't they."

The next two weeks were spent at three different country estates. Some of the guests had also been at Lord and Lady Haverslys' but the Von Haupts and Marjorie were not among them. Katherine wrote to Marjorie at her home, even knowing she wouldn't get the letters until her return. She missed her friend and was in such a state, she could hardly garner the energy to make new ones.

She spent far too many nights alone in her rooms, and her mother, thinking she was still upset about the affair, let her. She *was* upset about the affair. She looked back on her childhood and could not remember a single thing that suggested her parents were anything but happy together. They had not been demonstrative with each other, that was true, but how many older couples were? She couldn't remember ever seeing any of her friends' parents touching each other, unless it was to be helped down from a carriage or to walk in to supper together. Were all marriages frauds? Surely someone was happy.

They were heading out to yet another house party in Nottingham. Rufford Abbey was a home of little historic interest and less grandeur, but its owner was a colorful old bachelor who was well-liked among the ton. Sir John Stiley, Baron of Rufford, was unmarried and quite old—he was fifty-six—and Katherine hoped her mother had no secret hopes of a match. Goodness, he was older than her father by several years.

The Abbey seemed impossibly large, and, Katherine thought, rather ugly. It looked more like a hospital to her—a very large hospital—but the grounds were lovely and she supposed it was as good a place as any to stay until she was able to go home. Each time she mentioned returning to New York, her mother put on a sour face. No doubt because their departure would mean leaving the general behind. But for Katherine, it meant returning home and pretending England had never happened. She knew her mother still hoped she would find a titled gentleman, and she had a feeling her small respite from socializing was about to end. During this ride, her mother had chatted nonstop about who was supposed to be attending. Thankfully, Lord Avonleigh's name was not mentioned, and Katherine could not bring herself to ask after him.

It had been two weeks since she'd seen him. She'd had a brief glimpse of him through a window as he'd been talking with Lord Haversly. She could still remember what he'd been wearing—a dark gray jacket over a burgundy waistcoat—the way his hair had gleamed in the sun, how he'd bent his head just slightly to accommodate Lord Haversly's shorter stature. She hadn't said good-bye, though she had longed to. The last words he'd spoken directly to her were, "Don't think for one minute that I am not suffering. I am."

Was he? As much as she?

"Oh drat," Elizabeth said as they were stepping down from the carriage. She was watching as another carriage pulled up behind theirs. "The Von Haupts. Shall they plague us all fall? One would think now that the engagement is announced, they could return home and gloat there."

Katherine watched in near terror as first Mrs. Von Haupt stepped down, then Claudia. She stared at the door as the two women shook out their skirts, her heart beating madly in her chest, waiting for Graham to exit. But the footman closed the door, and Katherine nearly collapsed with relief. Or disappointment. No, surely it was relief.

Of course, Claudia saw them nearly at once and smiled and waved. Her mother said something to her and Claudia dropped her hand, but continued to wave secretly, her hand at her side and partially hidden by her skirt. Katherine couldn't help but smile. She truly wanted to dislike Claudia, but she couldn't bring herself to do it.

Despite Mrs. Von Haupt's obvious objection, Claudia escaped to come say hello while her mother kept busy directing the footmen and greeting Sir Stiley, an imposing man with a robust beard and impressively curled mustache.

"I've been dreadfully bored these past weeks," Claudia said. "English girls can be so snobbish. Even when they learned I was engaged to a marquess, they hardly would speak to me." She looked bewildered by this turn of events. "Mother says they'll be nicer when we're married, but I'm not so certain. It was purely awful. I do wish you were there. I could have used a bit of your bravery."

"Certainly Lord Avonleigh helped ease your boredom," Katherine said, hoping she sounded nonchalant. She was even more foolish than she could have imagined herself to be, but she couldn't keep herself from asking after him.

"Oh, I haven't seen him since the announcement," Claudia said, as if this wasn't a bit strange. "I imagine he'll be here, though. Mother said he's visiting a friend nearby. A Lord Braddock, I think."

The two girls followed their mothers in and headed up the stairs, following the housekeeper to their rooms.

"Come visit with me, will you?" Claudia asked.

Katherine hesitated before agreeing. She supposed keeping Claudia company was better than moping in her room and dreading the moment she would see Graham again.

"This is lovely," Katherine said, looking around the opulent interior and thinking the opposite. The room was done in dark reds and golds, with a large, heavily-carved bed, dark rugs, and velvet curtains that, while in fine shape, look like they belonged in another century.

Claudia wrinkled her nose. "It's rather . . ."

"Stuffy?"

Claudia giggled. "I miss my room back home. It's white and blue. My bedroom overlooks our garden and I do miss seeing my flowers bloom. I suppose most of them are dead by now." She walked over to the window, looked out, and sighed. "English gardens are so symmetrical. Have you noticed?"

"I have," Katherine said, joining her by the window.

Suddenly, Claudia began to cry, loud, wet sobs that seemed to have come from nowhere. She flung herself into Katherine's arms, her body racked by a grief that seemed profound.

"My goodness," Katherine said, rubbing Claudia's heaving back, "whatever are these tears for?"

"I want to go home," Claudia wailed. "I don't want to get married, and especially not to Lord Avonleigh. He doesn't like me, I can tell. He said the meanest thing."

Katherine drew back, thinking that Graham *could* be a bit mean when he wanted to be. "What did he say?"

Claudia shook her head as if it were too horrible to contemplate, and fished a handkerchief out of her reticule.

"What? What did that cad say?"

"That I couldn't convert the ballroom. He was adamant. He wouldn't even discuss it. He said a ballroom would be a frivolous expense and"—she sniffed loudly—"he said his first obligation was to his tenants. As if a bunch of farmers were more important than me."

Claudia's maid entered the room, ready to unpack Claudia's things, and Katherine vigorously shook her head, sending her away. "You must know how important Lord Avonleigh's tenants are to him," Katherine said gently. "He no doubt feels an obligation to repair their houses and make certain the roads are well-tended."

Claudia drew back. "But I'm his wife. Or will be. And the only thing I want is a ballroom so I can throw parties." Her face crumpled again. "Parties that no one will attend because they all hate me!"

Katherine didn't roll her eyes until she had again hugged Claudia, who seemed to be getting a second wind of misery.

"Father said he'd pay for the ballroom. But Lord Avonleigh refused. He hates me, too."

"He doesn't hate you, Claudia. He's simply very attached to the theater."

Claudia stepped back and wiped her nose. She was not a pretty crier, Katherine thought, then felt a bit guilty for that thought. Claudia sat down on the edge of the awful bed, looking like a young girl who'd just learned her birthday party had been cancelled.

"I don't want to marry him," she said softly. "I want to go home." Another tear slipped from her eye, which was more heartbreaking than the earlier sobbing. Katherine did feel sorry for Claudia.

"I want to go home, too," Katherine said with a small laugh. "If only they had titles in America, we wouldn't have to be here."

Claudia let out a sigh. "There's nothing I can do. I just have to marry him unless I can come up with a plan. Help me, Katherine. You're so smart, you can think of something."

Katherine could not believe what Claudia was asking of her. "What on earth can I do?"

"Something," Claudia wailed. "Please, just think. If you cannot, then I will manage somehow. Please, Katherine, promise me you'll at least try."

Claudia clutched at Katherine's hand rather painfully, and to get the girl to calm down and let go, she said, "Very well. I will try to come up with a plan. But I do believe you should try to make the most of this situation." Oh, she wanted to throttle the girl. Didn't she know how very lucky she was?

"Oh, thank you. I know you'll think of something. Otherwise, I'll have to live my entire life in that awful house without a ballroom, and with no friends. Nothing to keep me company but babies. And I don't even like babies. And do you know how babies are made? It's disgusting."

Katherine was so stunned, so flummoxed by the statement, it was all she could do to keep from laughing.

"I don't think it's entirely disgusting. Who said that it is?"

"Mother, of course." She wrinkled her nose as if she smelled something unpleasant. "She told me all about it." She sighed again. "He'll want an heir and I'll have to submit a few times, I suppose."

"Has Lord Avonleigh kissed you?"

"On the hand." She rubbed her right hand with her left, as if she could still feel his lips there—and it wasn't a nice feeling.

Katherine felt giddy with relief. "You'll grow to like one another, I'm sure," she said, feeling generous. Perhaps it was wrong and petty of her, but she was a bit pleased Graham would not share with Claudia what he could have shared with her. "You must, Claudia."

Claudia shook her head. "I'd do anything to stop this thing. But there's nothing I can think of. What can I do, Katherine?"

"Stop feeling sorry for yourself. That's a good first step," Katherine said, a bit more sharply than she'd meant to. But honestly, how could the girl sit here and complain about marrying Graham? She should be doing a jig, not crying.

"I'll feel better when I'm home. We're getting married in New York in the spring. At Trinity. Mother said it would be lovely."

A small bit of dread settled into the pit of Katherine's stomach. She'd be home in New York, as well, and it would be impossible to avoid news and gossip of what would likely be the wedding of the year. A thought suddenly occurred to her. Would Claudia invite her? Her mother would never include the Wrights on their guest list, but would Claudia insist? Her mother might be a bit more compliant to her daughter's requests once in New York. No doubt Mrs. Von Haupt would want to flaunt her daughter's success.

Yes, she would assuredly be invited and would be unable to come up with an excuse that her mother would believe. As much as her mother loathed Mrs. Von Haupt, she would see the invitation as a coup.

"I was wondering," Claudia said, looking earnest and too young to be marrying anyone at all.

"Yes?"

"Would you be one of my bridesmaids? Unless I can come up with a plan to stop the wedding, I will need a few. Mother said I could have twelve."

Perhaps by then, this terrible longing would be gone. Perhaps when she saw Graham during the pre-wedding festivities, she would feel nothing. She might even look at him and wonder what she had ever seen in him.

Or she might fall into hysterics.

"I'd be honored to be in your wedding party," Katherine said.

Claudia clapped her hands, all tears gone.

A knock on the door drew their attention, and thinking it was the maid returning to unpack Claudia's things, Katherine called out for her to enter. Instead of the maid, Marjorie walked through the door, all smiles.

"Thank goodness you are here," she said. "I fear we are the only people here who aren't ancient. Although more guests are expected in the next few days." She turned to Claudia. "Is your betrothed expected?"

"I don't know. I only know he's nearby visiting a friend. I imagine he will stop by."

"I'm certain he will, if he's so close," Marjorie said, looking about the room, and rubbing her hands on her arms as if chilled. She gave Claudia a long look, for it was obvious she'd been crying, but she said nothing. "I don't like this place. I remember staying here a few years ago. It seems oppressive to me. And cold, even though it's no colder than any other old house, I suppose." She turned toward Claudia and Katherine. "Do you know there's a ghost here? Perhaps even two? I've never seen them myself, but my mother swears she has."

Katherine was delighted. "Truly? What kind of ghost?"

"Don't tell me you like the idea," Marjorie said.

"Absolutely. At least there will be some excitement—even if it's all balderdash. Who is the ghost supposed to be?"

"Well," Marjorie said with an impish grin, clearly enjoying her role as a storyteller, "it's said there is a monk prowling about. He's so fearsome, a man once saw him and died from fright. I saw the church registry myself. It said something about a man seeing the Abbey ghost and dying. Can you imagine?"

Katherine laughed. "No, I can't. But imagine if there is such a thing? You said there were two ghosts?"

Marjorie waved a dismissive hand. "Oh, the other one is just a little old lady, not fearsome at all."

"But still, a ghost."

Claudia frowned fiercely. "I don't like the idea of sleeping here if there is a ghost running about."

"Don't worry," Katherine said, "it's likely just a lot of silliness. You know how people are. They hear or see something that can't immediately be explained and jump to the conclusion it was a ghost rather than the wind or a shadow."

"But don't you feel something odd here? Something . . . ominous?" Marjorie asked.

"Only the ugly décor," Katherine said, making Claudia laugh. Katherine was actually intrigued by the ghost, but she could sense Claudia was quite afraid, so she tried to make it all seem like silly old stories.

"At two this afternoon, Sir John is giving a tour of the Abbey," Marjorie said. "It should be great fun."

They all agreed to meet in the home's banqueting hall, where the tour was set to begin.

Katherine found the English fascination with history a bit amusing. Perhaps it was because everything in New York was so very new. Since they'd been in England, they'd toured churches, mansions, palaces, and ruins endlessly. They were all blending together in Katherine's mind, and the thought that she might actually stumble upon a ghost made this tour at least slightly intriguing.

Just before two, Katherine made her way down the stairs and followed the voices to a rather large group of visitors who had gathered for the tour. The banquet hall was a long, dark room, with heavily molded paneling, mosaic brick floors, and tapestries that looked as if they'd been hanging in the great hall for centuries. Sir John proudly showed them off, and those around her dutifully looked impressed. Or perhaps they actually were impressed.

"My father pieced together the tapestries himself," Sir John said with obvious pride.

"I think they need a good cleaning," Katherine whispered to Claudia, who giggled. Marjorie shushed them, and Katherine gave her a look of innocence. She knew Marjorie well enough to understand she would not have laughed at her joke. Marjorie took her Englishness very seriously, and her English history even more so.

"Oh my, look at that armor. It looks quite fearsome," Katherine said aloud.

"Indeed, Miss Wright," Sir John said, "the men who wore such armor were to be reckoned with. The armor itself is quite heavy. The mail alone weighs nearly thirty pounds."

At one end of the room was perhaps the largest fireplace Katherine had ever seen. She could have stood inside it and jumped up and down and not touched the top. She couldn't imagine why one would need a fireplace that large, unless it was to cook an entire cow at once. She made that comment to Claudia, who pressed her lips together to stifle a laugh, and earned another stern look from Marjorie. Katherine pulled a face at her friend, and Marjorie's body shook with stifled laughter.

While the banquet hall was impressive, Katherine couldn't help but whisper amusing quips into Claudia's ear until the poor girl begged her to stop. They visited a room where King Charles I and King Charles II once slept, and the chapel, musty-smelling and rather dreary. The walls were covered with more tapestries, and in the very center was a tomb, which Katherine found rather grue-some. It was dated 1309 and was for a monk. She couldn't help but picture a skeleton beneath her feet, its perpetual grin ghoulish.

It was when they were in the chapel that Katherine walked over to a window and looked out—only to see Graham dismounting from his horse. She doubted many people looking out that dirty, wavy glass would have recognized him, but she immediately knew it was he by the way he carried himself. Blood drained from her face and she turned away, breathing heavily.

"My goodness," Marjorie said, "it looks as though you've seen a—"

Katherine smiled and completed her sentence. "A ghost? No. I fear I'm simply starving. I just realized I haven't eaten anything more than a scone all day. I wasn't hungry at luncheon, and I'm paying the price now."

"Let's get you some sustenance. I'll have some food brought to you straightaway as soon as the tour is completed."

Katherine smiled weakly. "That sounds wonderful."

A few hours later, Katherine watched as her mother got ready for dinner. She looked on with a small bit of pique as her mother's maid dressed her hair in a new and elegant style. She looked pretty—or perhaps it was the glow of illicit love that made her so eye-catching.

"Mother," Katherine said, "when did you meet the general?"

Her mother looked slightly taken aback. "In London, dear, soon after we arrived. You remember, he was at a luncheon at Lady Chalmsworth's."

Katherine wrinkled her brow, trying to remember the general at the luncheon, but unable to place him there. It had been one of their first outings, and rather brief; Katherine couldn't imagine her mother and the general had formed any kind of attachment so quickly. It was only two weeks later that they were in Brighton, and

Katherine didn't think they'd been together then; her mother had been so ill . . .

A sudden flush filled her cheeks as she remembered their time in Brighton: her mother had claimed to be ill but had had a similar glow about her.

"Was the general in Brighton?"

Elizabeth, who had been putting on an earring, stilled, then smiled nervously. "As a matter of fact, he was."

"Oh Mother!"

Elizabeth turned, saying, "Oh don't 'oh Mother' me."

"But you claimed you were ill. You spent all your time abed and . . ." Katherine covered her face with her hands, muttering, "Oh my God."

"Do not take the Lord's name in vain."

"I'm not," Katherine snapped. "It's a legitimate entreaty for God to help me get this horrid image out of my head." Katherine realized that her mother's inattentiveness had led to her meeting with Graham. If her mother had spent time with her, had accompanied her on her walks, she never would have met him. And if she had, they would have met in far different circumstances and likely would never have spent so much time together. Her heart would not be breaking. She'd look at him with a bit of disdain, the poor titled gentleman forced to marry Claudia Von Haupt. Instead, she was being forced to watch the man she loved marry a girl she was actually becoming friends with.

"Do grow up, Katherine. I had a wonderful time."

Katherine was tempted to tell her mother all that had happened, all that her affair had wrought. No doubt her mother, seeing an advantage, would pounce on the information and claim she'd been compromised, forcing Graham's hand. For a fleeting moment, Katherine rather liked that idea, then immediately squashed it. She simply could not do that to Graham.

Katherine was thoughtful for a long moment and her mother went back to primping. "Mother."

Elizabeth raised a brow, waiting for her to continue.

"What happens when you return to New York?"

Katherine met her eyes in the mirror, and to Katherine's horror, her mother's eyes filled with tears.

"I don't want to think about that right now," she said.

Katherine couldn't bring herself to comfort her mother—she

was still too upset about the entire affair—but she did feel sorry that she was suffering. She would never want her mother to be sad.

"You said Father had been having an affair for years. Certainly he would understand if you had one of your own."

Elizabeth let out a watery laugh. "You are right. He would understand. But your father, despite all this, is very old-fashioned. He would be mortified if any one of his acquaintances knew of his affair. The two of them have been extremely careful because they both love their families, their lives. I know it seems as if I'm being too understanding. Perhaps I am. But I've had years to come to this understanding. And it's not as if I'm in love with your father. I'm not and probably never was. If I had been, it would have been intolerable. We are great friends, Katherine, and very aware of our place in society. Our worlds would fall apart if they publically proclaimed their love for one another."

"So you are not leaving Father?"

Elizabeth shook her head sadly. "No. I could never do that to him. A divorce is out of the question. And why should we, anyway? It's not as if either of us is unhappy."

"But you will be once you return to New York and the general is still in England."

Elizabeth smiled. "We live in a wonderful age, my dear. An age when one can travel across the ocean in a matter of days. We will not be apart for long. And as long as we are discreet, I can be very happy."

"I think it's taking an awful chance," Katherine said, still hating the idea of her mother cavorting with another man. "Will it be enough?"

"It must be." Elizabeth patted her hair. "Now, my dear, it is time for you to get ready. My goodness, I just realized you're not dressed. What gown are you wearing?"

"I thought the green velvet. It's quite chilly this evening."

Elizabeth smiled. "I approve. It does bring out the green in your eyes. Now hurry."

Katherine left her mother to get ready. Her hair was already done—or rather it was good enough for a simple dinner—so it was only a matter of changing her dress, and Clara was a wizard at fast changes. As she walked to her rooms, Katherine wondered if she could truly be happy with a life such as her mother was leading.

What if she married a man she didn't love? And what if one day she met up with Graham and he was equally unhappy? Would they engage in an affair? Could she possibly justify it the way her mother had?

When she reached her room, Clara was in a tizzy. "Where have you been, miss? We've only ten minutes to get you ready."

Katherine waved a hand. "It's all right, Clara. My hair is fine and we only need to change gowns."

"And underthings and jewelry and gloves and shoes."

"I'm wearing the green velvet, so I believe my underthings are fine," Katherine said on a laugh.

Clara eyed her critically, then nodded. "You're right. That corset will do nicely for the cut of that gown, though I may have to tighten it up a bit. That gown fits you like a glove, miss."

Katherine wrinkled her nose at the thought of her stays being pulled tighter, but Clara was right. She likely wouldn't be able to fit into that gown, at least not properly, with her stays so loose.

"Do what you must, Clara. And don't worry if we're a bit late. I don't want to go down anyway."

Clara gave her a knowing look. "I heard Lord Avonleigh is here?"

"Yes, he is. I was hoping he would forego this party, but alas, he is here and I will have to face him."

Katherine couldn't help but wonder what he was thinking at the moment. No doubt he knew she was here. She simply couldn't get his last words to her out of her head.

Graham eyed his form critically. It seemed his waistcoat was a tad looser than it had been not two weeks before. His trousers, too.

"Mr. Chase, I do believe I'm shrinking," Graham said.

"I find that does happen when one does not eat."

Graham frowned at his reflection. Since the Haversly party, he'd been working rather nonstop. Despite his lack of funds, he was able to buy materials and equipment on credit, thanks to his engagement. Men had already begun work on the Blackshires' cottage, and they would be able to move back to their home in a matter of weeks. And a good thing, too, for Mrs. Blackshire was expecting her first child.

He remembered Cook bringing him food, but he couldn't remember a single meal.

"I need a haircut, Chase," he said, frowning at the circles beneath his eyes. "And a good night's rest."

His time at Flintwood had done little to remedy that, for he and John had stayed up late nights with his father, much to Lady Willington's distress. No doubt she had been glad to see him ride away.

The time spent at Flintwood had been interesting, to say the least. He watched with a mixture of awe and envy how John dealt with his four young children. They adored their father, falling over themselves to be with him. And the man had absolutely no dignity when it came to his offspring, getting down on all fours and pretending to be an African lion. Graham couldn't imagine himself doing the same. Perhaps he could if he had a wife like Melissa, gazing at him as if the sun rose on his shoulders as he played with his children. For the life of him, he could not imagine Claudia doing the same. The idea was so foreign to him. He could hardly imagine Claudia naked beneath him, her mouth opened slightly in pleasure. Whenever he tried to conjure such an image—and he did try—she always turned into Katherine, with her red-gold hair spilled over the pillow while he brought her to ecstasy. Claudia stiffened just slightly whenever he touched her, and he hadn't even dared a kiss but on the hand. Truth be told, he didn't even want to kiss her.

And, he told himself with brutal finality, he did not want to kiss Katherine, either. He'd not seen her in nearly three weeks, and although he'd thought his obsession with her would have lessened to a far greater degree, he was pleased that the odd pressing pain in his chest had diminished considerably. He'd yet to see Claudia, and realized he wasn't looking forward to seeing her, but certainly wasn't dreading the encounter, either. Her mother was far more pleasant to him now that the marriage contract had been signed, and her father was in London and wouldn't be around to make him feel like a beggar. The interview with him had been humiliating; if not for the pressing problems at his estates, he would have walked from the room. He felt like a green boy being given an allowance by an overbearing father. The man actually had the audacity to point out that all funds would be immediately withdrawn if any large expenditures were made without prior consent.

"My daughter complains there is no ballroom at Bryant Park," he'd said, and Graham's stomach had churned.

"There is a ballroom, sir, but it is rather small. However, I've no plans for any large parties there at any rate. Country balls are so tiresome, are they not? I thought I'd reserve the large parties for when we are in Town." He had no London town house, as that had been sold long ago, but he would ensure any rented space would accommodate a large ball.

"My daughter was quite adamant," Mr. Von Haupt had said, but Graham stood firm.

"I'm afraid I will not budge on this point, sir." Graham swallowed, and watched the older man mull this over, his hand dangling over the contract that would mean his estate's salvation. And then he'd signed, and thrust the paper toward him.

He'd felt soiled by the entire ordeal. He wondered how his tenants would have felt to see him brought down so low. No doubt they would have counseled him to walk away and to hell with the estate.

It was a pure wonder how two such disagreeable but intelligent people had produced such a scattered-brained, flighty daughter.

"Sir?" Mr. Chase asked, pulling him out of his unpleasant remembrances.

"Yes, Mr. Chase."

"I've gotten a letter from Mrs. Alcourt. She reports they've started to interview for two new footmen, a cook's assistant, and four new maids. Everyone is quite excited about the changes to come."

Graham should have been just as excited, but all he felt was profoundly depressed. "I'm glad. It's been too long without some good news, eh?"

"Yes sir. And one more thing, sir." Mr. Chase took a bracing breath. "When I was downstairs eating luncheon, I recognized a maid I'd seen before. At the Lord and Lady Haverslys', sir."

Graham lowered his head as if a large weight had suddenly been attached to his chin. "Oh?"

"It was Miss Wright's maid, sir."

Graham closed his eyes briefly. "Thank you, Mr. Chase." He wiped a hand through his hair. He didn't know if he could face her without showing what was in his heart. He must. It would be cruel to both of them to offer even a bit of hope.

"Would you like to read the letter from Mrs. Alcourt, my lord?" Mr. Chase stood there, his eyes steady, silently admonishing him to forget Miss Wright for the sake of his people. He didn't need the old man to tell him his duty—but he found himself grateful for the reminder just the same.

He hesitated just a moment before holding out his hand to take the letter, and Mr. Chase visibly relaxed. "You needn't worry so, Chase. I am marrying Miss Von Haupt."

"I know, sir, but it doesn't hurt to be reminded about why now and again. Especially with Miss Wright here." Mr. Chase paused for a bit. "I know your heart was engaged, sir, but I do believe this is for the best."

"I know you do, Chase."

That answer didn't seem to sit well with the valet, but he remained silent.

Chapter 11

As he walked down the wide, stone staircase that led to the massive dining hall, Graham found himself profoundly grateful Mr. Chase had warned him about Miss Wright's presence. Had he not been prepared, the shot to his gut when he saw her no doubt would have been far more extreme. As it was, it took all his discipline not to stare at her like some wounded schoolboy with a fatal crush. My God, she was beautiful. She stood in profile to him, and he could make out the lovely shape of her jaw, the sweet curves of her form, as she chatted with Lady Marjorie and Miss Von Haupt. Her hair was piled atop her head in an artless fashion that allowed a few curling tendrils to trail down her back. He forced himself to look away, and spied his friend Lord Willington and his wife, Melissa. If Mr. Norris was here, it would have been a reunion of sorts. The last time they'd all been together, John had invited Norris and him to get a look at Melissa as a potential bride. The idiot was already in love with Melissa when he'd made the invitation, something that had been immediately obviously to Graham.

He walked directly to the couple. Lady Willington was already showing just the tiniest rounded belly, indicating she was carrying her fifth child.

"I can't believe you left Flintwood to come to this drafty old place," Graham said.

Melissa turned and smiled at him, holding out her hands in genuine welcome. Over the years, he'd gotten rather close to the couple, and would visit often. "Oh, I'm hoping to see the famous Abbey ghost. I fear I couldn't resist the chance. And the children adore playing with their cousins."

Lady Braddock, much to Lord Braddock's feigned horror, had produced three children within the first three years of their marriage. When Lord Willington was visiting his father, the household was utter chaos, with seven tiny lords and ladies running about. Oddly, Graham had found all those children and their nonstop chatter rather wonderful during his visit. The older children had put on a play, directed by Lady Willington, charming all the adults in attendance.

"I understand your betrothed is here," Melissa said. "When do we get to meet her?"

"Very soon. She's over by the fireplace chatting with some friends."

"Before I say this," said John, "I would like to preface it by letting you know, darling, that I believe you are the most beautiful woman in the kingdom. But is that stunning girl in green your fiancée, Avon?"

Graham knew immediately he was talking about Katherine. "No, the blond girl is my fiancée, Miss Claudia Von Haupt. The other one is Miss Katherine Wright, also of New York, whom I met in Brighton. And you know, of course, Lady Marjorie, do you not?"

John looked a bit sharply at Graham. "Is that the Brighton girl?" John said, rather too loudly, for the object of their discussion turned her head their way.

"Who's the Brighton girl?" Melissa asked, confused.

Oh damn. Graham had forgotten that he'd mentioned meeting a girl in Brighton. Good God, he'd even talked of wanting to make her his mistress. "Yes, but at the time I didn't realize who she was." He gave John a pointed look meant to shut him up.

"You were rather smitten with that girl, if I remember." Of course John would ignore his entreaty. "And it turns out she was an American heiress?" John burst out laughing, much to Graham's disgust.

"Who is the Brighton girl?" Melissa asked again.

"I am."

All three turned guiltily to find the lovely object of their conversation standing just outside their group. Behind her were Miss Von Haupt and Lady Marjorie, curiously looking on.

"Ah, Miss Wright, Miss Von Haupt, let me introduce Lord and Lady Willington. I believe, Lady Marjorie, you are already acquainted with the viscount and viscountess?"

"Yes," said Marjorie. "A pleasure to see you again. How are your children?"

"Well," Melissa said. "They very much enjoy visiting Flintwood."

Graham felt as if his right side was on fire, for Katherine stood next to him, silent, a pleasant smile on her face. He turned his head just slightly and took a deep, careful breath, hoping to catch her subtle floral scent.

"And this is your betrothed?" prompted Melissa.

Guiltily, Graham held out his hand to Claudia, forcing Katherine to step aside to make room. Katherine had yet to meet his eyes, but kept smiling at Lord and Lady Willington. "Yes, Miss Von Haupt is my betrothed." From the corner of his eye, he saw Katherine look sharply away at his words of introduction.

"And when is the date? Will you be married here?"

"Oh no," Claudia said. "We're getting married in New York. At Trinity. It's my hope to live in New York as much as possible. Father bought a small house on Fifth Avenue right next to theirs and he plans to tear it down and build a grander one for us. It's our wedding present."

Graham felt the breath leave his lungs and he looked at Claudia, stunned.

John laughed. "I take it you didn't know about this wedding gift?"

Claudia slapped her hand over her mouth, her eyes wide with horror. "Oh, I've ruined the surprise! After our wedding, Father was going to show it to you. It's to be completed by then. Father is hiring an army of workers to get it done on time, and it was to be the best of surprises."

"He certainly looks surprised," John said, with obvious controlled laughter. "Right next door, did you say?"

"Oh yes. It shall almost be like I've never left home. And when we have children," she said, blushing prettily, "my mother will be right there to help. It really is the perfect solution. I'm already so dreadfully homesick."

"I can't be away from my estate months at a time, my dear. Surely you know that."

Claudia waved a dismissive hand. "Oh, that's all right. I'll be fine in New York while you take care of your estate."

"Sounds lovely," Melissa said, giving Graham a searching look, which he studiously ignored.

"Wouldn't you rather be with your husband?"

This from Katherine, uttering her first words, which were like sharp little needles pricking his skin.

Claudia gave Katherine the oddest look, almost a "please shut your mouth" look, and one that seemed to amuse Katherine. "I mean to say," Katherine added, "if I was a new bride I would want to spend every minute of every day with my husband. Unless, of course, he was an onerous, humorless cad." She raised one eyebrow and glanced at Graham.

Claudia giggled. "You would never marry anyone like that."

"You're right," she said pleasantly. "I would not."

John cleared his throat uncomfortably, and Lady Willington looked a bit confused.

"When is the wedding?" Melissa asked brightly.

"Next spring. May, perhaps. New York is so lovely in the spring."

Sir Stiley clapped his hands at that very moment, calling for attention.

"After dinner this evening, I thought it might be great fun to play bridge," Sir Stiley said. "And as we have an equal number of men and women, we'll pair off as couples. We'll play two rounds, and after those two rounds, the couple with the lowest score will be eliminated until there are just two left. Champions will win these vases." With a flourish, Sir Stiley showed off two stunning, intricately painted vases. "I've assembled all names in a hat and teams will be formed randomly. I know some of you couples are a force to deal with and I wouldn't want anyone to have an unfair advantage," he said, to the laughter of several in the room. "Now, if you'll all proceed to the dining hall . . ."

Katherine felt a cloak of dread fall over her, which quite ruined dinner. Two long tables had been set up in the dining hall, and Graham had been seated at the other table, nearly as far from her as possible. It had been a blessed relief. How could she be expected to act as if he weren't in the room, as if his very presence wasn't making her heart physically ache? She had to pretend all was well, pretend she wasn't on the verge of tears, pretend she was looking forward to playing bridge, to possibly being paired up with him. If she was, she would plead an illness.

Earlier that evening, her mother had pointed out several young and not-so-young men with titles, ranging from an earl to a baron, but she had little interest. "You'd think you had a beau back home you were pining over, for all the attention you are paying to these men," her mother had said. "Your father has invested a great deal in this trip."

"I know. It's just that they all seem so . . . pompous."

"Not all of them. Lord what's-his-name over there seemed very pleasant." Elizabeth nodded to the young baron whose Adam's apple protruded rather disturbingly. He had, indeed, seemed pleasant, but Katherine wasn't certain she could get used to that thing on his throat bobbing up and down whenever he spoke.

"I will try, Mother. I know I haven't been putting forth an effort and I do appreciate this trip," she said, only to placate her mother.

Katherine had been seated next to a Mr. Robert Coulton, the heir presumptive to Viscount Newton. He was a pleasant enough fellow, with striking blue eyes that protruded just a tad and teeth that were slightly bucked, but he wasn't altogether ugly. He was also brilliant and talked with her as if she were an equal. How she loathed being patronized by men, but Mr. Coulton never once made her feel inferior. She found herself hoping she would be partnered with him for bridge, for they just might win.

After supper, they all assembled in a large parlor where several velvet-covered card tables had been set up. Though Rufford Abbey was a rather homely residence, its interior rooms were, with few exceptions, large and ornate. The parlor was well lit with gaslights, and a good thing, too, for the walls were all darkly paneled and the ceiling high above them. Sir Stiley had, perhaps, made an attempt to lighten the room with cream and gold-colored furniture, but Katherine still felt it had an oppressive air. Perhaps the monk was about, frowning upon their card playing.

Sir Stiley went to the front of the room and stood before yet another grand fireplace, and began drawing small cards from two baskets, pairing the couples for bridge.

Alas, when it came time to draw, she was paired with the general, but she was slightly gratified to see Mr. Coulton give her a look of disappointment. Katherine wasn't certain she could be civil to the general, given what he was doing with her mother.

But he was such a jovial, kind man it was difficult to maintain her anger. General Lawton had their opponents in stitches, which at first Katherine thought was a particularly astute strategy to distract the other players. Unfortunately, it soon became clear the man was dreadful at cards. Perhaps, Katherine suspected a bit later, it was his intended strategy to lose quickly. For her mother, an excellent bridge player, was out the first round after being paired with a put out–looking gentleman. She shrugged, then took the general's proffered hand, smiling up at him. Oh, the nerve of those two, Katherine thought. They'd obviously lost on purpose.

Graham and his partner, an ancient lady who appeared to be unable to read her cards correctly, were also victims of the first round. Claudia, however, displayed surprising and remarkable skill—and she'd luckily been paired with Mr. Coulton, who looked happy enough to be winning at bridge.

As each round passed, the losers milled about, forming small groups, but Katherine, not knowing anyone other than Graham, stood alone, acutely aware of Graham doing the same. With the weakest players removed, the games became far longer. Katherine was thinking she should go to her room. She couldn't wait there for an hour for the match to end with Graham standing not a few yards away from her. Katherine could feel him there, but she couldn't tell where he was looking, and, despite her better judgment, decided to sneak a look—and found herself staring directly into his eyes.

She smiled weakly at him, and he gave her a small bow. Letting out a sigh of defeat, she walked over to him and stood there a few moments in silence.

"How have you been?" he asked softly.

Miserable. I'm in love with you and you don't even know it. I want to throw myself into your arms and feel you hold me. I want you to know that I die inside every time I hear your voice. Instead, she said, "Fine and dandy."

"Good. I was afraid you were unwell. Forgive me, but you look tired."

"Oh, we've been going to parties nonstop. I'm weary from all the excitement and dancing and fun we've been having."

"I see."

Her heart felt like a ball of lead, her throat ached, and Katherine wasn't certain how long she could stand there pretending to be happy before she burst into tears. She wanted to shout at him, to call him a stupid clout for marrying a woman who didn't love him, even though she knew the marriage was the best thing for him. She wanted to tell him she loved him. Suddenly, a small bit of weight lifted from her heart. Yes. That was it. She would tell him. She knew it wouldn't make a bit of difference to him, but it would make a world of difference to her. "I need to tell you something," Katherine said, "but this is not the place."

Katherine looked up at him, then walked out of the room, praying he would follow. He should know that she loved him. It wasn't fair that he didn't know. She wanted him to realize fully how her heart was breaking. Perhaps he wouldn't care. And even if he did care, she knew it would not alter his course. But Katherine had the terrible urge to tell him. Maybe if she said the words out loud, they would cease to fester inside her; she would be purged of this awful feeling.

Katherine walked into the library and looked about, even though she'd been quite certain it would be empty. For such a large house, the library was relatively small, and lit only by a single gas sconce above the fireplace. The fire hadn't been lit and the room was a bit chilly, and Katherine rubbed her hands over her arms to warm them.

"What do you want to say to me?"

Oh, thank God. She turned, drinking him in with her eyes. All other men paled in comparison. His gray eyes looked almost ethereal in the dim light. She swallowed down the growing lump in her throat, praying she could get through this without crying. "I know it's not fair, and I know it changes nothing." She took a shaky breath. "But I love you." She smiled tremulously.

His brows snapped together. "What did you say? No, don't repeat it," he said when she started to open her mouth. He looked as if she'd just told him the most dreadful news.

"I thought you should know," she said softly.

"Why. Why should I know? So that I should be more tortured than I already am?"

"No. Actually, it was meant to make me feel better," she said miserably. "It didn't work." Her eyes filled with hated tears and she looked away from him, willing herself not to cry.

He stood there a long moment, several feet from her, looking at her as if he were angry. "I should go," he said, and she nodded. But neither moved. "I'm not going to kiss you again."

"I know."

"I'm not."

"I . . ." And then in two long strides, she was in his arms, crying out from finally, finally holding him against her. He kissed her ravenously, her face, her forehead, her lips, as if trying to make up for all those days they'd been apart and all the days to come.

"What are you doing to me?" he said, tucking her head beneath his chin and holding her tightly against him. She wrapped her arms around him, squeezing, trying to make him impossibly close to her.

"I'm sorry," she said, hating that she was making him so unhappy. He pulled back to look gently into her face.

"What are you sorry for?"

She shrugged and kissed him, letting him know how much she loved him, how much she would miss him. He deepened the kiss with a groan, one hand moving up to caress her breast, the other pulling her closer, against his arousal and the proof that he wanted her.

"I want to make love to you," he said, trailing kisses down her neck.

"Yes." *Oh yes, yes, yes.*

The neckline of her gown was just deep enough that he could push the material aside and expose one breast. She groaned as he did, and whimpered when he laved his tongue over her nipple. When he gently sucked, she nearly cried out from the sheer pleasure that shot from her breast to between her legs. He spent long moments making love to her breast, until she was liquid.

"Touch me," he groaned. She knew what he meant, and the

thought of touching him there was both thrilling and a bit frightening. "Please."

She moved her hand to the large bulge in his pants and watched his eyes drift closed as she did. He hardened even more beneath her hand, and she smiled at the wonder of it.

"Oh God, Katherine. If you knew what that felt like. You are unmanning me." He took her hand and guided it slowly up and down as his breath became more ragged. In a sudden rush, he dipped his head once more, taking her nipple in his mouth and sucking.

"Oh my God."

Graham's head snapped up and, with a swift movement, covered a dazed Katherine's breast.

Standing there in the door, eyes wide and mouths agape, were Katherine's mother, the general, Lady Summerfield, Sir Stiley, and Lord and Lady Willington.

There was no slow dawning of what Graham had just lost. No, it struck him with the force of a tidal wave, swift and painful. And suddenly, those words uttered by Katherine right before she kissed him took on a new meaning. "I'm sorry," she'd said without offering an explanation.

Now he knew what she'd meant.

Chapter 12

"Katherine, come here," Elizabeth said, in a tone that brooked no argument.

The small group entered the room, faces grim, as Graham's hopes for his people crumbled beneath his feet.

"What is happening?" Katherine asked. Surely she knew. Hell, from the happy gleam in her mother's eye, *she* certainly knew.

"Go with your mother," he said firmly.

"Graham, what is happening?"

"*Graham*," Mrs. Von Haupt gasped, coming on the scene, and Graham nearly groaned aloud. If there had been any hope of hiding this event, it was now lost. "How dare you use his given name!"

"Katherine, now," Elizabeth said, holding out her hand as if she were a recalcitrant child.

Graham watched her leave, his heart torn. Could she have been complicit in this? He could not believe it of her. He could not. He shut his mind away from Mr. Chase's words of warning. She'd looked stunned when they'd been discovered. Hadn't she?

When Katherine had been led away by her mother, most of the others followed. John and Mrs. Von Haupt, whose face had gone quite purple, remained. John moved into the room, giving his silent support by standing opposite the irate Mrs. Von Haupt.

"Tell me this isn't what I think it is," she said. "My daughter is not three doors away and you are in here cavorting with that little slut."

"Do not disparage Miss Wright," Graham bit out.

She let out a bitter laugh. "How pathetic that you defend that ambitious little whore. She has been well schooled, my lord, by a mother who knew precisely what she was doing. By a mother who nearly did the same to me twenty years ago. Did you know that? Ah, I see you did not. She was vying for my husband, and he nearly broke it off with me. But my husband was an honorable man and could not be swayed by a trollop. Don't you see, sir? This is her revenge, and her daughter knew all along what she was about."

Graham was stunned to silence. It could not be true.

Mrs. Von Haupt looked at him with disgust. "We're leaving in the morning. My husband will make certain to destroy that contract you so flagrantly violated." She went to turn, then stopped. "I do feel sorry for you. No doubt you are a proud man, and to be duped like this must be unpleasant. But you have hurt my daughter, sir. There will be reparation."

As she was leaving, Graham saw Claudia at the door and heard her say, "Is it true, Mother?" Her mother nodded, grabbing her daughter's arm and leading her away, and Graham distinctly heard Claudia say, "I can't believe she did it."

He knew he should run after them, apologize to Claudia, but he couldn't bring himself to. Instead, he walked woodenly to the nearest chair and sat down. "This cannot be happening," he muttered.

"She could be wrong about Miss Wright," John said. "The old hag was angry. Understandably angry." Graham shot his friend a look, and John smiled innocently.

Graham buried his head in his hands. "Oh my God, what have I done?" He sat, breathing heavily for a time, then stood and rushed to the window, threw it open, and vomited violently. When he'd recovered, John was there holding a glass of brandy, which he took and drained.

"You said Miss Wright is an heiress?"

Graham sat back in the same chair and nodded.

"Then she comes with money. Right?"

"Not nearly enough. I have let my people down. I have lost

Avonleigh and Bryant Park. People, good hard-working people, will suffer because of what I have done this night."

John hunkered down next to his friend and laid a firm hand on his forearm. "Perhaps I can help a bit. Perhaps not all is lost. Avon, listen to me. Let me look at your books. I'm a bit of a genius, it turns out, at cutting costs and making money. I've nearly doubled our barley yield at Flintwood. My father was stunned."

Graham nodded, but he doubted John could do much to save his home. "The thing is, the *worst* of it is, I love her."

"Miss Wright?"

"Yes. And if she's complicit in this, if she planned it . . ." Graham could not complete his thoughts. His eyes burned and he thought he just might vomit again. John put his arm on his back, and that gesture of kindness nearly was his undoing. He pressed the heels of his hands against his eyes and clenched his jaw against the pain.

"She didn't," John said firmly.

Graham took a deep breath. "No, she couldn't have."

"Mother, I can't marry him. He has to marry Claudia," Katherine cried. "He has such plans for his estate, to help his tenants. They are living in terrible conditions, and Graham is ashamed about the condition of their houses. He is such a proud man, and this will kill him."

"Oh, he won't die, I can assure you. I know it all seems terrible now, but if you do care for one another, you'll get by. You might think I found you with a stable boy, and not a marquess. Oh my goodness, you're to be a marchioness!"

Her mother's happiness over this horrid event was fraying the last of her nerves.

"He has to marry Claudia."

"Don't be ridiculous, Katherine. Mrs. Von Haupt is no doubt packing her bags as we speak. It wasn't as if I was the only one who saw the two of you. You did have quite an audience."

"Oh God." She'd been sitting on the edge of her bed, but at her mother's words, she threw herself back. She brought her hand up to touch the mermaid pendant she always wore and gasped. It was gone. She had no idea when or where she could have lost it. The pendant could be anywhere in the vast halls of Rufford Abbey and if any servant did find it, they would no doubt discard the cheap piece.

"Tell me, Katherine. Do you like him even a little?"

"I love him," she said miserably. She felt the bed dip as her mother sat down next to her. Then she lay down and gave her a much-needed hug.

"If that's true, you'll get through this. Does he love you?"

Katherine swallowed. "I think he might, though he's never said he does. I do know he didn't want to marry Claudia."

"How do you know that?"

Katherine's face crumpled as she remembered the pain in his voice that day at Lord and Lady Haverslys'. She wondered if she should tell her mother that she'd met him in Brighton, that they'd known each other far longer, and far more intimately than her mother could ever suspect. Oh goodness, that certainly would be a very bad idea. "After he announced his engagement to Claudia, he told me he was suffering." She turned her face toward her mother. "And now he's suffering even more. I don't want him to suffer," she wailed, and buried her head against her mother's shoulder.

"There, there, now, sweet pea," her mother said, using the endearment she'd used when Katherine was small. "Everything will work out just fine."

Graham sat in his room, a glass of brandy dangling from his fingers as he stared into the fire. It was eleven and the house was mostly quiet. No doubt everyone was in their rooms excitedly talking about what an idiot the Marquess of Avonleigh was. Or perhaps they were shocked by his indiscretion. Or his lack of honor. All of those scenarios were so far removed from any gossip that had ever been attached to him before, it was astonishing.

There was a soft knock on his door, and Graham wearily pushed his body up to answer it. He was stunned when he saw Lady Summerfield outside his door, her daughter, Lady Marjorie, slightly behind her. "Good evening, Lord Avonleigh. May we have a word with you? My daughter has something to say," Lady Summerfield said.

Graham nodded, and stepped back to allow the two women into his room.

"This is a terrible night for you, I'm certain, and my daughter is about to make it a bit worse, I fear," Lady Summerfield said ominously. "Tell him, dear. He needs to know."

"It will do no good now," Lady Marjorie said. "And I'm sure it's nothing."

"Please just say it," Graham said, nearly wincing at his sharp tone.

"I like Miss Wright. I truly do. But I hardly know her, not really. And given this evening's events . . ." She looked at her mother, who nodded for her to continue. "When we were at Briarbrook, during the picnic, Miss Wright said something that in hindsight seems rather . . . disturbing. I didn't think she was like some of those other American girls, but now I fear I may have been wrong. I feel so disloyal saying anything, but in good conscience, I believe I must. Do you remember when we were all walking along the lake and you and Miss Wright went into that clearing to see the deer?"

Graham remembered every detail vividly, and he nodded.

"I warned her that she shouldn't allow herself to be alone with you, with any man, that it could be dangerous and lead to a situation much like you are in now. And she said—I quite remember this because I was so very angry—that perhaps she would make such an event happen. That being married to a marquess wouldn't be so horrid."

That terrible hollowness in his gut grew exponentially. "I see."

"I'm certain she didn't mean it. I mean, not the way it sounds. She did say she was jesting."

Graham gave the young woman a steady look. "Then why did her words make you angry?"

Again, she darted a look to her mother. "I didn't think she understood the import of such a scandal. Of what it could mean for both of you. But the Katherine I know would not do such a thing," she finished in a rush. "Katherine has never given any indication that she wanted a title."

"But her mother certainly has, my dear," Lady Summerfield said gently. "Katherine may not be like all those title-hungry American girls, but I fear her mother is exactly like all those title-hungry mamas."

"Thank you, ladies," Graham said.

The two women left and Graham stood completely still for a long moment. Then, in one violent movement, he threw his brandy into the fireplace, shattering the glass.

* * *

Katherine awoke the next morning to Clara shaking her gently. She grabbed her pillow and covered her head, unwilling to face the day.

"The Von Haupts are leaving, miss," Clara said. "And Miss Von Haupt will not leave until she sees you."

Katherine threw off the pillow and sat up, horrified. "I can't!"

"You certainly can," Clara said firmly. "You've cooked your goose and now you must eat it."

Katherine scowled at her maid. "Very well. Is she coming up here or am I going to her?"

"She's waiting in the entry hall and her mother is already in the carriage, but she refuses to leave without seeing you. Here," Clara said, holding up her simplest dress, "put this on and let's get this over with."

Within minutes, Katherine was dressed and her hair piled in a simple bun. She looked at Clara, misery clear in her expression. "This is going to be exceedingly unpleasant. At least her mother is already in the carriage."

Katherine walked down the long hall and peeked over the balcony to see Claudia, charming in a lavender traveling outfit, waiting at the base of the interminably long staircase. What could she possibly say to Claudia? She'd ruined the poor girl's life.

She was halfway down the stairs when Claudia heard her descent, and she turned, a brilliant smile upon her face. What in all that was holy was Claudia smiling about?

As Katherine made it to the bottom, Claudia scampered over, holding out two hands in greeting. "I can't believe you did that for me," she gushed. "I feel like it's my birthday and Christmas, rolled into one!"

"What?"

"Oh, don't look so distressed, you silly girl. This is what I wanted. Did you think I'd be angry? It was my idea, after all. I just can't believe you would do that for me." Then, in a whisper, she said, "I think I'm in love with Mr. Coulton and I do believe he feels the same. We're going to London and he's following tomorrow. I might be a viscountess and he's ever so nice. Oh Katherine," she said, hugging her. "Thank you. Thank you."

And then, Claudia whirled away and left Katherine standing there, quite dazed.

Above her, watching that rather curious scene from the balcony, was Graham. Mr. Chase had come to him not moments before, having heard Miss Von Haupt was demanding to see Miss Wright before she left. Fearing a horrible and potentially scandalous scene, Graham had been on his way to attempt to stop the women from coming to blows, but stopped dead at the sight of the two women smiling at each other below him. Claudia looked radiantly happy.

How very odd.

Graham clutched the railing until his knuckles turned white as the meaning of what he was watching slowly dawned on him. He could not hear what the two women were saying, but it was obvious they were far from enemies. Indeed, they looked to be the best of friends. And when Claudia embraced Katherine, when she clearly said "Thank you" next to her ear, it felt like a hard blow to his gut, so much, in fact, he staggered backward.

Thank you? *Thank you?*

The blood drained from his head so quickly, he actually felt momentarily dizzy. My God, he was such a fool. Such a stupid, gullible idiot.

He turned blindly away from the railing, somehow making it back to his room, where Mr. Chase stood, his face registering immediate concern when Graham lurched in. Graham went directly to the window and threw it open, letting the misty, cool air bathe his skin.

"Sir? What is it? What has happened?"

"You were right about her all along, Everett."

"I'm so sorry, sir."

"I've been made a damned fool of. How could I have been so blind?"

Graham swayed at the window, and, growing alarmed, Mr. Chase rushed to his side, making Graham laugh bitterly. "Don't worry, Chase, I'm not throwing myself out the window. I'll face the music. I'll do my duty. But she will pay for doing this thing. She wanted a title? By God, she'll rue the day she got this one."

Chapter 13

"He's gone?"

Elizabeth's face was grim. "To London. To procure a special license and wait for your father. We're to go on to Avonleigh and await them both."

"Father is coming?" Katherine asked. "Of course, Father is coming. Is Lucy?"

"She's in school, dear. We can hardly take her out for a month to attend this wedding. Such as it is."

Katherine sat at a writing desk and her mother hovered behind her. "I . . . I want to apologize to you, Katherine. I have been inattentive, the worst sort of mother to allow this to happen. While I pray things will work out in the end, this is not the way it should have happened. These things do blow over, dear, but for now we shall do as Lord Avonleigh suggests."

Katherine clutched her hands in front of her, pressing her fists against her roiling stomach. "Where is Avonleigh?" she asked, sounding very much like a lost child, for that was precisely what she felt like. She had done this. She had acted recklessly, and now both of their lives were forever ruined. Graham would resent her forever for destroying his legacy, and she had lost her first love.

"In Northumberland, dear."

"And where is that?"

Elizabeth let out a soft laugh. "I haven't any idea. I imagine, given its name, it is somewhere north of here. I do know it takes several days' travel to get there, even by rail."

"Oh."

"I've heard . . ." Elizabeth hesitated slightly. "I've heard it's a bit rustic, dear."

"I shouldn't worry about that," Katherine said, hoping it was a hovel without any modern conveniences. It was only what she deserved. She wasn't such a martyr to lay all the blame upon her feet, but she had used no caution at all when dealing with Graham. How many times had they been alone? It was as if they had been playing a game of chance, one they were certain to lose. With so much at stake, how could they have allowed this to happen?

Katherine longed to talk to Graham so she would know how he was feeling. Angry, likely, with himself. Horrified, no doubt, to have lost everything because of one single act of weakness. But perhaps he was not altogether unhappy with the thought of marrying her. After all, though he might not have told her he loved her, she knew he desired her. That was something, was it not?

But he was gone and she would likely not see him until he reached Avonleigh with her father. Goodness, she wondered how that meeting would go. Her father had been opposed to this trip, even though he had agreed to fund it. Her mother had ultimately convinced him that Katherine's marriage to a titled gentleman would boost their social status, and that would lead to more prestige in the business world. If Father was anything, he was a driven and ambitious man.

Katherine's eyes burned, but no tears fell, for which she was grateful. She was sick of crying.

The women turned when a knock sounded on the door, and Elizabeth called out for whoever it was to enter. A man neither had ever seen before entered.

"Mrs. Wright, Miss Wright, I am Everett Chase, Lord Avonleigh's valet. I shall be accompanying you to Northumberland and assisting the staff to ready the house for his lordship's arrival."

Katherine stood. "You are the valet," she said, with a small smile, putting the slightest emphasis on the last word. "It is a pleasure to meet you, Mr. Chase."

The old valet gave her a curiously hard look before pulling out his watch. "We leave tomorrow morning. I do hope that gives you ladies enough time to pack."

"Yes," Elizabeth said. "More than enough time."

He gave them a small bow and departed, closing the door silently behind him.

"Oh dear, I fear Mr. Chase doesn't like me at all," Katherine said. "I shall endeavor to win him over, then."

Winning over Mr. Chase proved to be an insurmountable task. The man was exceedingly, almost painfully, polite. And yet through that politeness, Katherine suspected he disliked her. It shouldn't bother her so, as her mother pointed out, but it did. She knew, perhaps more than anyone, how important this man was to Graham, and the fact he disliked her was bothersome.

"What does it matter if the valet likes you or not?" Elizabeth asked, testy over the entire subject. They were sitting in a first-class train car headed north to Hexham, where they would have to take a coach to Avonleigh. It was a long and tedious journey, but the English rails were many, reducing the amount of time in a coach, for which they were grateful. Still, it seemed the train was constantly stopping to switch tracks or slowing for no apparent reason the two women could discern.

Mr. Chase was in a different car, but checked on the two women frequently. And politely.

"Can you not see how much he dislikes us?" Katherine said after one such visit.

"I have no idea what you are talking about, dear. He was exceedingly polite."

"It's more than politeness. I sense a coldness. And the other servants will follow his lead, you know. I am the downfall of them. No doubt they were making plans for improvements or adding to their numbers. With Lord Avonleigh marrying me instead of Claudia, they will be bitterly disappointed. It's only natural that they would despise me."

Elizabeth let out a heavy sigh, apparently irritated with the conversation. "They are hardly your friends, Katherine; they are your servants. I can't see that it matters."

* * *

Clara eyed the valet darkly. He sat next to Patty, Mrs. Wright's personal maid, whom she had always loathed. Because of her position as lady's maid to Mrs. Wright, she put on airs that were quite beyond what a lady's maid should. But she was old, so perhaps that was her problem. And perhaps Clara pointing out how lovely the silver looked in her brown hair annoyed the woman. She certainly hoped so. Clara smiled smugly to herself remembering Patty's look of thinly veiled dislike.

Mr. Chase made it quite clear he wanted nothing to do with either woman. All attempts at conversation were cleanly shut off like a dripping water spigot. But Clara, who was feeling a large amount of anxiety over this trip, persisted.

"What size is the staff at Avonleigh?" she asked. It was a normal enough question, but Mr. Chase looked at her as if she'd asked how much gold was in the coffers.

"Large enough to care for the home," he said without inflection.

"And the servants' accommodations, are they nice?"

"Certainly adequate."

"Is there a village nearby? In New York we were never without something do to on our day off."

"Yes."

"What size is the village?"

"Small." He said the word with a look that clearly said, "Now shut up." Which Clara finally did, even as her stomach twisted nervously.

She was beginning to get annoyed, never mind a bit frightened. When she'd set out on this trip, Miss Wright had assured her they would be returning home. And now she found herself traveling even farther away from her family, from her home. She knew Miss Wright was going to ask her to stay, but she wasn't sure what she was going to say. As much as she loved Miss Wright, she wanted to go home. She didn't want to spend the rest of her life in a foreign country where she could hardly understand what half the people were saying. But how could Clara abandon Miss Wright when she needed her most?

At least Patty knew she was going home, the witch. That was likely why she was sitting on the valet's side, looking so smug. She got to go home. But even if Clara went back with Mrs. Wright, she wouldn't have a job. Unless . . .

She smiled. Miss Lucy was getting to an age when she would need a personal maid. It was perfect. Lucy was a good girl and had the most beautiful blond hair. Just thinking about styling it made Clara's hands twitch. Yes, she would speak to Mrs. Wright and ask her about being Miss Lucy's maid. She pushed down a small amount of guilt for leaving Miss Wright. But why should she suffer for another's mistake?

Graham held the cable from Mr. Wright in his hand as he waited in his hired coach for the gentleman to disembark the steamship *Oceanic*. Anyone passing by his coach would have looked in to see a gentleman relaxed, his head back on the seat, his top hat pulled over his eyes as if he was taking a nap. In reality, Graham was trying to shut out the world and his thoughts and having very little luck. He'd met with his solicitor, who'd grimly given him an update of his finances. He had little choice but to lease Bryant Park—and that would put only a small dent in his expenses. Finding a tenant would be difficult, the gentleman had kindly pointed out, because so few updates to the home and grounds had been made. No wealthy merchant would want to live in a house with no ballroom and only partial gas lighting. Its close proximity to London might help, he'd said, but Graham got the distinct feeling the man was giving him a bit of hope when there was none. Too many other, grander, and more modern homes were available, so it was unlikely anyone would lease the run-down manor house.

Graham took his hat off and placed it on the seat next to him to look out the window for an angry father trying to find an interminably stupid fool. Good God, he could only imagine the man's reaction when he'd received Mrs. Wright's cable that he was to leave New York immediately to attend his daughter's hasty wedding. He had no idea what Mrs. Wright had written, and only prayed the cost of sending the cable had prevented the woman from going into too much detail. That night when he'd pressed against Katherine, when he'd tasted her, heard her sounds of pleasure, had been just ten days ago. Ten days of regret, anger, hurt, and doubt that combined in his stomach like a rotten stew, making eating nearly impossible. He looked like hell and felt worse. Even his solicitor had taken one look at him and inquired after his health. It certainly hadn't helped that he was using the hotel's valet instead of his own. But Chase was doing more good for him escorting his lovely bride to her new home than he could with Graham. Frankly, Graham wasn't certain he could have stomached the looks of disappointment from the man. Chase had warned him even in Brighton that he was taking the wrong path. Yet he'd persisted and persisted and now the entire future of his legacy was in jeopardy

Perhaps the worst of it was, before all the damning evidence against her had been presented, Graham had felt a large bit of joy over the prospect of marrying Katherine. As difficult as it would be to watch his legacy crumble beneath him, his heart had sung. Now? He battled with a heart that still loved Katherine and a brain that knew such love was misplaced.

A hundred times Graham had gone over every minute he'd spent with Katherine, from the day they'd met in Brighton to that terrible night at Rufford Abbey when he'd lost his head—and any chance he had at saving his estates. The evidence against her was damning, yes, but at nearly every turn he had been the one to pursue her. It seemed hardly likely that she'd planned it all from the beginning. Perhaps the idea had grown, like a virulent weed in her brain. Perhaps her mother had put her up to it.

I'm sorry.

What are you sorry for?

She hadn't answered. She'd kissed him and moments later they'd been caught. He could explain that away, even though she'd been the one to arrange that meeting. He could explain it all away, even Lady Marjorie's concerns, if he hadn't seen Miss Von Haupt hug Katherine and thank her. He could not envision a single scenario in which the woman who had been betrayed was *thanking* the betrayer.

Unless it had all been planned. Unless Miss Von Haupt had been involved, had perhaps helped formulate the scheme—as unlikely as that seemed. Claudia should loathe Katherine. Should have slapped her, screamed at her, cried. Instead, she'd hugged her and said thank you.

God, how could he have been so blind? How could he have fallen in love with such a woman? And he *had* fallen in love, if the way he was feeling now was any indication. His entire body hurt as if he'd been run over by a train.

He'd left Rufford Abbey, unable to face her without doing her bodily harm. In the last ten days, his anger had waned somewhat, turning away from her and toward himself. He'd always prided himself on his control, on putting his duty above all things. How he'd let a charming and beautiful woman sway him from his course, he didn't know. He was disgusted with himself and philosophically cold about Katherine. Why wouldn't a title-hungry girl do what she could to nab him? Being angry with her was the same as being angry with the fable's scorpion that stung the frog, drowning them both. It was her nature, he supposed, and he was the idiot frog who'd trusted her.

He simply couldn't believe he'd been so easy to fool. And there were times he couldn't believe it of her. She was either the greatest actress he'd ever known or she'd been as surprised as he to see they had an audience for their lovemaking. Or maybe he was simply blinded by lust and love.

Graham swore viciously, and then again as he saw a man who could only be Katherine's father standing still on the crowded wharf. Hell, the man was huge. He looked like a pugilist, not a successful businessman, even dressed as elegantly as he was. He wore a bowler pulled down low over deep-set eyes that scanned the wharf with purpose. Superfluous sideburns only enhanced the man's lantern jaw, which at the moment was clenched rather fiercely. But he didn't look angry, so perhaps Mrs. Wright's cable had been brief.

Graham jammed his hat on his head, climbed down from the coach, and walked toward the man he believed to be Bartholomew Wright.

"Mr. Wright?"

"I am. You are Spencer?"

"Yes sir."

The next thing Graham felt was a fist to his gut, and his vision momentarily went dark. Doubled over, trying to catch his breath, Graham swallowed down the bile forming in his throat. Good God, the man could punch. Apparently, Mrs. Wright hadn't been concerned about the cost of sending a detailed cable.

"All right, then. I didn't hit you that hard." Graham looked up at the man as if he were mad. He felt like he'd just been kicked in the gut by an angry stallion. "Let's get you married."

Graham tried to straighten to look the madman in the eyes, only to find Mr. Wright looking about as if nothing had happened. "I suppose I deserved that, but not much of a greeting, eh?" he managed to say, trying desperately not to vomit.

Mr. Wright gave him a curious look, as if wondering whether Graham had expected some other sort of greeting.

"My daughters are the lights of my life. It's best you remember that. And you also might remember that I'm in the ring toeing the line three times a week." He pointed to his rather mashed nose. "I didn't get this sipping tea and eating crumpets."

Despite himself, Graham laughed, gaining him the first non-murderous look of the day.

The two men immediately went to a nearby pub, which drew a small amount of attention, for it was the sort of place that rarely— if ever—attracted a titled gentleman. Graham needed a drink and it was the closest place that didn't look like it harbored gin-soaked cutthroats, and he had a feeling Mr. Wright wasn't the sort who would be comfortable in Brooks'. And St. James was too far to wait for a drink at any rate.

Mr. Wright ordered a whiskey and downed it like water, then ordered another before Graham had even taken his first sip. His stomach was still a tad sick after that hard blow. They sat silently at a table decorated with the rings of drinks long consumed, breathing in remnants of cigar and pipe smoke. The place was nearly empty, since it was early afternoon, and even the hardest drinkers had yet to venture in.

After downing his second glass, Mr. Wright broke the silence. "I kept wondering on the trip over here, what kind of man you were. Here you have a girl, pretty enough, who comes with a million pounds. That's more than a million dollars, you know. That's a lot of money for any man."

"And fifty thousand a year, you mustn't forget that," Graham said bitterly. Mr. Wright looked as if he just might punch him again, so Graham stopped talking.

"So here's this man, this broke, titled man, in desperate need of money. He's got his bird in his hand. He's ready to win the prize. Indeed, the prize is already his. This man, I'm thinking, is one lucky bastard. Beautiful girl. Lots of money that he hasn't had to work a minute for. He's in a good position now. An envious position.

"This man, this desperate man, loses it all"—he snapped his fingers—"just like that. I have a question for you, Mr. Spencer."

Graham didn't bother pointing out he wasn't a mister; he simply nodded and waited for the question.

"Did you ever in the course of these past weeks ever truly consider marrying my daughter instead of that Von Haupt girl?"

Graham swallowed, and as much as he dreaded feeling another blow, he told the truth. "No sir, I didn't."

Mr. Wright slapped his hand down so hard on the table, Graham couldn't help but wince. "That's what I thought," Mr. Wright declared loudly. "So, I'm thinking, why would a man take such a chance? He knows the rules. He knows if he gets caught dallying with this other girl—my *daughter*—everything will be ruined. All that money—poof." He gestured with his beefy, but somehow elegant, hands. "Why would a man do such a thing?"

Graham stared at the older man, briefly wondering whether that question wasn't rhetorical. He breathed a small sigh of relief when Mr. Wright answered for him.

"Is he a moron? I asked myself. Could be, could be." He looked at Graham as if assessing his intelligence or lack thereof. "Is he an immoral reprobate? Does he have no conscience? Is seducing innocent young girls a hobby of his?"

Graham felt his anger grow. "Sir, you have—"

"No need for a show of outrage, Mr. Spencer," Mr. Wright said, holding up a hand. "I know how you English feel about honor and whatnot. But you must imagine how difficult it is for me, the father of my lovely, *innocent* daughter, to imagine why a man—an engaged man with more than a million dollars at stake—would put his entire future in jeopardy. So is it stupidity or arrogance?"

Love. It was love, with a large dose of stupidity.

"Stupidity," Graham said softly. For wasn't falling in love with Katherine the height of stupidity?

Mr. Wright gave Graham a grim smile. "Now, why would I give a dime to a stupid man?" Mr. Wright said, his tone suddenly as cold and hard as stone on a winter's day.

Chapter 14

From a distance, Avonleigh took one's breath away. It was situated in a valley surrounded by brilliant green rolling fields dotted with sheep and backed by a thick forest. A small lake sparkled to the west, creating a scene that could be conjured for a fairy tale. Katherine looked up and felt her world tilt slightly. It was the strangest feeling, to look at a building she'd never before seen and feel as if she had come home. Her heart actually hurt, looking at Avonleigh. It was not the largest home she'd seen in England, but it was by far the prettiest.

Unlike so many homes they'd toured, it was not a hodgepodge of different centuries' architectural styles tacked together, but a lovely building with peaked copper roofs above mellow golden stone.

That was at a distance. As they grew closer, it became clear that what looked like a lovely garden—perhaps at one time it had been— was nothing more than an overgrown mass of flowers choked by weeds. The drive was rutted, and if it ever had been gravel, the stones had long been mashed into the ground to become part of the wild landscape. Weeds had even taken over the drive, poking up valiantly to brush against the horses' shins as they pulled the coach to the front drive.

No footmen appeared to help them from the carriage, and the women waited for Mr. Chase to slowly step down from his place next to the driver so he could assist them. He pulled down the steps and offered his gloved hand, grimly looking at his two charges.

"No wonder he wanted cash," Elizabeth said, when she'd exited the coach. She looked up at the home with no small bit of dismay. "It looks abandoned."

"He doesn't care about the house. It's his people he's worried about," Katherine said.

Mr. Chase furrowed his brow sharply at her words as he helped Clara and Patty from the carriage, and Katherine felt as if she'd said something unforgiveable. Did Mr. Chase think she was belittling Graham's need to help his tenants and the people who depended on this little town to thrive?

Just then, the front door opened and a man who appeared to be in his nineties peered at them with rheumy eyes.

"Ah, Mr. Stanfield," said Mr. Chase in a booming voice. Mr. Stanfield must be deaf, Katherine thought. "I suppose you did not get my cable."

"No, Mr. Chase," the ancient man said in a voice so thin as to almost be nonexistent. He sounded as if he were being choked. "No cable."

"We got a cable," a woman, who seemed not quite so ancient, said from behind Mr. Stanfield. "I knew you were comin' even if this old coot forgot." She tapped her head and rolled her eyes.

"Mrs. Alcourt, allow me to introduce Miss Katherine Wright and her mother, Mrs. Bartholomew Wright," Mr. Chase said. "Miss Wright is betrothed to his lordship."

Katherine couldn't help but give Mr. Chase a look of exasperation. The words themselves were innocuous, but it was the way he'd said them. He had the unique knack of making anything he said sound completely derisive.

"This is Clara, my maid, and Patty, my mother's maid. I've been looking forward to seeing Avonleigh, but for now, we'd like to go to our rooms."

"You're staying here?" Mrs. Alcourt said with horrified surprise.

Katherine shot a quick look to her mother. "Of course. This is where we plan to live. At least I do." Was the woman daft?

Realization finally registered on Mrs. Alcourt's face. "Oh my goodness, we're not ready at all. Not at all!" She glared at Mr. Chase, who seemed completely nonplussed by events.

"That is why I sent the cable, Mrs. Alcourt. To warn you of our impending arrival."

"All right, then, Mr. Chase. No need to get snippy, is there. We'll have their rooms right as rain in no time. Meanwhile, you can wait in . . ." A small bit of panic ensued, as Mrs. Alcourt apparently tried to think of an appropriate place to put the two women. ". . . the master's library," she finished triumphantly. "Mr. Chase, could you show their maids to the servants' quarters?"

It was soon apparent why Mrs. Alcourt had chosen the library, as it appeared to be the only room on the main level to have furniture. Their footsteps echoed ominously as they walked down a long, uncarpeted hall. Her mother whispered fiercely, "Why would he send us here? As bad as Bryant Park is, at least some rooms actually have furniture in them."

Even the walls had been stripped bare, the ghosts of paintings long gone the only adornment on the faded wallpaper. "I have no idea," Katherine said, but she was growing ever more alarmed. She could explain away why Graham had left Rufford Abbey in haste without saying good-bye, but how could she explain sending her and her mother practically to Scotland to live in a home that clearly was barely habitable? She knew he had to be bitterly disappointed about what had transpired. She felt purely awful that it had come to this—even as her heart celebrated. Every time a bit of joy filtered out of her, guilt for the consequences of her actions was close behind. During the trip here, she had resolved to make the most of it and make Graham as happy as she could. She might not come with one million pounds, but her dowry was impressive. Surely he could do much good with the one hundred thousand dollars she would bring to the marriage. It wasn't as if all was lost. He hadn't loved Claudia. So why did she feel as if she were being punished?

"I believe we've gone back in time," Elizabeth whispered as they followed Mrs. Alcourt down a series of halls. The walls held no gaslight, only naked candle sconces. She supposed even candles weren't needed in a home where no one lived.

"Here we are," Mrs. Alcourt said happily, pushing open a heavily carved door.

Katherine almost wept with relief. It was a lovely room, with rich carpeting, polished wood paneling, and windows that were clean and allowed sunlight to stream in once the heavy, velvet curtains were pushed aside. She noticed with pleasure that only the smallest amount of dust fell from the curtains when Mrs. Alcourt thrust them aside, and the room itself was immaculate.

"A lovely room, Mrs. Alcourt. Thank you."

Mrs. Alcourt beamed. "I'm afraid it's the only room below stairs that's been kept up, but it should be comfortable enough. His lordship eats in his rooms, you see. I expect he'll be here shortly?"

"I believe he's about a week behind us. He's meeting with Mr. Wright and they are traveling here upon my father's arrival."

Mrs. Alcourt was about to leave the room, then stopped. "The staff here is very excited about his lordship's marriage, Miss Wright. It's been a long time since we've seen him happy with all that's weighing him down."

Goodness, they must not know she was not the original American heiress. No doubt they'd all been quite excited about the prospect of having funds in the coffers again. She'd let Graham explain things to them and said only, "I look forward to a long and wonderful life here, Mrs. Alcourt."

When the housekeeper was gone, her mother collapsed onto the nearest chair, looking as if she were in shock.

"I had no idea," she said. "I cannot allow you to stay here, Katherine. It's completely out of the question."

Katherine forced a smile. "It only needs a bit of furniture. It's a lovely home."

"A bit of furniture? Lovely! It has no gaslight, no carpets, no paintings. No staff to speak of. I hardly think a house this size can be run properly with two elderly people. I wouldn't be surprised if they handed you a chamber pot."

Katherine sighed. "I'm actually fairly certain this home doesn't have water closets. I'll just make do. Goodness, Mother, if a chamber pot is my biggest worry, I daresay I shall be quite happy here."

"You're not staying. My daughter will not stay in a home without adequate staff or furniture."

"Perhaps you should have thought of that before forcing me on this trip to hunt for a title." Katherine continued even as she registered the shock on her mother's face. "I don't know if you've noticed, Mother, but a very many titles in need of cash have homes much like this one. They want to marry an heiress so they can update their homes. At least Lord Avonleigh is not so self-involved to only care whether he has pretty paintings on the wall. I'm quite certain that every penny he made from selling it all off went to his farmers and the village. And I'm glad of it. You have no idea what that man has endured, how seeing his people suffer has hurt him. If I have to use a chamber pot for the rest of my life, that's what I'll do." Her mother looked as if she were about to have an apoplexy, and Katherine was about to burst into tears, but the sudden appearance of Mr. Chase acted like a stopper. She swallowed and composed herself, excruciatingly aware she'd just been talking about chamber pots. "Yes, Mr. Chase?"

He stared at her a long moment and raised one eyebrow. "Your rooms are being readied, Miss Wright, Mrs. Wright," he said. "I'll send Mrs. Alcourt when they are nicely turned." He gave a small bow, then left the room.

"No doubt we'll be sleeping on the floor," Elizabeth said darkly.

And that's when Katherine burst into tears.

Graham had never been so tense in his life. Bartholomew Wright was one of the most intimidating men he'd ever met, and the memory of that beefy fist sinking into his stomach was never far from his mind during their long trip north. He supposed he'd imagined Mr. Wright as an elderly businessman, a bookish gentleman who spent his life behind a desk. He could not have been more wrong. He couldn't fathom how a man like Wright could have produced a beauty like Katherine.

Long silences as they sat together on the interminable train trip north were often interrupted by pointed questions in which Graham felt every syllable he uttered was being judged. Numerous times he had to squelch the urge to point out Katherine's duplicity, for this constant barrage of animosity, when he was the true victim, was getting wearing.

It was after one long silence on the train when Mr. Wright asked—or rather demanded, "How did you meet my daughter."

"It's a long story."

"We have time."

And so, leaving out only the details about how he'd kissed

Katherine and was actually considering asking her to be his mistress, he told him their story. Every time Mr. Wright's brows snapped together, Graham braced himself for a massive blow, but it never came.

"You mean to say to me you asked a young girl to meet you at midnight?"

The way Mr. Wright said it sounded so sordid. Graham supposed it was. He hadn't been in his right mind. If one were to write down the facts, they would be quite damning. Everything he'd done, every action he'd taken was improper—on both their parts. He knew why he'd carried on so; he'd been completely enchanted by her. But why had she met him?

"Yes sir, I did. I know it was wrong."

"And she did? She met you?"

"Yes sir. At the time we blamed it on the sea air. But in hindsight I think it was because we were both anonymous. It was very much like going to a masquerade where your identity is completely concealed. I've noticed that people do things at a masquerade that they would never do in their normal life."

Mr. Wright scowled at him. "I cannot imagine Katherine doing such a thing. And where was her mother?"

"I couldn't say, sir," Graham said, his eyes shifting away.

"This entire debacle is maddening. My daughter, who's never done anything more rebellious than wear a red scarf when she should wear brown, would not do the things you say she did. But she obviously did do them—and with a man she thought to be a valet. When did she realize who you were?"

"It must have been two weeks later that we met at a house party. We immediately recognized one another—and immediately realized we'd both been untruthful. It was at this same house party that my engagement to Miss Von Haupt was announced."

"And you took up with Katherine again?" Mr. Wright said.

"We were at the same house party. It was inevitable that we should see one another. I . . ."

"You what?" the older man spat.

"I thought I'd never see her again after Brighton. In my mind, she was a maid and completely unacceptable."

"My daughter," Mr. Wright said with steel in his voice, "is the most acceptable girl you'll ever meet. Don't you ever forget that, you pompous prig."

Graham was stunned. But he took the epithet like the earlier blow, figuring he deserved it. And to Katherine's father, he probably did sound like a pompous prig. He did wonder how many blows he'd be able to take before he struck back.

It was worse than she'd thought. If Katherine had been born in 1790 instead of 1852, Avonleigh, despite the lack of furniture, would have been charming and quite up-to-date. In fact, based on English standards, it was rather modern, architecturally speaking. She didn't mind the lack of a designated water closet; there were still many homes in England that did not have them. But she did mind that she needed to carry a candle or lamp about in the evening, and reading by the fire became just that—reading by the flicking light of the one fire burning in the house in the library.

Four rooms were furnished, if one could call them furnished. The library seemed to be the only room in the house that hadn't been completely stripped. Two bedrooms—what Katherine presumed to be Graham's and one other adjoining room—were furnished sans paintings and carpeting. A third bedroom had hastily been put together by the home's skeleton staff—or rather the staff's children who still lived in the area. These "children" were men and women in their sixties, who still had quite a time bringing the bed from the attic where it had been stored. A large wardrobe dominated her room, a piece of furniture so huge and so heavy, Katherine had no doubt why it remained in the room. Katherine took the smaller bedroom and gave the other one adjoining the master suite to her mother. With her father on the way, another room would have to be prepared, but the poor movers were so done in by their task, she didn't have the heart to tell them a fourth room needed to be set up.

If it broke Katherine's heart to see this beautiful home stripped nearly bare, she could only wonder what Graham thought about it. It was clear he had cannibalized every bit of what he owned to pay bills. How awful it must have been to watch his things disappear one by one.

Unlike Bryant Park, the ballroom in Avonleigh was stunning. She was half-tempted to scrape all the gilt paint from the walls to help Graham restore the rest of the home. Three magnificent chandeliers hung from a high sky-blue ceiling, trailing dust from their crystal chains, pendaloques, and intricate scrollwork. A large fireplace, of pink Italian marble, dominated one end of the ballroom, its ornately carved mantel a work of art. Certainly at one time this family had had a huge amount of money. Where had it all gone?

Katherine, staring up at the strings of dust blowing in some unfelt breeze, heard a scuffling sound behind her and turned. "Hello, Mr. Chase. I was just admiring the ballroom. It certainly is grand."

"It is that, miss."

"I imagine it makes you sad to see the home like this. It makes me sad and I have no history here."

"It may not be the largest home in England, but it is certainly one of the prettiest," Mr. Chase said, surprising her. Up until that moment, his responses to her queries had been taciturn and painfully concise.

"I wish I could have seen her in her glory," she said with a wistful smile.

"It was the tin, miss."

"Tin?"

"Northumberland used to be a large producer of tin and the old lord invested heavily in it. That and copper."

"What happened?"

"They found large deposits of tin in the Malayan rivers. They were scooping it up from the riverbanks, getting more tin in a day than the mines here could get in a month. Prices dropped. Income dropped. And then very much the same happened to copper."

Katherine took in the gilt painting, the beautiful marble flooring, and understood then how fragile it all was. One discovery and all was lost.

"Then it wasn't neglect. It was chance. That makes it so much worse, somehow," she said. She suddenly imagined what it would have been like to discover everything you had was on the brink of disaster. It would have been devastating. How would a man react to the news that he was about to lose everything he possessed, that the legacy generations had built, was teetering on the edge? "Mr. Chase, when did all that happen, the discovery of the tin and copper?"

He stiffened just slightly. "I believe it was about ten years ago, miss. Just after the old lord had passed. It was a difficult time for his lordship."

So, not only did Graham have to deal with his father's suicide, he was left to watch his world crumble around him. "How awful," she said. "And right after his father . . ."

"After his father died, yes," Mr. Chase said, his voice gone cold once more. But Katherine realized this was only to mask his pain.

"I know how his father died, Mr. Chase," she said softly. "And I am so sorry for both of you."

Mr. Chase looked both horrified and shocked. "He told . . . I see."

"It must have been a terrible time."

Mr. Chase nodded, his eyes filled with raw pain. In a matter of moments, he composed himself completely, as if the discussion had never taken place. "I do apologize, Miss Wright. I came in search of you for Mrs. Alcourt. She would like to discuss dinner with you."

"Is Mrs. Alcourt also the cook?"

"In a manner of speaking, yes."

His words were spoken without inflection, but Katherine was certain she detected just the slightest sparkle of humor in his eyes, so she smiled. "Thank you, Mr. Chase, for the warning."

"She is waiting in the library."

Of course she was. Where else in this house could she be waiting?

Chapter 15

The sense of relief Graham felt when the coach finally pulled up in front of Avonleigh was akin to that of a man being told he was not going to die in the gallows this day—or any day. He wasn't certain he could take another minute of Mr. Wright glaring at him, examining him, interrogating him. He had the distinct feeling the man found him wanting in nearly every category, likely because Graham refused to make excuses for the facts. Yes, he was broke. Yes, he'd made a horrible decision to put all his money with a single investor. Yes, he'd compromised the man's daughter by agreeing to meet with her privately. Yes, he'd lied to Katherine when they'd first met and met her time and time again secretly. He had no defense. He was guilty—and the man knew it.

But knowing he was at least partially to blame did nothing to ease the pain in his heart that Katherine had planned all along to trap him. Well, he thought, looking up at Avonleigh's shabby exterior and knowing it was far, far worse inside, Graham hoped she enjoyed what her actions had wrought.

"So," Mr. Wright said, looking around him at the rutted drive, the paint peeling on the door, the overgrown garden, "this is where my daughter is to live."

"Yes sir."

They'd passed through the small village that desperately needed an influx of cash, and it seemed as if Mr. Wright's eyes missed nothing—the silent textile mill (the water wheel was in disrepair), the men who should be working sitting outside empty shops, the land that was uncultivated. This was sheep country, and many of the farms were dedicated to raising sheep wool or meat. But without a working mill or slaughterhouse, it was too expensive for many of the farmers to make a good living. Outside mills charged too much, and shipping the raw materials ate into their profits.

By the time they reached Avonleigh, Mr. Wright had a very good idea of the enormity of the problems facing the estate, Graham had no doubt.

Graham stepped from the coach, breathing in the sweet Northumberland air, grateful to finally have Mr. Wright's attention drawn away from him. In his breast pocket, he held the special license, which he hoped to utilize the very next day. He wanted this over. He wanted the Wrights gone. He needed to meet with his solicitor and reexamine what he was to do, what he could do to create some sort of cash flow. Getting the mill operational was his first priority, but the repairs would have to be done on credit. Negotiating such a project with carpenters who knew he had no money would not be an easy feat. Already he'd had some work done on the promise that he was marrying an heiress. When word got out that the heiress had disappeared, it would be near impossible to get any more work or materials on credit.

Still, with all his worries, it was good to be home, good to look out and see the rolling green hills of Northumberland. The door opened a crack, revealing Mr. Stanfield, looking out, clouded brown eyes squinting to determine who was in the courtyard. Graham had to smile at the absurdity that the old gent was still the butler—as he had been for more than fifty years. He'd started his tenure as butler when Graham's grandfather was still marquess.

"Ah, Mr. Stanfield, good to see you. Where are our guests?"

"Guests, sir?" he asked in his frail voice. "We've no guests."

"Oh, for goodness' sakes, Mr. Stanfield, we do have guests."

"Mrs. Alcourt. This is Mr. Wright. I do hope you can escort him to Mrs. and Miss Wright. No doubt they are in the library."

Mrs. Alcourt's eyes widened. "Mrs. Wright is indeed in the library. But Miss Wright is out and about somewhere with Mr. Chase."

"Out and about?"

"Who is Mr. Chase?" Bartholomew boomed.

"My valet," Graham explained calmly, though why on earth Mr. Chase should be escorting Katherine anywhere was a bit of a mystery.

"She seems to be drawn to the company of valets," her father said darkly.

"I believe they are visiting the poorhouse today," Mrs. Alcourt said.

"I see." He found it a bit odd that Mr. Chase had agreed to take Katherine to the poorhouse. Perhaps Katherine had browbeaten him into it, though he found that even more unlikely.

Avonleigh's poorhouse was not nearly as crowded as some, and Graham had ensured it was run fairly and properly. When he'd first inherited his title, one of his first actions was to petition the government to have the house's warden fired. He'd personally hired the current warden, who was dedicated to the cause of improving the life of the poor. But, like everything in Avonleigh, the home needed physical improvements. Though the government paid to run the home, it had always relied on extra attention from Avonleigh, which he had continued to provide even when his own finances were thin. Each child celebrated a birthday. Each Christmas the residents would have gifts. They worked just ten hours a day as compared to their London counterparts, who worked thirteen. He was only able to get away with such leniency because Avonleigh was so very far from London and rarely attracted the attention of the inspectors from the Local Government Board who oversaw the poorhouses. The local poorhouse committee, of which he was chairman, had been criticized in the past for its "lenient and harmful policies" of allowing workers to toil fewer hours than was standard, but Graham simply could not stomach forcing children and the elderly to work from dawn to dusk.

The news that his daughter was visiting a poorhouse alarmed Mr. Wright, who had no doubt read *Oliver Twist*—as so many people had. But the Avonleigh House for the Poor was nothing like that depicted by Charles Dickens—though many in England were still as bad or worse.

"Our poorhouse is well-run and quite unlike what you may have heard about workhouses here," he assured Mr. Wright as they walked inside. "Katherine has nothing to fear, and she is in good hands with Mr. Chase, who has often visited the home and is well-known there."

Bartholomew stopped dead in the entrance. "Have you been robbed?" he asked.

"No sir," Graham said, only slightly amused by what he assumed was a joke.

Bartholomew proceeded down the hall, stopping to open every few doors, before finally saying, "Is there any room in this house that is furnished?"

"The library. And my bedroom. I do hope the servants were able to scrounge up enough furniture in the attic to create sleeping quarters for your wife and daughter."

"I hope you know this is not acceptable," Bartholomew said, turning fully toward him, and Graham had to stop himself from taking a step back.

"I agree."

"So what are you going to do about it?"

"I had planned to marry a great heiress, but those plans went awry," Graham said pointedly. He was sick to death of taking all the blame for what had transpired. Yes, he'd been foolish to get caught, but he was not the one who'd set the trap. If his daughter had to live with a bit of inconvenience, Graham figured that was just punishment for what she'd done.

The older man glared at him and Graham glared right back. "Your daughter . . ." Graham stopped, shaking his head. It was not gentlemanly at all to blame the woman—even if the blame was hers.

"My daughter what . . . Do go on."

"Your daughter will adjust," Graham said finally, deciding Mr. Wright would certainly give him another blow if he said what he'd meant to: "Your daughter is to blame."

Mr. Wright thrust out his jaw and let out a sharp breath through his nostrils, reminding Graham of an angry bull. Graham gave the man a level look, then held out his arm, indicating Mr. Wright should proceed down the hall to the library.

When they reached the room, Graham watched with interest how husband and wife greeted one another, and was surprised by the warmth the couple displayed toward each other.

"I'm so sorry," Elizabeth gushed. "This is all my fault. You have no idea how wretched I feel." Elizabeth threw herself tearfully into her husband's arms.

Graham looked on, slightly annoyed that the two of them were carrying on so. It wasn't as if their daughter was marrying an ogre and about to be held in a tower room. She was marrying a good man with a lofty title whose only flaw was an empty bank account.

"How is she holding up?" Bartholomew asked, much to Graham's dismay. How was she holding up? She had everything she wanted. Oh, perhaps the condition of Avonleigh had been a bit of an unpleasant surprise, but the girl couldn't be that shocked, considering she knew he needed to marry Miss Von Haupt for her vast fortune.

"As well as can be expected," Mrs. Wright said, looking over to Graham. "Lord Avonleigh, I apologize for my tears, but this has been upsetting. I do hope you understand."

Actually, he did not. "Of course," he said tightly. The woman was a consummate actress. He had no doubt where Katherine had gained her skills.

A sound at the door drew all their attention, and Graham's heart pounded painfully when he saw Katherine standing at the library entrance, a wide smile on her face. She looked even more beautiful than he remembered, her eyes shining brightly, her hair upswept with tendrils curling about her neck. Graham took a step back from her and looked away until she ran across the room and threw herself into her father's arms. Graham couldn't stop himself from wishing she had thrown herself into his arms—even as he realized how foolish that thought was.

"It's so good to see you," she told her father, and Graham watched as she was swallowed up in the man's embrace. Bartholomew looked directly at him over his daughter's shoulder and Graham schooled his features to remain completely impassive. After the embrace, Bartholomew pushed his daughter gently away and, holding her by her upper arms, said, "You don't have to do this thing. You can come home."

"For God's sake," Graham muttered. They should be celebrating their coup, not acting as if someone had just died.

Katherine looked at Graham and gave him a shy smile, which he could not bring himself to return. Her smile slowly faded, replaced by confusion, before she looked back to her father. "Mrs. Von

Haupt was there, Father. I cannot go home to the gossip she will no doubt spread if I do. You know how she is."

"No one will have her now. She'll be completely cut off from society. Lucy's reputation will suffer, too, you know," Mrs. Wright said dramatically. "Katherine's prospects are completely ruined."

Graham had had enough. "Katherine's prospects? She's managed to trap a marquess into marriage. You should all be doing a victory jig, not acting as if she's being forced to marry a stable boy."

"Trap!" Katherine said, looking shocked.

"Oh, don't pretend otherwise," he snapped.

Her delicate brows furrowed. "What are you talking about?"

Graham clenched his jaw. "This is a discussion for another time. I do apologize," he said, giving the small group an overly formal bow. "I will allow you to visit while I make arrangements for the wedding tomorrow. We dine at eight."

He heard Katherine call his name, but he continued through the door, unable to stand looking at her one more moment.

"Welcome home, sir," Mr. Chase said as Graham walked into his room.

"Thank you." Distracted, Graham handed Mr. Chase his coat, which he'd been hanging on to since entering his home. He'd been worried that if he'd handed off his coat to Mr. Stanfield, the poor man would have collapsed beneath the weight of it. He went to the adjoining room and looked in.

"Mrs. Wright is there. Miss Wright thought her mother would be more comfortable in it and said it would be improper for her to take the room next to yours until you are married."

"It's a bit late for propriety, but all right. Where is she?"

"Down the hall. We had some beds taken down from the attic."

Graham poured water from a pitcher into a basin and splashed it on his face, getting rid of at least some of the grime from his travels. What he truly needed was a bath, but he could hardly ask Mrs. Alcourt and Mr. Stanfield to prepare it. When he'd come home in the past, he'd simply taken a bar of soap and gone to the lake to take a breath-stealing bath in the cold waters. When he was done drying his face, he braced his hands on either side of the washstand and stared into the water at his reflection. "I understand you took Miss Wright to the poorhouse. How went that visit?"

"Very well, sir. She now knows you walk on water."

Graham chuckled. He was a rather popular fellow there, especially after Stanley Bosh showed up telling them horror stories of a poorhouse in London that he'd "escaped" from. With every tale he told, the esteem the residents held for Graham increased until he was now deemed the most benevolent of men.

"I wish her father thought so. He loathes me."

Mr. Chase was aghast. "Why would that be, sir?"

"I suppose from his perspective, he's a right to his anger. I did compromise his daughter. And now she is forced to live here. With me. Even if it was entirely Miss Wright's idea, he doesn't know that. He's put the blame fully on me."

"About that, sir . . ." Mr. Chase paused as if uncertain whether to continue.

"Yes, Mr. Chase?"

"It's only that for a girl who cares only for a title, she seems terribly aware that you have been wronged."

"Of course she's aware of it. She did wrong me."

Chase shook his head. "Let us say I understand how you were charmed. After spending some time with her, I find it increasingly difficult to dislike her," the old man said, blushing a bit.

Graham looked at his valet and grinned. "Succumbed to a pretty face, did you?"

Chase gave him a withering look.

"It doesn't matter, for she is marrying me tomorrow, unless her father whisks her away. He just might at that." The thought sat like a lead ball in his stomach. He wanted to remain angry with her, but seeing her today only confused him more. She didn't look triumphant when she'd seen him or even fearful. She'd looked happy.

Why would she look happy when she knew he must be angry?

Katherine pushed her fork into her over-buttered, under-salted turnips. She should have declined the root, but the old butler had had such a time getting the serving plate steady enough for her to take a portion, she felt she had to take a bit. And then, just as she was about to remove a small portion, he shifted and she'd ended up getting far more on her plate than she wanted. Now it sat, a congealing turnipy blob, waiting for her to take a second bite.

"I imagine one of the first things you'll do, Katherine, is find a proper cook," Elizabeth said, after a long bout of chewing the stringy, tough roast beef. If it ever had been a good cut of beef, any goodness had been cooked right out of it.

"Mrs. Alcourt does try, Mother, but it is not her strength," Katherine said, shooting a small smile toward Graham. He had yet to look her in the eye, and her heart fell another notch. Why was he being so cool toward her? Was he so very disappointed that he was being forced into this marriage? She understood he was bitterly disappointed about the money—and she could not blame him for that—but she'd thought he at least liked her enough to be mildly pleased. She looked back to her plate, feeling her eyes burn slightly. Her father always ate like a man angry about something, sharp, jabbing movements that often amused Katherine. But tonight she sensed true anger in his manner and she wondered what had made him so. Every once in a while he'd glare at Graham, so it became quite clear to Katherine that her father was angry with him.

"How long are you staying after the wedding?" Katherine asked.

"We're leaving immediately," her father said, staring at the wine with distaste. Her father didn't care for wine, and the watered-down stuff they'd been served was particularly awful.

"But surely you can stay for a time. You've only just arrived in England."

Her mother gently put her fork down. "Your father and I are traveling to London to spend a week there to take in the sights, then we're returning home. We want to get home before the seas get too rough, and we don't like being so far from Lucy. By the way, has Clara said anything to you about leaving with us?"

Clara leaving, too? "No, she didn't," she said in a small voice.

"Well, dear, she feels just terrible about it, but she never thought to stay in England. Her life and family are in New York. And I do think she's sweet on Harrison."

"She is?" Clara had never told her, and she'd never suspected. Why had she thought that her life would become Clara's? She'd always thought of Clara as more of a friend than a servant, but obviously the divide between them was far greater than she'd believed. Of course Clara would want to go home. Katherine shook her head at her own thoughts. "She was probably afraid to tell me. She knew

I'd be sad." She swallowed against a growing lump in her throat and forced a smile. "But I shall get on well enough. I'm sure there's a girl in the village who will do nicely."

She looked at Graham for his agreement, but he continued to stare at the half-full wineglass dangling from his hand.

While the others at the table continued to force the food into their mouths, Katherine gave up and laid her fork by her dish. Everything was wrong. Her father shouldn't be angry. Graham shouldn't be so cold. Clara shouldn't be leaving.

Tomorrow was her wedding day, not her funeral, but that was what it was beginning to feel like. She'd been looking forward to seeing Graham again, to talking to him to see how he felt about everything that had transpired. But it had been impossible to be alone with him with her mother and father watching over her—and Graham pointedly keeping his distance.

To Katherine's horror, her eyes filled with tears and no matter how hard she tried to blink them away, a single tear fell with a small *plink* onto her plate. Her head down, she prayed no one knew she was crying; it would only upset her parents, who already were distraught about this hurried marriage. She gripped the fork and forced herself to take a small bite of beef, hoping the distraction of chewing would stop any more tears.

"I do apologize," Graham said, pushing his chair from the table abruptly. "But I fear the trip here has done me in. I hope you will excuse me."

Katherine kept her head down as if the food on her plate was of utmost interest, but she was keenly aware of Graham walking toward her on his way out of the dining room. As he passed, he pressed a handkerchief into her hand and left without a word.

Like the house itself, the tiny chapel on the grounds was utterly charming. Everyone had pitched in to clean it for the wedding, and when Katherine entered the building, the midmorning light shined through sparkling stained-glass windows. There was no organ music, no attendants, no observers but Mrs. Alcourt, Mr. Stanfield, who appeared to be sleeping, and Mr. Chase. Graham stood stoically at the small altar as the vicar, a young man with frightfully red hair, rocked heel to toe while he waited. Right before walking down the short aisle, her father forced her to look at him by placing his hands gently on each side of her head. "You don't have to do this."

Katherine lifted her chin. "I want to do this, Father. I love him."

Katherine nearly laughed at the look her father gave her. "Did you truly think I would marry a man, no matter what the circumstances, if I did not love him?"

"Oh Katy," he said, his voice ragged. He hugged her to him as if what she'd said broke his heart.

Katherine gave him a searching look when he pulled away, but he'd put on a stoic expression as if, indeed, he were leading his daughter to the gallows with as much dignity as he could muster.

Before she knew it, for it was quite a small chapel, Katherine was standing next to Graham. He darted her a quick look before turning to the vicar, who'd apparently been instructed to perform the briefest ceremony possible. For before Katherine even knew what had happened, the man was pronouncing them married and Graham was leading her to the side where they could both sign the license. They hadn't even been instructed to kiss.

Mrs. Alcourt, bless her, tried to serve a wedding luncheon, but it was as unpalatable as the dinner the night before. Katherine heard her father mutter something to the effect it was a good thing they were leaving later in the day because he was about to starve to death.

Graham removed himself from their group almost immediately following the meal, leaving Katherine both depressed and dismayed.

"Father," she said when he was gone, "did something happen between the two of you? Graham is quite unlike himself."

"I made it no secret I don't like him, if that's what you mean."

"Why? Graham did nothing wrong. If anyone is to blame, it is I. I'm the one who had him follow me into the library."

Her father looked stunned. "I didn't realize."

"And Graham didn't tell you?"

"No," her father said, shaking his head thoughtfully. "But that doesn't excuse his actions. He told me about meeting you in Brighton, about pursuing you at that house party. That was inexcusable behavior for a man who was engaged."

"He wasn't engaged at the time."

Her father frowned down at her. "Was there not an understanding between Miss Von Haupt and him?"

"Yes, but . . ." Katherine shrugged her shoulders. "We were both foolish. We rather liked each other, but as is obvious, Graham desperately needed an heiress. I knew that, but it didn't stop me from falling in love with him. Or acting very, very foolishly."

"And has he told you he loves you?"

Katherine furrowed her brow. "No," she said softly.

"I thought not. I have two things to tell you, Katherine. One is that I love you and don't want you hurt. No father wants to see his daughter living like a pauper. But I cannot stomach giving that man one penny of my hard-earned money. I'm sorry, Katherine, but I've made up my mind."

Katherine felt the blood drain from her face. "You'll give us nothing? You cannot be so cruel."

"You will receive enough allowance to keep you in pretty dresses, but *he* will receive nothing. And if I find that you've been giving it to him, I will cut you off."

"But I don't care about pretty dresses. I only care that Graham can do at least some good to help his people. He can do so much with so little. I visited the poorhouse today and you should have seen what he's done there. They practically worship him. You saw the town, the house. These people depend upon him for jobs. They need his help." Katherine looked to her mother. "Mother, you cannot let Father do this. All along I've counted on that dowry. You promised it to me. I've got the title you wanted, now I want the money I'm due. You cannot do this. At least with my dowry we could have done a little good."

"If he was so desperate to help his people, then he should have been a bit more careful with his money. And kept himself in check and married the Von Haupt girl."

Katherine gasped, outraged by her father's stand. "You have no idea what he's been through. If you did, you wouldn't do this thing."

"Bart, really, must you be so stubborn," Elizabeth said.

"It is not stubbornness. I simply refuse to reward immoral and reckless behavior."

"You of all people should understand how he felt," Elizabeth said. At his look of dismay, she quickly said, "Don't worry, Katherine knows. And don't look at me that way. She's a grown woman."

Her father glared at her mother, and for the first time in her life, she saw raw pain in both their eyes. "I loved Janice. It is not the same at all."

"How can you be so certain Lord Avonleigh does not love our Katherine?"

"Because he told me himself. He had no intention of marrying Katherine even though he was trying to seduce her. A man in love would never . . ." He stopped and Katherine's mother finished for him.

". . . marry a woman he didn't love?" She raised one eyebrow.

"It's not the same and you well know it. I loved her and she knew I loved her. It's not the same."

As there were very few rooms in the house to look for Graham, Bartholomew found him easily enough. Graham looked up and grimaced when his new father-in-law entered his room looking like he had murder on his mind. He'd been talking quietly with Mr. Chase, reminiscing about when he'd been a boy and had often disappeared for hours into the forest surrounding Avonleigh.

"If you'll excuse me, sir, I'll see to your boots, shall I?"

Graham gave his valet a fond look. "Of course. Thank you, Chase," he said, putting soft emphasis on the words to let him know he was thanking his valet for far more than polishing his boots. When Chase was gone, Bartholomew immediately went to the point.

"We're leaving shortly. But before I do, I'm going to tell you what I told Katherine. There is no dowry. Nothing. I will give my daughter an allowance, but you are not to touch it."

One more devastating blow, which Graham took in stride. Why not?

"You've nothing to say?"

Graham shook his head. "You owe me nothing and it is your prerogative to withhold Katherine's dowry."

"Damn, you're a cold bastard," Bartholomew said with disgust.

Graham stared at the older man and gave a small, mocking bow of his head.

"So, you don't care about money suddenly?"

"I do, but I also recognize the futility of asking for it," Graham said, walking to the window to look out.

"Something's been bothering me. When you met my daughter, you were not engaged."

"No."

"Did you pursue her?"

Graham looked at the older man, and shook his head slightly even as he said, "Yes, I did. It was unforgiveable but, yes, I did."

Mr. Wright moved his jaw as if he were chewing his words before letting them out of his mouth. "Why?"

"Why? Because, forgive me, sir, but your daughter is lovely and . . . I was drawn to her, I suppose. I knew nothing could come of it, but I persisted."

"You didn't answer my question. I want to know what is in you that made it permissible to pursue my daughter when you were for all intents and purposes, an engaged man." Graham could see the rage building in the man, but he knew no answer he could give would make him happy.

"I have no answer for that."

Bartholomew looked annoyed by this response. "Think, young man. Why?"

"I tell you I don't know."

"You do," Mr. Wright shouted. "Why? Why pursue her? Are you a rake bent on seduction?"

"No," Graham said, horrified by the notion.

"Are you without morals? Do you make a habit of seducing innocent girls?"

"No sir."

"Then why, damn it. Why?"

"Because she made me happy," Graham shouted, anger and frustration pouring out of him.

Bartholomew crossed his arms with a satisfied grin on his smug face, and Graham barely held himself back from striking the man.

"Now, was that so difficult to admit?"

God, yes. "It is no excuse for what I did. I knew I could not marry her and yet I couldn't stop myself. I am . . . ashamed." When he said those words, a wave of regret washed over him. Perhaps Katherine had schemed, had trapped him, but by God, he had walked almost willingly into that trap.

"You love her." It almost sounded like an accusation.

Graham stared out the window, and tapped one knuckle against the cold pane. "I suppose I do."

Bartholomew gave him a hard look that softened just slightly before leaving the room.

The Wrights were leaving, and so Graham stood dutifully by his new wife as they said their good-byes. Mr. Wright shook his hand grimly. Oddly enough, he stopped in front of Mr. Chase and shook his hand, as well, before embracing his daughter.

"I'll leave you to your good-byes," Graham said, before turning to Katherine. "I'll see you later this evening."

"Of course."

Graham strode to his room, feeling as if he were about to tear apart. She'd looked so damned sad, he'd wanted to pull her into his arms to comfort her. But, God, what if it had all been a game to her?

For a man who had never had a problem making love to a woman, Graham was decidedly at loose ends. Perhaps "filled with dread" was a more fitting description. Katherine was a virgin—and would be his first. He took a deep breath. That was it, of course. This feeling had nothing to do with the cold block of despair that sat where his heart had once been.

Graham looked in the mirror and laughed aloud at that thought. Had he ever gazed upon a bigger fool?

Since his father's death, Graham had tried with all his being to control his life. After all, it had been his actions, his words, that had led to his father's suicide. He'd tried ever since then to prove to his father that he was worthy of the title, but again and again, he failed. Logically, he understood his father was a tortured man and suicide was likely inevitable, that the discovery of tin and copper could not have been foreseen, the fortune lost with the experienced American investor was beyond his control. The fact remained, it had all happened. And now, one million pounds were gone simply because he'd fallen in love with the wrong woman—a woman who likely had manipulated him into complete financial ruin. Worse was that he couldn't wait to bed her—virgin or not.

Several hours after the Wrights had departed, Graham donned his robe over his naked body and walked to his room's adjoining door, pausing only when he noticed just how badly his hand was shaking. Clenching his fist, he knocked on the door with perhaps a bit more violence than he intended.

* * *

Katherine jumped nearly a mile when the knock sounded on the door. She sat in bed wearing one of her old nightgowns, a virginal affair with a high neck and ruffles. There hadn't been time to get a more appropriate wedding nightgown. The lamp by her bed had been turned up, but she quickly put the flame down before calling out for her husband to enter.

"Come in." She swallowed when the door opened, revealing the silhouette of Graham, wearing a deep blue velvet robe and, she suspected, little else. Her eyes drifted down to his naked legs lit only by the lamp and the low fire in the hearth, then up to his face, her cheeks heating with a sudden blush.

He walked over to her bed and sat down at the edge, the mattress sinking beneath his weight.

"Your mother told you what to expect?"

She nodded, searching his face for any emotion. Since they'd been caught together, they hadn't shared more than a few polite words in front of company. He'd hardly looked at her. This was the first time she'd been alone with him in three weeks. She felt as if he were a stranger, this stern man who sat on her bed. With her, Graham had always been charming and relaxed. But the man sitting on her bed was tense, his expression hard and unwelcoming.

He leaned over to her lamp and lowered the flame until it went out, leaving only a curling bit of blue smoke in the moonlit room. The fire from the dying embers in the hearth offered little light, and he looked over to her window as if he wanted to shut the shades.

"All right, then," he said, and he stood and dropped the robe, a whisper of sound.

Even though they had kissed and touched most intimately, even though her mother had given her the basics in an extremely awkward thirty seconds, Katherine found herself a bit frightened by what was to come. This is Graham, she told herself. But in the dark, with only shadows, he could be anyone. He didn't speak, but laid his palm on the side of her head and gently drew her forward until they were kissing.

"Oh," she said, so glad to have him kissing her, so glad he was familiar and no longer the cold man he'd been since Rufford Abbey. She opened her mouth to him and he deepened the kiss with a primordial groan, easing himself over her. The bedclothes and her own nightgown still separated her from his body, but she could feel the heat of him, feel his arousal already jutting hard against her thigh.

He moved one hand to her breast and she melted against him, remembering the exquisite feel of his hand and mouth against her nipple. She arched into him, silently telling him what she wanted. He pulled the covers down, then touched the hem of her nightdress, pushing it up over her thighs. In the dim light, she knew he was looking at her, but she couldn't tell what he was thinking. She wanted him to say something, to tell her he loved her—or even that he liked her a bit.

Instead, he bent his head and took a nipple in his mouth, through her nightdress. He tugged and bit gently, and a piercing shard of pleasure shot to her core. "Oh God."

With a small grunt, he leaned up and unbuttoned the top few buttons of her nightdress, just enough so that both breasts were exposed, and he made love to them with his mouth and tongue until she was writhing beneath him, wanting him to touch her between her legs, wanting him inside her. How odd to want something with near desperation that she'd never before experienced.

Her eyes had adjusted to the dim light of the moon and embers, and she could just make out a golden glow on his skin. He was beautiful, a living, breathing statue bathed in golden-red light, as if the last bit of a spectacular sunset was touching him. She watched him, his eyes closed, as he tugged his mouth against one nipple, as his thumb moved over the other, slowly and with exquisite care.

"Good. So good," she said into the silence.

At her words, he brought a hand to her inner thigh, caressing, moving higher toward where she was wet and throbbing for his touch. When he finally, finally touched her, she lifted her hips in celebration. He moved his finger, back and forth, creating such a heat she didn't know what to do with it. It was nothing like she had ever felt before; a hundred times greater than what she'd experienced with him before.

"Please, please," she said, moving her head back and forth, moving her hips up and down, unaware she was even doing so. He inserted one finger into her body, *inside her*, carefully, slowly, exquisitely. And then, his thumb, his talented thumb, moved against her as his finger moved inside of her and she arched against him, her hips jerking, as a rush of raw feeling flooded her, making her body burn as never before, a pulse of pleasure that caused her to cry out.

Graham, his breath ragged, withdrew his finger and kissed her as he positioned himself between her legs. She felt him, large and hard and velvety soft, press against her where his finger had just been. Slowly, slowly, as his breath became more shallow. Finally, he lowered his head and kissed her hard as he thrust inside her all the way.

She let out a small sound of pain and he stilled, dropping soft kisses on her lips, her cheeks, her neck. He moved inside her and she burned, not with raw pleasure but with something decidedly less pleasant. He moved, thrusting in and out, and she wrapped her legs around him, not knowing what else she should do. His movements became faster and then his entire body tensed and he let out a moan, deep and harsh.

He lay atop her, resting most of his weight on his knees and elbows as his breath slowly returned to normal. He kissed her one last time before withdrawing and sitting with his back to her, on the side of the bed.

She wanted to lay her hand on his back, slick with sweat. She wanted to get on her knees and pull him toward her, to nuzzle her mouth against his neck. But his head was bowed and Katherine sensed he didn't want her touch.

"Are you all right?" he asked finally.

She nodded, then realized with his back to her he wouldn't see. "Yes. Of course. That was . . . lovely."

He let out a small laugh and stood, grabbing his robe as he did. "I'll see you tomorrow, then. Good night."

Katherine watched in dismay as he left the room and closed the door silently behind him. Perhaps this was what marriage was like in the aristocracy. A couple took their physical pleasure of each other then said good night. Perhaps that was what most couples had, but Katherine didn't think it was what she wanted—or would accept.

Graham closed the door quietly, then pressed his back against it and slid to the floor, covering his eyes with the heels of his hands. Hell, was he a woman? he thought as a wrenching sob shook his body. He pressed his hands harder, trying to push back the pain he was feeling.

She was beautiful, exquisite, and he'd wanted to love her forever. He'd wanted to lose himself in her, taste her, make her come over and over. He wanted to hear her say she loved him, because, God curse him for a fool, he still loved her. She'd been so damned responsive, he couldn't imagine how good it would have been if he hadn't been trying so hard not to care.

"Sir?"

Graham let out a curse.

"Did things not . . . go well?" Chase asked hesitantly.

Graham dropped his hands and laughed aloud. "Things went swimmingly, Chase. Can't you tell? I was moved to tears."

"I was preparing your clothes for the morning. I didn't realize you'd be done so . . . quickly." Mr. Chase closed his eyes briefly in an agony of mortification. "Of course, that did not come out as intended, my lord."

Mr. Chase always got formal when he was embarrassed. "Do not worry yourself, Mr. Chase. All is well." Graham stood up and held his hands out to his sides as if to prove he was hale and hearty.

"As you say, sir," Mr. Chase said, giving him an annoyingly long, assessing look.

But of course, nothing was well and Graham wondered if anything in his life would ever be well again.

Chapter 16

Something was terribly wrong. It wasn't that Graham was cruel—he wasn't. He was all that was kindness, inquiring about her day as he read the *Times*. What did she have planned? Did she enjoy her outing with Mrs. Alcourt to find a new cook? Had she made any inroads finding a lady's maid?

And at night he would come to her and they would make love and he would leave. While they made love, she felt loved. But after he left, she always felt like crying. Was it her or was it him or was this simply the way it was for everyone who was married? He hardly looked at her—while making love or not—and when they spoke it was almost always about things that could spark no real debate.

If she hadn't known better, she would have thought someone had taken the passionate, funny man she'd fallen in love with and replaced him with a colder, sterner version of himself.

"Graham."

He lowered the newspaper—only two days old by the time they got it—and raised an inquiring chin. His eye flickered to hers briefly, then settled on the plate before him. "Yes, Katherine."

"We've received an invitation to Sir Peter McAllister's for the fourteenth of November. Do you think we might attend?"

"Unfortunately, we'll have to send our regrets as I plan to leave for London on the twelfth."

The lump that had become a permanent fixture in her throat began to throb. "I am to stay here?"

"I see no reason for the expense of two of us going. I'll be in business meetings with my solicitor and visiting Bryant Park to ready it for leasing."

Katherine's mouth fell open slightly. "You are leasing Bryant Park? Why?"

He made an infinitesimal shake of his head, as if he couldn't quite believe how obtuse she was. In that moment, she saw just the slightest slip in his maddeningly even composure. "Oh, of course. You must feel awful about leasing the place."

"Not really. I don't intend to spend much time in London. I need to do some work to get it ready, paint and some repairs." The newspaper rose up again, blocking her from view.

She looked down at a sausage on her plate and felt the overwhelming urge to throw it at the newspaper. She didn't, for they purchased the meat from the local butcher and it was the only edible bit of food on the table. "How long will you be gone?"

"Not certain. But you may have some company. My sister wrote and mentioned she might come for a visit." This was slightly muffled for he hadn't even bothered to bring the paper down.

Staring at the paper, she picked up the sausage and held it like a cigar, pretending to puff away at it. "I should like to meet your sister." Silence. "The sausage is quite good, isn't it?"

"Yes."

"The kippers, though, I have to say I don't care for them." She pretended to blow smoke rings, imitating her father, who had a talent for the trick.

"Hmmm."

"I wonder if I might borrow one of the horses and ride while you're gone."

"Hmmmm."

"I'll probably take your black for a ride." The black gelding was a nasty creature that would only let Graham ride him. The stable master wouldn't even let her near the horse when she'd ventured in during her first week at Avonleigh.

"That's fine."

Katherine narrowed her eyes as she pretended to puff away at the sausage. "And then I'll go to the horse auction. I imagine he'll bring a pretty penny. If I sell him, perhaps I'll be able to buy myself a new ball gown."

"Fine."

"Graham," she said loudly. He finally lowered the paper and looked slightly annoyed. "How much do you think we'll get for it?"

"Get for what?"

"The black gelding you just gave me permission to sell," she said succinctly.

"I did no such . . ." She took another phantom drag on her cigar. He looked as if he wanted to laugh, but no sound came out. "My apologies, my dear. What were you saying?"

"Nothing of import."

That night, when Graham entered her room, she pretended to be asleep. He stood by her bed for several long minutes before turning to go. After she heard the door snick closed, Katherine gave in to the tears that had been threatening all day.

The next morning, she went to breakfast in her dressing gown, her hair gathered atop her head and allowed to rain down upon her shoulders, making her look much like an urn with ivy bursting from it. Graham was already at the table and he greeted her with a perfunctory "good morning." He actually raised his head and looked in her direction, but apparently not long enough to take in her appearance. Katherine smiled grimly.

"Graham, attire is more casual in the country, is it not?" she asked as she selected that day's breakfast offerings. More sausage, certainly, and perhaps some browned potatoes.

"Yes."

"Then I won't have to change when I go into the village?" She turned to him, only to find him hidden by the *Times*.

"Not at all. You're perfectly fine."

One eye began to twitch as she pressed her lips together. Her hands went up to her dressing gown and she unbuttoned the top four buttons. Thank goodness the house didn't have footmen waiting on the sidelines to assist them.

Instead of walking to the other end of the table, she put her plate adjacent to his, getting small satisfaction when he tensed—even if she didn't draw his attention away from whatever riveting article he was reading.

"Are you certain it's not too . . . casual?" she purred, bracing two hands on the table and leaning toward him. A bit of her ridiculously cascading hair brushed his hand, finally drawing his attention.

"What the—" His eyes snapped from her breasts, which were very nearly spilling from her gown, to her face and silly hairdo, and back down. "Good God."

Katherine shoved away from the table and sat, buttoning up immediately. He placed a hand on hers, stilling her movements while she still had two buttons left to go.

"What is this about?"

"Do you hate me?"

He looked away and her heart tumbled. "Of course not."

"Then why can you not look at me?"

"Eat your breakfast, Katherine." He sounded both weary and impatient.

"I want to know, what is wrong with you? You are acting so different and I don't know why."

"Don't you?"

"No," she shouted. "I do understand you are unhappy about the money. But I thought you at least *liked* me. You act as if you cannot stand to look at me."

Even now, Graham found he could not look at her. It hurt too much. He'd thought if he made love to her in the dark, he wouldn't see her lying eyes. He'd get his release, he'd block his heart from feeling anything. But it hadn't worked. He wanted her more and more.

"Eat your breakfast and meet me in the library. And for God's sake, put on some clothes," he said. He didn't mean to sound so harsh, but it was all he could do not to drag her into his arms and make love to her on the dining room table. Did she not know what she did to him? How much he loathed himself for loving her still?

As he waited, he paced back and forth, stopping only when he heard her enter. Her eyes were red-rimmed and she'd obviously been crying. He should be glad for her tears, but they only made him feel abominable. At least if he had married Miss Von Haupt he would have had all that money. Now, he had nothing. In a way, Graham felt sorry for Katherine. She had what she thought she wanted only to discover it wasn't so wonderful, after all.

"Please sit down," he said softly.

She did as he asked, looking up at him. "What is wrong, Graham? I don't understand what happened, why you seem so different."

He ignored her question, ignored her pleading eyes, ignored that small but growing voice in his head that told him he had to be wrong. "I have one question for you. I thought I could move past this, accept what happened, but I find I cannot. I do not enjoy being cruel to you, Katherine. Clearly, you are as unhappy as I am."

"Only because you are so different from the man you were, not only in Brighton, but at Briarbrook and Rufford Abbey. It seemed that you were rather fond of me then, and now it's almost as if you hate me."

"Do you really not know?"

"No," she said, sounding exasperated.

"All right then. Why did Miss Von Haupt thank you as she was leaving?"

She gasped and grew slightly pale before her cheeks bloomed with color. "Wh-what?"

He knew then. He had his answer, but he wanted to hear it from her lips. He wanted her to tell him she'd planned it. "Why," he said, his words as sharp as cut glass, "did Miss Von Haupt embrace the woman who betrayed her and then thank her?"

"Oh God. You . . . It's not what you think."

"Tell me why she thanked you. *Tell me,*" he said, slamming his palm against a table, making her jump.

"She thought I had planned it all. That I planned to get caught with you." Tears filled her eyes, but this time Graham was immune to them.

"Now, it seems to me that if she *did* believe you planned it all, she would have been quite angry. Livid, to have been humiliated not only by her fiancé but also her good friend. But instead of getting angry, she thanked you. And embraced you. Why did she thank you?" he asked, ending on a shout.

"Stop shouting," she said, tears streaming down her face.

"I apologize," he said with a mocking bow. "And while we're on this topic, you should know I had a conversation with Lady Summerfield and her daughter. It was quite enlightening."

"With Lady Summerfield," she repeated, sounding muddled.

"Oh yes," he said pleasantly. "It seems Lady Marjorie was quite upset about what happened at Rufford Abbey. So upset, in fact, she felt compelled to tell me about a conversation the two of you had. Let me think," he said, tapping one finger against his chin. "I believe it had something to do with your hoping to get caught in a compromising position. With me."

"Oh my God." Katherine looked at him blindly, shaking her head back and forth. "It's all misunderstandings. All of it."

"Do tell."

"Stop being that way. It's hateful."

He tilted his head as if in commiseration.

"I was joking with Marjorie. She was angry with me for being alone with you by the lake. She told me it was dangerous and could have led to a forced marriage if we'd been caught doing anything untoward. I joked that it wouldn't be so bad being forced into a marriage with you. That's all it was, a joke between friends."

She pulled out a handkerchief, the same one he'd given to her on their wedding day, and blew her nose rather indelicately. At one time, he might have been charmed, but today he found her display of tears not quite believable.

"Fair enough, you were joking. And, after all, it was my idea to lead you into the clearing. But it was not I who manufactured the meeting at Rufford Abbey." He stared at her, wishing with all his being that he was wrong about her, that she hadn't planned to be caught with him. But she'd offered nothing to make him think otherwise. "You planned that meeting in the library. And there they were, a neat little crowd to bear witness. How did you pull it off? Or was it your mother?"

"I didn't plan anything. I truly only wanted to tell you that I—"

He held up his hand, his head jerking to the side, eyes briefly closing, stopping her because hearing her say those words again was unbearable. "Then why did Miss Von Haupt thank you? Why, when we were first discovered did she happily say, 'She actually did it.' Why, Katherine? Why?" He didn't care if she heard the agony in his voice or saw the pain in his eyes.

"Because she didn't want to marry you," Katherine said, sobbing now.

"And you did."

"Yes, I did," she shouted. "Though now I realize what a fool I was."

*   *   *

Katherine spent that night in her room, quietly crying. The evidence against her was damning—and all true, except for the most important fact: She hadn't meant to force a marriage. She had led him to that room. She had said—and even thought to herself—that being forced to marry Graham wouldn't be so awful. She'd longed for a way for them to marry, even though she'd known they could not. How had all her silly, girlish dreams turned into this nightmare? He would never believe her, not having witnessed Claudia embracing her and thanking her. No wonder he'd seemed so angry. And hurt. No one could have been more shocked than Katherine when the silly goose had done that. Claudia had actually believed Katherine had gotten caught with Graham on purpose simply to save Claudia from an unwanted marriage. Oh, why hadn't she pushed her away and set her straight?

And what must Graham have felt to have seen that embrace, to hear Claudia say, "Thank you"? No wonder he was angry. It was like being caught standing over a body with a knife in one's bloodied hands and then claiming innocence. Even the fairest person on earth would think her guilty of subterfuge.

"Now he'll never love me," she said aloud, wincing at how pathetic she sounded. She didn't even have Clara to cry to. And she felt as pathetic as she sounded, so why not give in to her misery for just a little while?

Now, with her father withdrawing her dowry, they would have nothing. How Graham must hate her. Even though it was unjustified, she still understood it. She vowed she would tell him the truth, every detail, in hopes he would believe her. She didn't know how she would convince him, but convince him she would.

Chapter 17

Graham felt like death. At least if he'd drunk himself silly the night before, he would understand why, but he hadn't touched a drop. He was too depressed even to drink. His general feeling of fog and the raging headache that made opening his eyes to the dull morning excruciating could only be explained by one thing: regret.

What sort of cad treated his wife so? One who believed she had betrayed him, he thought stubbornly. The evidence be damned, he just didn't believe it of her, not entirely. But the doubts that plagued him made his head and heart hurt in equal measure. He almost wished he'd never made love to her. That way he wouldn't have the tortuous memories of how she felt, how hot and tight she was, how her nipples puckered when he sucked them. The sounds she made when she came. Just thinking about it made him unbearably hard—which did little to help his pounding head.

Chase was shuffling around his room pretending he wasn't trying to wake him, no doubt unsurprised to find him in his own bed. Alone. The old coot should be happy, but he looked worried, casting surreptitious looks his way every few minutes.

"Just say it," Graham said, his voice still raspy from sleep.

"Say what, sir?"

"Whatever it is that is making you skulk around my room hoping I'll wake up."

Chase neatly folded a towel. "It wouldn't be my place, sir."

"Since when has that stopped you?"

He put the towel aside and turned toward Graham. "I believe I was wrong about your lady, sir. And I am filled with remorse that I ever said a word against her."

"Oh God," Graham groaned, pulling a pillow over his head.

"I know it does appear that she schemed to marry you, but I am convinced it was simply an unfortunate series of events that led us to draw the inevitable, but mistaken, conclusion."

Graham pulled the pillow from his head. "I am quickly coming to the same conclusion," he said. He sat up, wincing slightly.

"Do you need headache powder, sir?"

"Indeed I do."

"I didn't notice any brandy missing," Chase said as he busied himself getting the powder and a glass of water. He handed Graham a small spoonful of the white, bitter powder, looking over him like a mother hen as he took the headache remedy.

"I didn't drink. I came by this pain naturally. Or perhaps God is punishing me. I just hope this powder doesn't make me even more ill as it did the last time."

Chase took the spoon and now empty glass from him. "You simply have to decide which is worse, a headache or stomachache."

Graham lay back down, pressing the heels of his hands against his eyes to relieve the pain. "Chase?"

"Yes sir?"

"About Miss Wright, no, it's Lady Avonleigh now, isn't it? Good God. Lady Avonleigh. My question is, Chase, why did you change your mind about her?"

"Because she so obviously loves you, sir," Chase said offhandedly, as if such a thing were common knowledge.

Graham tried to control his heart, which found those words remarkably uplifting. "Even so, she still appears guilty of manipulating me into marriage."

"No sir."

Graham dropped his hands to look at Chase. "No?"

"No."

"And you say this because . . ."

"Because she was so very angry with her father. You know I'm not one to eavesdrop," Chase said with utmost dignity. "But the lack of furniture and carpeting in this home allows sound to carry quite well. And I happened to overhear enough to convince me that even though she loves you, sir, she is deeply unhappy that you were unable to marry Miss Von Haupt."

"Oh? Pray tell, what did she say?"

Chase cleared his throat, obviously uncomfortable to be repeating something he'd overheard. "Something to the effect that she had little need of pretty dresses when you so desperately needed money to help your people. I believe it was during the conversation in which her father informed her there would be no dowry forthcoming, but that he would provide for her to have pretty things."

Graham smiled slightly. "She was angry, was she?"

"Yes sir. She . . ." Chase paused, and his voice was suddenly filled with a strong emotion. "She said her father could never know what you'd gone through and that you deserved to be able to help your tenants."

"She said all that."

Chase nodded. "You told her about your father."

Graham looked up at Chase, and then blindly at the foot of the bed. "Not all of it, but yes."

Chase nodded sharply, then tugged down his waistcoat. "If that will be all, sir?"

"Yes. Thank you, Chase."

Katherine spent the morning alone, wandering the grounds and trying to imagine what the garden had looked like when it had been kept up. No matter where she was on the estate, whenever she looked up to the house, she smiled at the beauty of it. Even if Graham abandoned her in Avonleigh and returned to London, she would be happy here. Alone. Wandering the grounds like a ghost from a gothic novel.

Mr. Chase had told her Graham was ill—too ill to go down to breakfast, but Katherine was fairly certain that was just an excuse. He simply couldn't stand to be in the same room as she. For the first time since their marriage, he hadn't come to her the previous night. Even though she'd convinced herself she'd feign sleep again, she was still bitterly disappointed he hadn't even tried.

Mr. Chase had been quite apologetic; the old man had been so kind to her of late. She thought of Chase's new attitude as The Great

Thaw of 1874. She didn't know why Mr. Chase was now so agreeable, but she was glad he was. If only she could have the same effect on her husband.

Katherine stayed out of doors for as long as possible, even though it was a dull and misty day, until her stomach began some strident grumbling, forcing her back inside for luncheon. She'd worn a warm coat and sturdy boots, and had been quite happy traipsing about, feeling the cool, fresh air fill her lungs. She loved the rolling green hills, the tall evergreens that surrounded Avonleigh, and especially the lake that attracted all kinds of water fowl. A folly stood at one end of the lake, but that was a trip for another day.

With a frown, she wondered what Mrs. Alcourt was preparing. If her father did send her an allowance, she vowed to spend it on a cook. Certainly, having sampled Mrs. Alcourt's cooking, he couldn't complain about that expenditure—even if it meant Graham would also benefit from good cooking.

As she had for breakfast, Katherine sat alone at the dining table, which had been rescued from the attic along with the extra beds. The table itself was an ancient pockmarked affair that had been once used in the servants' quarters. It did nicely with a new cloth on it, and no one was the wiser when a piece of fine linen was draped across it. Still, the table was far too small for the large dining room, and the fact that such a poor table had been saved made it clear this was a house with frugal servants. With the sky so overcast, it hardly looked like day outside, and the maid had lit candles to lend some brightness to the otherwise dark room.

Luncheon was cardboard-like pork covered in thick, brownish, floury paste that Katherine assumed was supposed to be gravy. She adored a nice succulent pork loin, but alas the meal on her plate was only a poor relation. She did her best, because she didn't want to see the look of worry on Mrs. Alcourt's face when she saw the still-full dish. The day maid, for they had no footmen and Mr. Stanfield was likely napping, removed the plate.

"Is there anything else you'll be needing, my lady?"

My lady. Goodness, that sounded silly. "No, thank you, Sarah. And please thank Mrs. Alcourt for a wonderful meal."

The maid looked at the plate skeptically for a moment, then gave her a quick curtsy before disappearing into the shadows of the room.

Katherine was about to leave the dining room when she stopped dead. A strange and quite lovely woman stood at the entrance, her hair the color of pale gold.

"Hello," Katherine said, trying to recall if she'd met the woman before. But instead of returning the greeting, the woman stared at her, her cold gray eyes assessing her without a trace of warmth.

"You are the American who forced my brother into marriage."

Katherine was slightly taken aback by this greeting from her new sister-in-law. "Well, I don't recall holding a gun to his head," Katherine said, smiling uncertainly. "But yes, I am Katherine Spencer, your brother's wife. You must be Juliana." Despite the cold greeting, Katherine decided to be pleasant and welcoming.

"Lady Spencer, yes."

Katherine walked over to her but stopped short of offering her hand in greeting. Juliana seemed more statue than woman. Her hair was flawless, her perfectly fitted gold silk gown only made her look even more inanimate, and her cold stare was beyond disconcerting.

"I am curious about you. What did you hope to gain by marrying my brother?" Though her words were like shards of glass thrown with precision, Juliana's face was completely devoid of expression. How did one master the particular art of aristocratic disdain quite so well? Katherine wondered.

"I beg your pardon, but you don't even know me. How can you say such a thing?" Katherine asked calmly, even though inside she was raging.

"I know your type. I don't need to know more."

Katherine had never in her life been the target of such calmly delivered venom. Juliana used the same tone of voice Katherine had heard some women use with their beleaguered servants—dismissive and demeaning but cloaked with civility. "And I'm very much afraid I know your type, as well. And as such, I don't believe we have anything more to say to one another."

Juliana lifted her chin slightly. "You didn't answer my question. What did you hope to gain?" Juliana's eyes swept over her form, her nose wrinkling in distaste, and Katherine was suddenly made conscious of her wind-mussed hair and mud-stained hem. "It must have been quite a shock when you saw Avonleigh for the first time. What did you think? That you would become some sort of princess? That everyone would be bowing and scraping before you? You

Americans. You think you can marry a title and you magically become one of us."

"I wanted nothing else but to be happy with Graham. Since I cannot convince you that I am anything other than what you believe me to be, I won't waste either of our time." Katherine was proud that her voice was so steady, for it felt as if her entire body were trembling with anger—and no small amount of hurt. "Good day, Lady Spencer." She started to leave, then stopped. "I had been so looking forward to meeting you. I had to leave my younger sister in New York, and I miss her desperately. I was hoping to have a sister here. I see now that I was terribly mistaken."

Katherine fled, leaving Juliana staring after her, the smallest furrow appearing between her eyes.

"I think I've made a grievous mistake," Juliana announced.

Graham, who was trying desperately not to vomit, carefully nodded at his sister. Not only had the headache powder not taken away his pain, he was terribly nauseated and not in the mood for conversation. "And what mistake was that?"

"I met your new wife," she said, as if that were enough explanation.

"Oh God, what did you say?" Graham pressed his hand against one eye. One side of his head throbbed incessantly, and he could hardly keep his eyes open even in the gloom of his room. He wanted nothing more than to lie down with the pillow over his head—in complete silence.

"Of course I based my opinion on what I've heard and your own letter to me. I must say I was expecting Miss Wright to be far different from the woman I met."

"Lady Avonleigh," Graham muttered.

"Oh really, Graham. Fine. Lady Avonleigh."

"What did you expect her to be like?" He pulled the pillow over his head.

"Like Miss Von Haupt, I suppose. Silly and vain. It's not how she looked," she added, "but rather what she said. I asked her what she'd hoped to gain by forcing you into marriage. I must say she didn't like that, but she seemed as hurt as angry. I thought that a bit strange, to be honest with you. And then there was her answer."

"What did she say, Jules?" Graham said, his voice muffled by the pillow.

"She could be lying, but I don't see why she should at this point. I mean to say, she managed to marry you and get the title. She told me she only hoped to be happy."

Graham let out a low groan.

"Are you quite all right?"

"Other than the fact my head feels as if it might explode and I'm trying not to vomit, I'm just ducky," Graham said. "Also, I fear I was wrong about my wife and am now regretting some things I said to her. And the way I've treated her. If I am wrong, I'm the worst sort of husband a girl could want."

"Oh dear. If we're wrong about her, I fear we both need to apologize," Juliana said. "But, Graham, how can you be wrong about her? Based on what you wrote to me, it seems fairly likely she did trap you."

"I know it seems that way, but I'm beginning to think it's all circumstantial, horrible bad luck." He pulled the pillow from his head, wincing at the dim light. "And she's won Mr. Chase over."

"No," Juliana gasped, clearly impressed. "That settles it then, Graham. We must apologize."

"I'll talk to her when I can sit up without the room spinning about. Leave me be, will you, Jules? I think if I lie here completely still and silent, this blasted headache will go away."

Juliana moved to the side of the bed and looked down fondly at her brother. She'd never do anything as demonstrative as kiss his cheek or even pat his shoulder, but she did give him an encouraging smile before taking her leave.

Katherine walked blindly for quite a distance, her mind racing. Was she doomed to live for the rest of her life with a man who thought she was a scheming liar? She thought back on the line from *Hamlet*: "The lady doth protest too much, methinks." It was ridiculous, but the more she tried to explain herself, the more she sounded like she was lying. She could not prove she had not planned to get caught in a compromising position, and so had to accept that Graham would never love her.

She stopped, depressed and a bit tired from all her walking. She was completely coated with a fine mist, her cloak and skirt hanging heavily from the damp. Looking about, she tried to see Avonleigh, but a thin misty fog made seeing farther than a quarter mile impossible. The mist hung heavily near the ground, thinning as it rose, making Katherine feel as if she were the only human in England. The air was still, and the only sound was the bleating of some sheep somewhere to her right. A lichen-covered stone wall, the moss seeming impossibly green against the grayness surrounding her, separated her from the sheep that she could barely make out in the pasture next to her.

Katherine had no fear of getting lost, for she'd remained on the same road since leaving Avonleigh, so she decided to walk to the next rise before turning back. She had no idea what time it was as it was impossible to determine where the sun was in the sky. She wished she could walk forever, and wondered if Graham would even care if she walked all the way to Scotland and never returned. Probably not, she thought in a bout of self-pity.

She trudged ahead to the top of the rise, fully intending to turn and go back to the house when the bleating she'd heard earlier began sounding a bit more frantic. Her mind instantly went to the old story about the boy crying wolf. He'd been a shepherd, hadn't he? And hadn't that story taken place in England? Were there still wolves in England? Oh, the poor sheep sounded quite desperate. She walked ahead, fear making her spine tingle, as she tried to peer through the mist to where the bleating seemed to be coming from.

Then she saw it. A little thing, probably born just that spring, stuck in a muddy pool of water. A few other sheep were milling about looking completely unconcerned that the little fellow was struggling so.

"Oh, you poor little thing," she said, and climbed over the stone wall. Her skirt snagged a bit and she gave it a good yank, ripping her hem a bit. No matter, it was her oldest dress.

Having been raised in a city, Katherine was quite unfamiliar with farm animals, and she looked at the sheep warily. They somehow seemed much larger than she'd thought they were. The lamb in the mud pit wasn't as small as she'd thought, either. She edged toward the muddy pond, and the lamb's bleating became ever more frantic as it tried to heave itself out of the mud. "Now how on earth did you get yourself in there?" Katherine asked softly, hoping the soothing sound of her voice would calm the animal. It seemed as if the more the sheep struggled, the deeper he got. She looked about, hoping to see the farmer coming to the rescue, but the pasture was as still and silent as before. The lamb was making less noise now, and Katherine feared it was getting itself tired out. Perhaps she could walk and try to find someone to help the little lamb. A sound idea, except she hadn't met a soul or seen a cottage in quite some time. The fog was so thick now that she'd likely walk right by a cottage even if there was one.

There was nothing to do but let the poor thing perish in the mud or rescue it herself. It somehow didn't matter that rack of lamb was one of her favorite meals; she simply could not let this lamb die.

"Hello, lamb. I'm going to save you. I hope. You don't bite, do you?" She stopped at that thought. Did sheep bite? She'd never heard of anyone suffering from a sheep bite, but then again, she'd never lived near sheep.

Katherine looked down at her boots, which had sunk perhaps an inch into the thick, black muck. The smell emanating from the mud was extremely unpleasant—so unpleasant she wondered if there was more than one sheep carcass in it.

"I truly do not want to go in there and get you. Can't you try one more time?" The sheep stared at her, its mouth slightly open, revealing its pink tongue. She held out her hand the same way she would coax a dog, by pretending she had a treat for it. It didn't work. The lamb looked at her blankly, gave a small effort to disengage itself, then went still.

With a grimace, and holding her nose, Katherine inched forward. If she could grab its scruff—did sheep even have scruffs?—she'd be able to pull it out without going in too far herself. "Come on, you silly creature," she said, stepping further into the mire. She reached out toward its head and it jerked away from her. "Oh, you ungrateful wretch."

She stood, hands on her hips, and glared at the lamb. With a sigh, she realized her dress would be completely ruined, and she took one tentative step into the mud. Without warning, Katherine felt herself pushed violently from behind. She let out a screech as she realized a ram had butted her and managed to turn just in time to avoid falling face-first onto the lamb. She landed instead on her back, arms flailing, with a near silent *splotch*.

"Oh, oh Lord. Oh yuck." She sat up to watch the lamb, frightened by the flailing human, heave itself out of the mud and safely onto solid ground. "You scoundrel," Katherine yelled miserably. It stood there on dry land as if nothing had happened. "You're welcome," Katherine muttered as she pressed her hand down into the muck in an attempt to gain leverage to pull herself out. She crawled to the edge of the mud and stilled. The ram stood guard over her like some medieval gaoler. It snorted and took a menacing step toward her, and Katherine scurried back a bit. Suddenly the mud seemed like the better place to be.

Sheep *attacked*? She'd had no idea. The ram, which from Katherine's perspective looked nearly as big as a horse, stood its ground and stared at her. Whenever she made the slightest move, it would rear up slightly on his hind legs and stomp its front legs into the moist earth.

And then, the skies opened up and it began to pour. "Oh, lovely," she said, blowing water from her mouth. Katherine had heard stories of sheep drowning in torrential downpours, too stupid to turn away from the rain. But this rain seemed to have no effect on the ram. "Go away," Katherine yelled. She picked up a glob of mud and threw it at the creature. It shied away, giving Katherine a glimmer of hope. But when she began crawling out again, the darned thing lowered its head as if it were about to ram her again.

"I hate you," Katherine said darkly. And then she began to laugh. It was just too, too funny. She would die here, in a stinking mud puddle guarded by a crazed ram, and Graham would never know what had become of her. "Woman killed by sheep," the headline in the *Times* would read. She laughed until tears mixed with the rain. At least, she thought grimly, she'd die laughing.

It was perhaps an hour from dusk when Graham was able to sit up without fear of vomiting. He could even tolerate the sound of the rain beating against his windowpane. His head still ached, but it was a much more manageable pain—one that was far secondary to his need to see Katherine.

Graham pulled his bell cord, and not five minutes later Mr. Chase appeared in his room. "I need to get dressed, Chase, and I'd like to look my finest whilst eating crow. At least that's what I believe I'll be dining on this evening."

Mr. Chase smiled—a rare thing, indeed—and with an extra

bounce in his step, gathered Graham's clothes and pulled out his shaving supplies. Thirty minutes later, Graham looked more like himself and was ready to search out Katherine. It wouldn't take long as there were only so many places she could be. Graham started with her room, knocking and then entering, for he thought she just might be so angry she wouldn't answer at all. But her room was empty. The library, where a fire cheerfully glowed, was also empty. And so it went until he began to experience the smallest bit of panic.

"Where is she?" he said aloud, standing in the entryway. He went to the kitchens, thinking perhaps Mrs. Alcourt would know where she was—or was perhaps even now meeting with Katherine. He found the old housekeeper in her rooms, sitting by a fire and knitting.

"I'm sorry to disturb you, Mrs. Alcourt, but do you happen to know where Lady Avonleigh is?" It was embarrassing, but at this moment, Graham was beginning to get concerned, even though he told himself that concern was unwarranted.

Mrs. Alcourt looked a bit surprised by the question. "Oh no, sir. I haven't seen her since luncheon. No, no. It was before that, even. Perhaps breakfast?"

Graham pressed a thin smile on his face. "Thank you, Mrs. Alcourt."

"Should I gather the others and begin a search?" she asked, standing and with real concern in her voice. Then the realization that the "others" included only Mr. Stanfield and Mr. Chase obviously struck her. "No, I don't think that would be of much help. Perhaps she went for a ride. She has gone for a ride nearly every day. Usually in the morning, but . . ."

Suddenly, the image of Katherine lying cold and still on the wet ground hit him like a blow and he nearly staggered. "I'm sure she's fine, sir," Mrs. Alcourt said, for it was clear the same grim thought had entered her mind.

"Yes. I'll go out to the stable and see for myself if a horse is missing." Graham left Mrs. Alcourt worrying her hands together and began to run. Outside, he went directly to the stables, where his groomsman was sitting near a stove repairing a bit of tackle. At his entrance, the man stood, putting aside his work. A quick count reassured him that all horses were accounted for, and he nearly collapsed from relief. But if she hadn't taken a horse and she wasn't in the house, then where was she?

"Carl, have you seen Lady Avonleigh this afternoon?"

Carl squinted his eyes a bit, then nodded. "I did, m'lord. Saw her take off down the drive just past noon. 'Twasn't rainin' then, sir, so I didn't think it odd. On the days she doesn't ride, she takes walks. Has she not returned?"

"No, she has not. At least not that I can determine. Thank you, Carl."

Graham hurried back to the house and called out to Katherine. He went to each floor, calling her name continuously. Perhaps she'd been exploring the house and had fallen ill? That made no sense, but Graham wasn't thinking sensibly at the moment. He stopped outside his father's study, locked from entry all these years. He tried the doorknob, relaxing when he found it locked still. He called out Katherine's name anyway, just in case she'd somehow made her way inside.

His sister appeared, drawn out of her room by the commotion. "Whatever is wrong?" she asked.

"I can't find Katherine. She's not in her room nor the library. All the horses are accounted for. I'm going out to search for her. Will you continue searching inside?"

"How long has she been gone?" Juliana asked, worry etched on her face.

"Since luncheon," Graham said heavily.

Juliana paled. "Oh Graham. If anything has happened, it will have been my fault. I was horrid to her and . . ." She paused, closing her eyes briefly, gathering her emotions. "I'll make a thorough search. We will find her. If she wants to be found."

"What the hell do you mean by that?"

Juliana, faced with her brother's anger, took a step back. "Only that she may have gotten it into her head to leave you after all the things I said to her."

Graham immediately dismissed the notion. "She would never run away. And besides, all her belongings are still in her room. Just look for her, Jules, will you?"

"Of course, Graham. Of course I will."

Graham hurried to his room and fetched his coat and hat, for it was chilly outside and raining still. And soon it would be completely dark. He decided to look for her on foot, concerned that in the dark his horse might run over her if she'd collapsed on the road. On foot, he could go places he couldn't on horseback. Fear and helplessness gnawed at him. He had no idea where she'd gone. If she'd walked down the drive, she could have turned left or right when reaching the main road, or she could have wandered off along one of the many footpaths before reaching the road. She could be anywhere, hurt, bleeding. Shivering in the cold. Or worse.

"Please, God, let her be all right," he said as he started down the drive, rain beating loudly against his beaver hat. He pulled his collar up and trudged onward, oblivious to the fact he was wearing his finest shoes.

When he reached the main road, he turned left. He decided he'd walk a ways, and if he saw no sign of her, he'd double back and go the other way. She'd been upset, and no doubt wouldn't have wanted to run into people. He guessed she'd gone the opposite direction from the village and prayed he was right.

It was nearly full dark when he thought he saw a human shape in the distance, and his heart began a painful beating in his chest. He began running toward the shadow, slipping in the mud more than once. It was clear as he got closer that the shape was definitely human and obviously a woman.

"Katherine?"

The shape stopped still.

"Oh God, please." And he began to run, heedless of the rain beating down and the muck on the road. It was she, standing drenched and bedraggled, hair streaming down her face in thick clumps. She was the most beautiful sight he'd ever laid eyes on. "Katherine, thank God," he said, and pulled her limp, cold body toward him. He smiled down into her adorably scowling face, and kissed her hard on her lips, shocked by how cold she felt. "You're freezing," he said, kissing her cheeks, her nose, her mouth. "Oh God, you're all right. You're all right." Then he stilled. "My God, what is that stink?"

"I hate sheep," she said darkly.

"And you hate me, don't you? I deserve it," he said, pulling off his coat and wrapping it about her shoulders. "What happened, love?" He drew her toward him and they began walking back toward Avonleigh. She was shivering violently, and so he heaved her up against him. It was too far for him to carry her, and he wished now he had brought his horse.

She was shivering so violently, she could hardly talk, so he hushed her and they walked on. "Juliana is quite sorry for the way she acted, you know. But we'll talk more when you are dry and warm, shall we?" He pulled her closer, half-carrying her down the dark road. When they reached the drive, he heaved her up and into his arms, and she clutched his neck tightly, burying her head against his shoulder, still shivering uncontrollably. If anything happened to her, if she became ill, he would never forgive himself.

Avonleigh was lit as it hadn't been in years, with light coming from nearly every window. Good ol' Jules, making a beacon in the night in case Katherine had been out there, lost in the dark.

"W-why is the h-house all l-lit up?"

"So you could find your way home, love," he said, pulling her closer to him. His arms were burning from the effort of carrying her, but he trudged on, his eyes on Avonleigh. When he reached the entry, Juliana was there holding the door open. Graham immediately brought Katherine to the kitchen, knowing it would be the warmest room in the house. Mrs. Alcourt, brilliant woman, had already begun heating up water and had somehow managed to drag a tub to the large kitchen.

"Oh, the poor dear," Mrs. Alcourt said, clucking her tongue. She pulled out a chair, putting it close to the stove, and Graham placed the still-shivering Katherine upon it. He took his now-soaked coat off her shoulders, then began working on hers. His fingers, stiff from the cold, could hardly manage the task, and he let Mrs. Alcourt take over.

"I think the coat may be a lost cause," he said, wrinkling his nose at the thick mud that still clung to it. "You may throw it away, Mrs. Alcourt." He looked down at Katherine and gave her a small smile. "I think I can handle the rest of Lady Avonleigh's needs. Thank you."

"Just call me if you need me, sir." She gave Katherine one final worried look before leaving the kitchen.

"I am more sorry than I can say, Katherine, for the terrible things I said to you," Juliana said. She stood with great dignity, clasping her hands in front of her. Only Graham knew just how upset Juliana was. Her cheeks were flushed, her always perfect hair in disarray, no doubt from running about the house lighting lanterns. The tub was made of copper, and heavy even when empty. He could only imagine the struggle Mrs. Alcourt and Juliana had had trying to drag the thing into the kitchen. No wonder Juliana looked so completely disheveled.

"You did say terrible things," Katherine said, her voice steady now that her shivering had subsided. "But I understand it was only because you love your brother."

Juliana frowned, as if she were displeased that Katherine was being so kind. She gave a nod. "I do hope you will feel better soon. Good night."

Once his sister left the room, Graham got down on his knees next to Katherine and grasped her still-cold hands. "What happened? I was worried out of my mind."

"I'm sorry you worried," Katherine said. "I was angry and your sister was quite awful. I just wanted to get away from . . ." She closed her eyes briefly. ". . . everything. And then I saw a lamb stuck in the mud and thought I'd help it out and this other very large sheep butted me from behind and I fell into the muck and the lamb got out and then it started to rain and the nasty sheep wouldn't let me leave."

Graham tried to maintain his look of concern, he truly did, but the image of Katherine being sent sprawling into a large mud puddle was too much. He burst out laughing.

Katherine scowled at him, and then joined him. The entire episode *was* funny.

"I'm sorry, love, but now that you're safe and sound—" He stopped, chuckling again. "Really? You were attacked by a sheep? Are you all right?"

"No, I'm not all right. Do I look all right to you? I'm covered with stink, I'm cold, and no doubt I have a very large bruise on my backside." She pretended to be miffed by his question, but truly, it was rather nice to have Graham look at her with concern, to have had him hold her and kiss her. She'd thought she might never see him look at her like that again. What had happened? Was it only that he'd been concerned?

Graham laid a hand aside her face and smiled gently at her. "And you've never looked more beautiful to me."

Katherine narrowed her eyes, suspiciously. "What is wrong? Why are you being so nice to me?"

Graham stood, stepping back. "I am torn. I think that perhaps I may have made some erroneous conclusions."

Katherine studied him, and realized he wanted to believe her. He did look quite awful, Katherine thought. His gray eyes had dark circles beneath them and his hair was mussed, the edges damp and curling from the rain. Suddenly, it became impossible to go on as they had a second longer. She loved him. She had to make him believe her.

"Oh Graham, I swear to you. I swear I didn't plan to be caught. You *must* believe me."

Graham pulled out another chair and sat down, looking weary, and Katherine's heart leapt. "God knows I want to believe you, Katherine. When I thought you might be out in that storm, hurt or ill, it made me quite mad. I can't control my heart, you see. I have tried, but the blasted thing still loves you. So, tell me everything."

Katherine closed her eyes briefly and gave a small prayer of thanks. He loved her; he'd just said so. But it was just as important that he believe her. "It turns out Claudia Von Haupt is a very silly thing, but I do like her. I cannot believe I'm saying that, given our history together, but not liking her would almost be the same as not liking a lost puppy. Even though I would be happy to strangle her at the moment."

Katherine went on to tell Graham about Claudia's fears of marriage, how she was uncertain she even wanted to marry and live in England. "She was telling me all this and it broke my heart because she didn't know how lucky she was to be marrying you. I won't lie and tell you I didn't wish every day that it was me and not her marrying you. But I knew you had to and I cared enough for you to want that for you, too."

Graham studied his hands a moment before looking up. "Why did she thank you, Katherine? I was under no misapprehension that Claudia was marrying me for any other reason than that her mother wanted her to in order to garner a title. My feelings in this matter are not relevant as they were not engaged."

Katherine took a deep breath. "It all happened at Rufford Abbey. We, of course, didn't know the Von Haupts were going to be there. And Claudia was so happy to see me. I still feel guilty about it. It is astounding to me that she could have been so completely unaware of how I felt about her. She asked me to her room and then she started crying. Sobbing, really. She didn't want to marry you, she said. She was frightened of you. Isn't that silly?" Katherine asked.

"Not particularly. Many people are. Go on."

Katherine gave a small shrug. "She begged me to help her. And I have to say, this made me angry. Here she was, getting everything I wanted, and all she could do was complain. I know you don't want to hear it, Graham, but I was in love with you even then and when she went on and on about how miserable she was, I wanted to slap her. I told her she was lucky to have you and she'd get used to you. She wouldn't give up. She wanted me to come up with a plan to get her out of the marriage and I told her I'd think on it, simply to make her stop crying."

Graham narrowed his eyes. "That's it?" He was clearly skeptical. "I told you she's a ninny."

"I find it difficult to believe even Miss Von Haupt is that stupid."

For some reason, Katherine felt compelled to defend her. "She's not as stupid as she is very young."

"You two are practically the same age."

"Yes, but for some reason I think of her more as my sister's age."

Katherine reached out and clutched at his hand. "I am so sorry about the money, Graham."

He let out a small laugh. "To be completely honest with you, I haven't given it a thought since the moment we got married."

"Truly?"

"I've been rather distracted by other thoughts." The slightest mischievous look came into his eyes, and Katherine's heart soared.

"Do you believe me, then?"

"I'm afraid Chase insists on it. How you won him over, I will never know."

"I adore Chase. And he's a very good judge of character, you know."

Graham looked down at their joined hands, his brow furrowed. "You are telling me the truth. If I find you are not, Katherine, I fear it could very well destroy me."

"I swear to you, Graham. I wanted to marry you, but I was resigned to the situation I found myself in. It was horrible to be in love with you and pretend otherwise. To encourage Claudia to go through with it when in my heart of hearts I only wanted you for myself. But I knew it could never be."

"I'm not completely unhappy, Katherine," Graham said, a small smile touching his beautiful mouth.

"Tell me you believe me. Tell me that you know I never planned to compromise you. Tell me."

He drew her face to him and kissed her. "I believe you."

Katherine threw herself against him with a sob, kissing him over and over. Then she pulled back and frowned at him. "You put me through a terrible time, Graham. From the moment I met you, you've been just awful."

"I know. You bewitched me," he said, grinning.

"Don't you smile at me. It won't work. What on earth were you thinking, trying to seduce a girl you thought was a maid?"

"If I'd been bent on seduction, Mrs. Spencer, I would have succeeded. I've asked myself that question a hundred times. And I still haven't come up with an answer. I was going to ask you to be my mistress."

Katherine's mouth opened in shock. "Mistress! You scoundrel."

"Indeed. Mr. Chase was even going to arrange it for me."

This shocked Katherine even more. The staid and proper Mr. Chase, arranging for Graham to have a mistress at the same time he was negotiating an engagement with another girl? "Why would Mr. Chase do such a thing?"

"Because, my darling, he knew I was in love for the first time in my life."

Oh, that did take away some of her bluster. Rather all of it. "You were in love with me back in Brighton?"

"Desperately. And when you disappeared, I was a bit lost. And then, there you were, the American heiress I couldn't have. It was torture. I know what I did was wrong, but how could I stay away from the woman I truly loved?"

Katherine raised one eyebrow. "You could have married me. At least then we'd have some money from my father."

"I felt my happiness didn't matter as much as the well-being of my people. I still believe that." He gave a small shrug.

"I know it had nothing to do with greed," Katherine said. "Perhaps my father will come around someday when he sees what a wonderful husband you are." Katherine furrowed her brow as a thought came to her. "Did you ever tell my father of your suspicions about me?"

"No, I did not."

"So you accepted blame for what happened."

"Of course," he said, as if the very idea of laying the blame upon her was absurd.

"Why? I did draw you to that room. You fully believed I had set a trap. Why not tell my father that?"

"I saw no need to have your father angry with you. He clearly adores you and it seemed to me rather poor of me to blame you. You didn't force me to kiss you, after all. If it had been a trap, I went quite willingly."

"It wasn't a trap," Katherine said darkly.

He grinned. "I know that now." Graham let out a breath. "Now, if you don't mind, I fear my nostrils are singed enough from that smell emanating from you. What say we get you cleaned up."

Katherine eyed the tub, still steaming and terribly inviting, then looked down at her still-soaked and muddied dress.

"I'll be your lady's maid this evening, shall I?"

The question was casual, but when Katherine looked up at Graham, her face flushed from the heat she saw there.

"No funny business," she said.

Graham gave her an innocent look.

"At least not until I'm clean." Graham let out a growl and kissed her breathless.

"I'm sorry, love, I cannot make any promises," he said as he hunkered down to remove her mud-caked boots. "Here, stand up and let's get this dress off you. And throw it in the rubbish."

Katherine stood and let Graham unbutton her dress, smiling, her eyes drifting partially closed as his knuckles skimmed her breasts. She was trying to control her breathing, but the sight of his hands slowly undoing her dress was incredibly erotic. When all the buttons to her waist were free, he pushed her gown off her shoulders and kissed what he'd just revealed as he drew her mud-caked dress down and over her hips.

Graham swallowed heavily, the sight of her in her corset and chemise, both still wet, causing a surge of heat. Stepping behind her, he moved her hair—stiff from the mud—aside and made quick work of the loosely tied corset. Off it went, joining the ruined dress on the floor. When he returned to her front, his eyes dipped to where her dusky nipples were clearly showing through her chemise.

"I'm not certain I can do this without ravishing you," he said, his voice husky.

"Do try, I feel positively filthy. Look at my hair," Katherine said, pulling up a clump of hardened locks. "Just think of the stink."

Graham chuckled. "I've an idea. Let's rinse your head before you get into the bath. If you wash your hair in the tub, you'll soon be washing in a mud puddle."

He led her to the sink and she leaned over, giving him an enticing view of her backside. He simply could not resist placing his palm against her delicious bum. Katherine let out a little squeal and straightened. "Please, Graham, do try to resist my charms at least until this muck is off me."

She bent over again and Graham squeezed his eyes shut. Had she no idea what seeing her bent over the sink, her lovely cheeks clearly visible through her damp bloomers, was doing to him? His arousal grew painful, and it was all he could do not to press himself against her just to relieve some of the building pressure. But he knew doing so would do nothing but torture him. With a sigh, he began pumping the water, smiling when she let out a small scream as the cold water hit her head. He continued to work the pump with one hand while she rinsed the mud away, but he couldn't resist placing a hand on her neck and caressing her there. Katherine finally squeezed the water from her hair, stood, and threw herself against him.

"You are a cad," she said, then pressed her mouth against his. His hands immediately went to her lovely bum, and he pulled her against him. My God, he would never get enough of her. He'd wanted this feeling since the day he'd met her, this feeling that he could have her whenever he wanted, that he didn't have to hold back, that he could truly love her without being ashamed.

"Take your bath. Quickly, love. And then we're going to bed. And you're going to stay in my bed all night. And all day tomorrow. And I'm going to make love to you a hundred times."

"That seems excessive to me," she said with a smile.

"No. It doesn't," Graham said. "In you go. Take off that chemise and those silly bloomers and get clean." Graham turned his back, only because he knew if he watched his wife disrobe completely, she'd never quite make it to the water. Instead, he focused on other things than the fact Katherine was behind him, stripping herself completely. He heard the wet plop of each garment hitting the floor, the sound of the water as she dipped one leg, then the other, and her sigh as she sank into the still-warm water.

"Oh heaven," she said. Graham, not two feet away from his naked wife, would not describe his current predicament as heaven, but he knew the faster she got clean, the faster he'd have her naked and in his bed. Finally.

He turned. If God had been standing there with a chastising frown, he still could not have resisted. "My God, Katherine." It was all he could manage, seeing her sitting upright, her uptilted breasts wet and soapy, her skin impossibly smooth and white. With a siren's smile, she slowly lowered herself into the water until she was completely submerged with only her shiny knees poking above the surface. When she emerged, still smiling, her hair was slicked back from her forehead.

"Come wash my hair, Lord Avonleigh."

Mrs. Alcourt—or perhaps it had been Juliana—had left a small pot of hair shampoo on a table next to a towel. He held it up to his nose and smiled. "Nice," he said, dipping his hand in and scooping up a small bit onto his fingers. Katherine leaned back and sighed when he began massaging the soap into her hair, but frowned when he felt the grit on her scalp from the stubborn mud. "Did you take a bath in that mud puddle?"

"I very nearly did. You ought to train your sheep better," she said.

"It's very nearly mating season, love, and that ram perhaps saw you as a threat to his territory."

"But I'm a girl!"

Graham chuckled, loving the feeling of her silky hair beneath his fingers. "I don't think that ram knew it. But I do," he said, letting his soap-slippery hands drift slowly down until he cupped her breasts. He moved his thumbs over her nipples, and she arched upward, much like a cat when it's petted. In fact, the sound she let out resembled a purr. He watched, one side of his mouth lifting as she slipped beneath the water, rinsing her hair and rising up so suddenly, some of the water sloshed over the edge.

"You, madam, are clean."

"One more time." And she disappeared again.

"Are you done torturing me?" he asked when she came up again.

"I think you deserve a bit of torture for treating me so shabbily. Shame on you for believing such a horrid thing of me." She said the words lightly, but Graham knew she was hiding a deep hurt.

"I'm sorry. Come here. Stand up and I'll dry you off." She stood and he wrapped the towel around her. She looked up at him, her eyes dark, her long lashes spiked from the bath water, and he could see the doubt in them, the worry. "I *am* sorry," he said. "I didn't want to doubt you, believe me. I thought I was every kind of fool for loving you still."

Tears filled her eyes and his heart hurt just to see them. "I thought I'd lost you forever," she said. "That there was no way you would ever believe me. I couldn't prove my innocence. What changed?"

Graham stared at her lovely face, wishing he could point to a moment when he'd realized fully she never could have betrayed him. "I don't know. I only know I could no longer go on *not* believing you. It never made sense to me, and yet I felt I was a fool to believe my heart."

She got up on her toes and kissed his jaw. "I don't blame you for doubting me. The evidence *was* damning. I only wish you'd come to your senses a bit earlier."

She looked adorable wrapped up in the towel, her feet bare on the cool tile. "As do I," he said, then scooped her up, ignoring her squeal.

"What are you doing?" she asked, laughing.

"Carrying you off to my lair to ravish you."

"Oh good," she said, and kissed his neck. "I rather like being ravished."

It seemed as though he flew up the stairs, her body molded to his, arms wrapped tightly around him. "How would you know? You haven't been ravished yet."

She pulled back and gave him a skeptical look. "I haven't? I quite remember *feeling* as if I'd been ravished."

He stopped right before entering his bedroom, his heart nearly bursting. "You have not been ravished. Not properly. But that is going to change tonight."

Mr. Chase was in his room when they entered. They startled the old gent, who appeared to be dozing on a chair set in one corner.

"No need for you this evening, Mr. Chase," Graham said, throwing back his covers with one hand before depositing a giggling Katherine on the bed.

Chase stood with great dignity and nodded. "Very good, sir." But just as he was closing the door, he smiled and gave Katherine a wink.

"You have him wrapped around your finger, don't you?"

Katherine shrugged. "I have no idea what you are talking about." She went to turn out the lamp, but Graham stopped her.

"Tonight I want to see you."

Katherine lay back, her head propped against the fluffy pillows. It was the first time she'd been in her husband's bed and she rather liked it. His was much finer than hers and his pillows softer. It would be a pity to return to her own lumpy mattress and skimpy pillow.

Graham started to undress right in front of her, and Katherine realized she was about to get her first look at her husband completely naked. And she, other than the towel, was also bare. On other nights, her room had been nearly dark, with only the dim light from the fire lighting her room, and she'd never been unclothed. He disrobed quickly, giving his ruined shoes a grim look before tossing them aside.

And then he was naked, every glorious inch of him. He had a fine form, a well-muscled chest sprinkled with a nice amount of manly hair and a firm, flat stomach. She couldn't quite bring herself to look below that enticing line of hair that seemed to point directly to his . . . man part. Though she did want to take a look at the part of him that had been inside of her. His body was so unlike hers that Katherine was fascinated by it. She took a shaky breath, darting a look to his arousal, jutting forward, then up to his face. He looked slightly bemused and very intense. She'd missed seeing that heat in his eyes when he looked at her. He came forward to stand beside the bed, his member nearly even with her head. Goodness, it was so . . . male.

"Touch me, Katherine."

She darted a look to his face, then back down, knowing he meant for her to touch his member. Holding out one finger, she touched the very tip, startling a bit when it moved. He took her hand gently and wrapped her hand around him, squeezing, showing her how he wanted her to touch him. As she explored, amazed at the silky hardness of him, a small drop glistened at the tip and she touched it with her index finger.

Graham groaned, and Katherine smiled, glad to finally be giving him such pleasure.

"Kiss me, Katherine," he said, his voice strained.

"Here?" She looked doubtfully at his cock.

"God, yes."

She gave the very tip a delicate kiss, and he moved subtly toward her, his breathing harsh, his entire body taut. And when she opened her lips and took him slightly into her mouth, he cried out. In one smooth movement, Graham lay atop her, then rolled until she was on top of him, the towel unraveling and leaving her naked, his mouth hungry on hers. His hands moved down her body until they cupped her bottom, moving her against him. She could feel his arousal, hard against her stomach, as pure heat flooded through her and pooled between her legs.

He rolled again, and Katherine thought he'd do what he always did, enter her. Instead, he kissed her, then moved to her breasts, loving them with his mouth and tongue, creating an intense heat that Katherine knew would end with that wonderful feeling she craved. She moved her hips and he chuckled as he suckled on one nipple, then the other.

Graham sat back on his haunches and smiled down at her. "You are so damned beautiful." He skimmed his hands down her body, to her outer thighs, then to the soft and sensitive inner thighs just inches from where her body throbbed for release.

"Do you want me to touch you?"

"Yes." Katherine almost didn't recognize that voice.

He put his hand between her legs, his eyes intent on her as he touched her, moving his thumb back and forth before inserting a finger into her. She closed her eyes as the need grew nearly unbearable. God, he knew what she wanted, knew how to help her find release.

"Do you want me to kiss you?"

Her eyes flew open.

"I want to kiss you, Katherine. The way you kissed me. Here." He moved his thumb against her swollen nub.

She couldn't respond, but he must have seen the need in her eyes, so he dipped his head, his eyes on hers, as he licked her. "Oh my God," she said, her hips pushing up toward him. How could something feel so good?

This was what Graham had meant when he'd said he wanted to ravish her. She felt ravished. She felt loved. He made love to her with his mouth and his fingers until that wonderful feeling burst through her, more intense, more overwhelming than anything she'd ever felt before. She cried out, long and hoarse as her body jerked in pleasure.

She was still pulsing when he entered her, and she welcomed him by lifting her hips against him. He moved slowly, as he kissed her breasts, her neck, her mouth. It was carnal and wonderful and more than she ever dreamed making love could be. And when he moved his hand down between them and touched her again, she cried out, a sudden rush of pleasure making her arch her back and find release again. His thrusts became more urgent, harder, as if he'd also been overcome with need. He kissed her, thrusting his tongue against hers before arching his back and finding his own release.

Graham stayed inside her a long time before he could bring himself to withdraw. He wanted to stay like this forever, feeling her hot, tight body around him. Finally, he withdrew and lay on his back, pulling her to him and kissing the top of her head.

His wife snuggled close to him, kissing his shoulder now and then as if to remind him she was still there. After a time, she said, "Should I go to my room?"

He pulled her closer and kissed the top of her sweet-smelling head. "This is your room."

They woke near dawn and made love again, then slept until the sun was alarmingly high in the sky. Graham woke first and gazed down at his still-sleeping wife, thanking God for giving her to him and for helping him to realize his mistake. He was sickened by how he'd treated her, and could not purge from his memory the looks of hurt she'd given him over the past few days. He'd make it up to her forever.

They would be poor. They might never have gas lighting or proper bathrooms, but they would be happy. Perhaps he'd overlooked something, perhaps his extremely competent solicitor had come up with a plan. Maybe he could finally find a bank to give him a loan so he could repair Avonleigh's textile mill. It seemed all his problems were smaller now that Katherine was in his life and in his bed.

The morning's sun, edging across the bed, finally touched her face and Katherine slowly opened her eyes.

"Good morning, love," Graham said, kissing her.

She smiled and drew her arms around him. "A very good morning." Then she frowned. "Today is November twelfth. You leave in two days."

"You are coming with me."

She narrowed her eyes and he kissed her again. "I thought you said we couldn't afford for me to come with you."

"We can't. But I can't spend that much time away from you. Not now. Probably not ever."

"You are so smitten," she said, grinning.

"Far more than smitten. I'm completely in love. It's extremely disconcerting."

She kissed his mouth, but since they were both smiling, it lost much of its effect. "And why is that?"

"The Miserable Marquess is not used to feeling so ridiculously happy. I think it's giving me indigestion."

Katherine laughed and sat up. "Speaking of indigestion. I am starving."

"So am I," Graham said, drawing her back down and showing her a hunger of a different kind.

Chapter 18

The two of them were quite disgustingly in love. That day and the next, when they weren't in bed making love, they were going for long walks and gazing at each other like fools. Mr. Chase was ecstatic.

Everett Chase prided himself on being an honorable and honest man, something Mr. Wright had seen almost immediately. Either that or he was a gambling man with few options. Before the Wrights had left, Mr. Wright had handed him an envelope and directed Everett to give it to Lord Avonleigh "on the chance I'm right about the lad and he turns out not to be a rascal."

It had been a surprising meeting to say the least. Mr. Wright had sought him out the morning they were due to leave. The house had been shrouded in misery, and Everett had been feeling more than a bit depressed. His lordship, who was more son to him than master, was despondent, feeling betrayed by the only woman he'd ever loved. And feeling the weight of all he had lost.

For years, Everett had tried to direct him, tried to make him realize that his father's death was not on his hands. But it had been a difficult task to convince Graham that his words to his father had not led to his father's suicide—for they likely had. Everett had known for years that the old marquess was . . . different. Though the marquess had been discreet, it was nearly impossible to keep such a secret from his valet. And though he was personally disgusted by the notion of a man loving another man physically, Graham's father was such a good man, Everett had overlooked this one characteristic.

To a young man, discovering his father with another man had been both shocking and devastating. Graham had said things he no doubt regretted. Everett hadn't heard the exchange, but he knew what had happened for the marquess, heartbroken, had told him. Graham had discovered him with his longtime companion, and the marquess had been destroyed by his son's horrified reaction. Of course, he hadn't expected any other reaction, but had foolishly thought his son would never find out. Everett would never forget the raw pain he'd seen in the marquess's eyes that afternoon. He had feared for his lordship's life, had even gone so far as to hide the key to the old marquess's gun cabinet. But it hadn't been enough for a determined man.

It was early afternoon and Graham had been gone for about an hour, when Everett heard the gunshot, his entire body jerking at the sound. He knew what he would find—at least he thought he'd known. Instead, he saw Graham running toward his father's study, crying out when he saw the marquess. When Everett entered the study, Graham was holding his father's body, rocking back and forth, and crying over and over, "I'm sorry, I'm sorry." He'd known then the weight the young man would bear for the rest of his life.

Graham had been inconsolable. He'd loved his father unconditionally, but that love had been tested by one moment, one exchange that could never be taken back. Had Graham's father not killed himself, Mr. Chase had absolutely no doubt that the two of them would have talked things out and come to an understanding. The fact that Graham had returned to get the pen given to him by his father told Mr. Chase that.

Mr. Chase sighed and stared at the sealed envelope Mr. Wright had given to him. He'd written "Mr. Spencer" on it. Cheeky American. And Mr. Chase was only to give it to Lord Avonleigh should Graham prove to Mr. Chase that his daughter was truly happy in her marriage, that Graham had demonstrated love and devotion.

If their heartening display of affection was proof, then indeed, Lord and Lady Avonleigh were quite, quite happy.

Graham was happier than he'd been since his father's death. He'd never imagined such a feeling of complete contentment. He was whistling—*whistling*—as he took off his cravat when Mr. Chase entered the room. Katherine was in the room next door, packing for their trip to London.

"Sir, I have a letter for you from Mr. Wright. He gave it to me before he left with instructions to give it to you now."

Graham looked at the envelope curiously, smiling a bit when he saw the inscription. "Do you know what this is about, Mr. Chase?"

"No sir."

Graham cracked open the seal and took out one small slip of paper.

You've made my daughter happy. There is five hundred thousand pounds in Baring's Bank in your name. Keep her happy.

Graham read the letter again. Then again. "Are you certain this is from Katherine's father?" he said, afraid to hope too much. It was an obscene sum.

"Yes sir. Is something wrong?"

"No, Mr. Chase. Something is very, very right. Katherine!" he shouted. She appeared at his door almost instantly, brought quickly by the urgency in his voice. He handed her the note. "Did you know about this?"

She took the note, a furrow forming between her eyes. "What is it? Who is it from?"

"Your father."

Katherine's mouth dropped open. "My *father*?" She read the note again, her hand shaking slightly. "But this is far, far more than . . . I don't understand. Oh my, Graham. Do you know what this means?"

"It means Avonleigh is saved. It means I can do nearly all that I planned." He hugged her and the two of them bounced up and down in their joy as Mr. Chase looked on, a smile on the old man's face—despite Lord Avonleigh's rather undignified behavior.

No one closely observing Lord and Lady Avonleigh would ever believe they had just acquired a great fortune. They were frugal in nearly everything they did, agreeing that most of the funds in Baring's would be used to improve Avonleigh and create jobs for the local population. Only when the mills and factories were profitable would Graham feel comfortable spending money on their own comforts (although the two agreed their home did need a bit more furniture). Bryant Park would be leased, but now they had the funds to make proper repairs and hire adequate staff for its upkeep.

The idea that Lord Avonleigh had once been dubbed the Miserable Marquess was noted by the members of the ton who witnessed the man's nearly constant grin as the newlywed couple strolled down Regent Street.

Katherine had immediately cabled her father, thanking him. He had replied, saying she ought to also thank Mr. Rockefeller for purchasing his steel factory for an extremely favorable price. He'd ended the brief cable with: I knew he was a good man the moment I met him.

Graham read the cable over her shoulder and snorted. "He punched me in the stomach the moment I met him."

"He did?"

"Rather hard, actually."

Katherine grinned. "If you could take one of his punches, you no doubt impressed him."

On the evening before departing London, they were to attend a small gathering to listen to London's most famous soprano, Thérèse Tietjens, in Lady Gartner's Mayfair town house. Katherine had been looking forward to the evening, for it was the first social function they'd attended as a couple and she'd never had the chance to hear the well-known singer.

No doubt rumors about their forced marriage had swirled about the ton in the weeks since their marriage, and Katherine was glad to be able to show everyone how happy they were to find themselves shackled together for life. Those were Graham's words, and they made her smile every time she thought of them.

"How am I to keep my hands off you when you look so lovely?" Graham asked once she had her formal gown on. She had yet to find a lady's maid and so Graham had been acting as such. To a certain extent. Oftentimes, with good intentions, he'd start to help her don her corset, only to have it off again before it was fully laced.

"I really must find myself a proper maid, else we'll be late to every engagement," she'd said, laughing after he'd thrown her down onto the bed and kissed her senseless.

"I don't think we should ever get you a maid. And I thought I was getting rather adept at the job."

"More at the taking off of things than the putting on, sir," Katherine said. Sometime later, Graham successfully demonstrated his ability to dress his wife. And now she stood before him, ready to depart and feeling a bit nervous about the evening to come.

"You may save up all your desire and spend it this evening when we return," she said saucily. "Now. How do I look? Matronly?"

"Like a siren."

She gave him an exasperated look.

"Fine, you look very boring and very matronly."

She frowned. "I do?"

"Of course you don't, love. Before we go, I have a gift for you."

"Oh?" Despite their frugality, Katherine couldn't help but enjoy receiving gifts.

Graham pulled out a thin case and presented it to her. She opened the case and gasped. "I thought I'd lost this."

"I found it on the floor in Rufford Abbey's library."

Inside was her mermaid pendant, looking quite lovely against the velvet case. A little too lovely.

She picked it up and felt the hefty weight, realizing quickly that this was not made of cheap metal and paste, but gold and real gems. But every other detail was precisely like the original, which Graham held dangling from his hand. "Just in case you also wanted the real thing. For sentimental reasons."

She threw herself into his arms and kissed him. "Oh Graham, it's perfect. The most perfect gift."

Graham grinned. "Let's put it on," he said, and gently placed it around her neck. He looked down at her, a wicked gleam in his eyes. "Is anyone looking?"

Katherine smiled, remembering that day on Brighton Beach when he'd put on the original necklace. "Why?"

"Because if I don't kiss you, I fear I shall perish."

Katherine laughed and kissed her husband until they both were tempted to forgo the evening's activities.

"Come now," Graham said, drawing back reluctantly. "We're already a bit late. You know we cannot enter the parlor if the performance has already begun."

As it happened, they arrived in plenty of time to see the famous soprano, for she wasn't scheduled to perform until midnight.

"Do you think we'll see anyone we know?" Katherine asked, trying not to sound as nervous as she felt.

"No doubt we shall," Graham said, then gave her a curious look. "Are you nervous?"

"A bit. After all, the last time we were at a social gathering, it was a bit scandalous."

"Yes, but we are married now. London society will forgive our indiscretion."

Graham's prediction was correct. If anyone remembered or even thought about how they'd been married, no one gave any indication. They greeted the new couple, if not warmly, then politely. Katherine was secretly amused when Graham put on his "aristocratic air" as she called it. "My goodness, no wonder everyone thinks you're so fearsome," she said after one exchange with a Lord Whippet.

"You're the only one who hasn't thought so," he said, slightly miffed.

She laughed, and he looked down at her and smiled. They were oblivious to the near collective sigh of all the unmarried girls and unhappily married matrons who could not miss the look of total adoration Lord Avonleigh was giving his new bride.

Katherine recognized a few faces from the house parties she'd attended and was beginning to relax when she saw Marjorie standing with Charles Norris. Katherine looked about for Lady Summerfield, but didn't see the older woman.

"Let's go to the refreshment table," Katherine said, even though her glass of punch was still half full. But it was too late. Marjorie had spotted her and was making her way toward them, with Mr. Norris following behind almost reluctantly.

"Hello, Lady Marjorie," Katherine said pleasantly.

Marjorie looked terribly distressed and Katherine tried not to be affected. She'd counted her a friend, and even though she understood why Marjorie had told Graham about her words, she still felt betrayed by her actions.

"Please, may we talk privately?"

"Go on, Katherine," Graham said. "I'll keep Norris occupied while you two talk."

Katherine gave Graham a small smile of gratitude, then followed Marjorie from the crowded room and into a small hall. "I cannot say how sorry I am for what I did," Marjorie said. "I am so glad to see that you are happy together. It was my mother. I mentioned, in passing, what you'd said to me after you'd been caught with Lord Avonleigh. And only because she'd seemed so enthusiastic about a match between the two of you. I could not have predicted her reaction. She was incensed and demanded that I tell Lord Avonleigh what you'd said to me."

"It's all right. Everything is fine now and we're very happy."

"You didn't plan it, did you?"

Katherine shook her head. "No. I didn't."

"I *knew* you didn't. But . . ."

"I understand. Graham and I never were very discreet. It was bound to happen. And now we're both very glad it did."

"Oh, that's wonderful," Marjorie said. "I was going to write, but I didn't know quite what to say."

"Please, you are forgiven. You only did what you thought was right. And what of you? Are you here with Mr. Norris?"

Marjorie looked slightly taken aback. "No," she said quickly. Then, "Yes. No. Well, yes."

Katherine laughed. "Which is it?"

"Yes. But we're not a couple. Not really. It's a long and very ridiculous story. I find him extremely onerous, as a matter of fact."

"He *is* handsome. And rich."

"No title," Marjorie pointed out with a laugh. "And besides, he's half in love with someone else."

"There is always Lord Mandeville," Katherine said.

Marjorie laughed at the mention of the doddering old widower. "I'm so glad you're not angry."

"I *was* angry," Katherine said. "But that lasted only until Graham came to his senses."

The two women returned, arm in arm, to the parlor where Miss Tietjens would soon sing. Katherine immediately spotted Graham off to one side still talking to Mr. Norris. He looked up and smiled, then scowled at something Mr. Norris said.

When the two women reached the men, Mr. Norris said, "Lady Avonleigh, did you know that your husband once made a mockery of me for having the audacity to fall in love?"

Katherine pressed her lips together to stop from smiling. "It does sound like something he would do."

"What in heaven's name did you do to him, my lady?" Mr. Norris asked.

Katherine looked up at Graham, her eyes shining. "I made him smile."

Jane Goodger lives in Rhode Island with her husband and three children. Jane, a former journalist, has written and published numerous historical romances. When she isn't writing, she's reading, walking, playing with her kids, or anything else completely unrelated to cleaning a house. You can visit her website at www.janegoodger.com.

The Mad Lord's Daughter

She couldn't resist...

JANE GOODGER

What forbidden lady can say no...

When A
Duke Says
I Do

JANE GOODGER